Land *and* Blood

CARAF Books
*Caribbean and African Literature
Translated from French*

Renée Larrier and
Mildred Mortimer, Editors

MOULOUD FERAOUN

Land *and* Blood

Translated and with an Afterword
by Patricia Geesey

UNIVERSITY OF VIRGINIA PRESS
Charlottesville and London

Cet ouvrage publié dans le cadre du programme d'aide à la publication bénéficie du soutien du Ministère des Affaires Etrangères et du Service Culturel de l'Ambassade de France représenté aux Etats-Unis.

This work received support from the French Ministry of Foreign Affairs and the Cultural Services of the French Embassy in the United States through their publishing assistance program.

Originally published in French as *La terre et le sang,*
© Éditions du Seuil, 1953; foreword © 1962

University of Virginia Press
Translation and afterword © 2012 by the Rector and
Visitors of the University of Virginia
All rights reserved
Printed in the United States of America on acid-free paper

First published 2012

1 3 5 7 9 8 6 4 2

LIBRARY OF CONGRESS CATALOGING-IN-PUBLICATION DATA

Feraoun, Mouloud.
[Terre et le sang. English]
Land and blood / Mouloud Feraoun ; translated and with an afterword by Patricia Geesey.
p. cm. — (CARAF Books)
"Originally published in French as La terre et le sang, (c) Editions du Seuil, 1953"—T.p. verso.
Includes bibliographical references.
ISBN 978-0-8139-3220-0 (cloth : alk. paper) —
ISBN 978-0-8139-3221-7 (pbk. : alk. paper)
1. Kabyles—Algeria—Fiction. 2. Families—Algeria—Fiction.
3. Land tenure—Fiction. 4. Villages—Algeria—Kabylia—Fiction.
I. Geesey, Patricia, 1961– II. Title.
PQ3989.F4T413 2012
843'.914—dc23

2011038355

Contents

Foreword to the
1962 Second Edition

On the morning of March 15, 1962, at El Biar in the hills of Algiers, Mouloud Feraoun attended a meeting as part of his duties as inspector of social centers. Shortly after 11:00 AM, armed men entered the administrative offices and ordered the room's occupants to stand against the wall with their arms raised. After searching them, they called out seven names. One of the individuals called was absent. Among the six others was Feraoun. In a pleasant voice, the leader of the assassins assured the men they would not be harmed, but that they would just record a statement into a tape recorder. They thought it was going to be an O.A.S. "pirate broadcast."

The six victims were led outside single file to a space between two buildings where other armed men were waiting. These men took away their identity cards. The massacre followed. With his chest crushed by a hail of bullets from a machine gun, Feraoun was the last to fall. His body landed on top of his friend Ould Aoudia. It was 11:15 AM. In a nearby field, an old woman and some children had witnessed the slaughter.

Feraoun had been obliged to leave the town of Fort National, where he was teaching, due to an incident with a bureaucrat known for his cruelty. He accepted the position of principal at a school close to Algiers in Clos Salembier, because it would be close to me. At that time, I was living in a neighboring district. In spite of the friendship we showed him, he still missed Kabylia. He did not like Algiers, where, in all honesty, he felt uprooted.

Then Feraoun received, as we all did, the first threatening letters. Far from intimidating him, these anonymous letters appeared to make his convictions even stronger. He hoped for an Algeria where there would no longer be the victors and the vanquished, but only men delivered from an "age-old injustice."

These threats added to his anguish. They were a sign of the madness that would amplify the misery of others, a symbol of the insanity that would kill him in a springtime of death. In any event, these threats drove him to take action and to bear witness. He was seen in Algiers at the podium of a liberal demonstration. His lucid and thoughtful messages were read in Paris. He had already laid out his position on the Algerian uprising in an open letter dated February 22, 1956, addressed to the Teachers' League. Here are a few excerpts from that letter: "I have for Kabylia a filial tenderness that I have tried to express in my books. I have given it a sympathetic image, but it is not a deceptive one. What can I write now as anguish chokes me? Should I speak of her suffering or her rebellion? . . . One must understand this unanimity in the rebellion, why the divorce is so brutal. The truth is that there never was a marriage! The French remained apart. They believed that they were Algeria. . . . What would it have taken to fall in love? To come to know each other, first of all. For an entire century we lived side-by-side, curious about each other. The only thing that remains is to reap this studied indifference that is the opposite of love. . . . The price to pay is the recognition of our right to live, our right to education and progress, and our right to be free."

Mouloud Feraoun is buried in Tizi Hibel, the village where he was born, in the small cemetery I know well and that he himself described as being located across from the convent workroom of the Soeurs Blanches: "There where the paved road ends . . . and his tomb will blend in with all the others because it won't have any inscription and, as soon as spring arrives, it will be covered with delicate grass and white daisies."

Emmanuel Roblès
Académie Goncourt

Mouloud Feraoun was born in Tizi Hibel, in upper Kabylia, in 1913. After studying at the Ecole Normale d'Alger, he taught for several years in Algeria and was named inspector for the

Centres Sociaux. His works include, among others, L'anniversaire, Le fils du pauvre, *and* Les chemins qui montent. La terre et le sang *received the 1953 Prix du Roman Populiste. Mouloud Feraoun was murdered in Algiers, on March 15, 1962.*

Translator's Acknowledgments

I wish to acknowledge the support of a University of North Florida Summer Faculty Research Grant, which allowed me to begin this project. I am grateful to Professor James D. Le Sueur of the University of Nebraska for suggesting that I undertake a translation of Mouloud Feraoun's novel. I also wish to express my appreciation to Professor Alek Baylee Toumi of the University of Wisconsin, Stevens Point, for his help in compiling the Arabic and Berber glossary and for providing information on Kabyle social and political structures.

Land *and* Blood

I The following story really happened in a corner of Kabylia accessible by road, with a tiny school, a white mosque, visible from the distance, and several two-story houses. No doubt it would be thought that such an ordinary setting could only be witness to banal lives, since the main characters whose story will be told here are not the least bit exceptional. (The reader must be informed of this at the outset.) At most, one might be surprised that one of these characters is a Parisian woman. Indeed, who would have thought that in Ighil-Nezman a Frenchwoman from Paris could be tucked away?

The village itself is rather unattractive, it must be said. Picture it planted on top of a hill, like a big, whitish-colored dome, fringed by edges of greenery. The road snakes around awkwardly before it arrives there. This same road begins in the city, and it takes two hours to make the trip, if the car is in good shape. The first leg is covered in gravel and is well maintained, and then it ends. The town's boundary line is crossed. Depending on the weather, the next stretch of the road is dust or mud, and it climbs and climbs and zigzags crazily above the chasms. The car has to stop to rest. The tires are blocked to keep it from rolling, and the tank is filled. Then it climbs and climbs some more. Normally, after passing dangerous curves and narrow bridges, one finally arrives. A noisy and triumphant entry into the village of Ighil-Nezman is made.

It was in this fashion, on a spring afternoon, that the Parisian who caused such a commotion in the village arrived. Yet the event was no more important than others that, from time to time, importunely aroused people's curiosity and shook the village out of its torpor. The children rushed to surround the rare taxi. Then, without much ado, they escorted the couple, leaving the tall, bearded driver wearing a leather vest and a *chéchia* like their own to depart. The beautiful lady smiled at them like a condescending queen. She said to her companion: "So, here are the Kabyles!" It was an invitation to follow her. The gentleman was well suited to the lady; he too was good-looking, although his complexion wasn't very light. He did not have a mustache or a hat, but the children knew who he was as soon as he met up with the men of the village. The first to come to greet him, with a kiss on his head and hand, called him by the name of Amer-ou-Kaci. He said Amer's mother was going to be very happy to see him again and that she was lucky not to have passed away before she could see him once more. He hardly bothered to glance at the lady, who was still smiling. It was clear that she did not understand the Kablye language.

Amer-ou-Kaci was becoming more and more timid, blushing even more at every encounter, and it seemed as if he wanted to apologize to all of the elderly men, the very men he had abandoned, God knows how long ago. (With the younger men, he was more at ease.) The children understood that this impressive gentleman was none other than the lost son of old Kamouma. He then dropped quite a bit in their esteem, but they took pity on the beautiful lady, and their gaze became gentler. The men seemed more annoyed than astonished to see a *tharoumith* arrive in their village; those who stopped by left again, hiding their mockery under lowered eyes with a faint expression of disapproval at the corner of their mouth.

The young women who happened to pass by stared boldly at the lady; next they were overheard whispering and laughing. Two old ladies went on their way again after having embraced Amer and favored his companion with a big hello. They planned to warn Kamouma, and they quickened their steps with all the strength in their old bodies, making their faded old clothes flap on their dried-out legs.

The couple made their way through the village with circumspection because they were now entering the main street. If it couldn't be guessed as to what, exactly, the lady was thinking, or what was causing her shyness, it was possible on the other hand to understand Amer's embarrassment. He hadn't thought about public opinion, and now he hesitated; he didn't want to confront it head on. No, it is not the public garbage dump forming an enormous mound right in front of them; it isn't even this poor, rough, narrow, rutted, and muddy road. It is not the sight of these things that makes him blush in front of his wife.

He wouldn't mind that! Besides, he had already described all of that to her. But there it is, his "back is to the wall!" He feels as if even these objects reproach him for something. The bluish muck seeping out in rivulets from under the houses, the piles of dung rotting off to the side, these half-crumbled walls, patched in places with bundles of reeds, these minuscule, smoky, and dirty shacks are all angry with him for letting them be seen up close like this by an outsider.

Still, the man, the woman, and the procession of children pressed and resolutely went down a dark alley in order to get to Kamouma's house.

Amer was born in that house, and it is where Kaci died ten years ago during the prodigal son's absence. It had hardly changed, Amer told himself at the sight of it; a bit older, no doubt, the worm-eaten door had only one side left; he would have to get it repaired, he thought. The little courtyard seemed small and dirty, the front of the stable was falling apart: he would have to get used to it. Old women and relatives blocked the doorway to the home; he tried to recognize his mother among all those weathered faces, amid this impossibly dark and tangled pile of *gandouras*. She came forward, timid and happy; he drew her to him and placed a kiss on her head.

"It's my mother," he said in French.

The Parisian embraced Kamouma warmly, and the old lady gave her noisy kisses in exchange, kisses she would have liked to give to her son. Kamouma laughed with her whole toothless mouth. She is dark-skinned and impressive, as tall and dried-out as ever, but now stooped and fragile like a hollow reed. Wisps of wooly hair poke out from underneath her scarf, her large dark eyes are cloudy and her gaze is blurred, her eyelids red and bare. She puts her wrinkled face right up close to the beautiful smiling face of the Frenchwoman, who returns her gaze without fear. Kamouma stares a moment and blinks, then moves aside to make way for the other ladies. They take hold of the woman, greet her with kisses on both cheeks, tug on her clothes, and look at her with admiration, caressing her like a doll. Amer is only given the usual kiss on the back of his hand; the women are a bit reserved and distant with him. He crosses the threshold of his mother's poor house and puts a big suitcase down near the loft stairs—the rest of the day will be spent greeting people. Everyone comes to say hello. It's the rule. No point in getting impatient with it, since, on the contrary, it would really be annoying if no one at all came to greet him and fuss over him upon his return. But just why, exactly, would the villagers ignore Amer, even though he himself never gave his relatives a thought during his absence? Now he is happy to have the crush of visitors at his home. This proves to the Parisian woman that he is well liked here. He sits down on a round bench built into the pillar that holds up the loft and notices a small black goat staring at him with wide-eyed surprise. He pats the animal distractedly, thinking to himself how useful the small creature will be: milk, offspring, and manure for the garden . . .

"And my mother is still able to keep a goat! She always had milk."

This observation lessens his remorse; he even feels a small sense of relief in his heart, his gaze brightens, and he looks into the courtyard.

"They won't let go of me," the lady calls out to him, as she glances back into the dark interior of the house.

"Be patient! It's the custom. There are no introductions with us, you kiss everybody," he explained.

But as other ladies were arriving, Kamouma led the woman away and left her next to her son. She ran to the pile of bedding and took a woven mat and placed it on the floor, then scattered some smoky-smelling wool blankets and cushions and made the woman sit down there. With resignation, the Parisian sat down awkwardly, as if on a pile of dirty laundry.

"We could be getting a visit from just about anybody, now," Kamouma explained.

II   When a Kabyle returns to his mountain after a long absence, the time he has spent in another place only seems like a dream. This dream can be good or bad, but reality can only be found in his own land, at home, in his village.

The village is a collection of houses made of stones, earth, and wood. They hardly even look as if human hands had anything to do with their construction. They could have sprouted there by themselves, sitting there for the taking as if by a miracle on this hostile land. The homes are practically indistinguishable from the terrain; it is the same land upon which everyone in the village passes their life, only to be laid to rest under a shale slab at the end of that life.

Here, one cannot find a solid, grandiose, or beautiful and complex work of man, capable of outlasting the centuries and attesting to an admirable past anywhere. Instead, in this region one sees the isolated effort, a bitter, unprofitable, and ceaseless struggle that poor men undertake in order to survive. At the same time, one sees that this constant effort cannot outstrip life itself. Consequently, the legacy left to the next generation is minimal; each generation must start over, striving only for itself.

The oldest houses in Ighil-Nezman, which appear to bear the patina of centuries with their blackened roofs, their loose mortar, their bowed walls, and their broken roof tiles, actually only date to the grandfather's era. Two generations, and they must already be rebuilt! Families faced with the problem of rebuilding have a specific goal in life, and in a sense, it is always good to have a plan to follow. But sooner or later, everyone finds they need to rebuild, yet the village's appearance really doesn't change. The new homes follow the same pattern as the older ones; sometimes the interior is altered a bit, but no attempt is made to expand toward the street. As a result, the street is never widened either. It is condemned to remain the same. A few newer houses look better; some pleasant dwellings are going up outside of the town. This is reassuring, since, in short, one might say that the village is growing and that grandsons are worthy of their ancestors. Even the construction methods are improving. Not only is a plumb line used nowadays, but a real beam replaces the haphazard, knotty oak support in the roof, the roof tiles come from the city, the door is brightly painted, and a few red-tiled, peaked chimneys poke up from the roofs.

The day after his return, Amer-ou-Kaci notices these changes with real pleasure since, after all, this is the village where he was born, always ready to welcome home without reserve one of its prodigal children. He has felt this welcome himself, already accepted back into the fold, as a mysterious web of threads envelops him in its texture, threads made up of specific memories and vague feelings that now flood back to his mind, re-creating a familiar atmosphere. In short, Amer understands that he is once again becoming a child of his country. His long absence already has no other significance than that of a giant parenthesis, one that cannot really alter the basic meaning of his life. But while he makes sense of all this, other observations come to mind. What will he do now? He will be judged according to his accomplishments. He will soon have to act like everybody else in his family.

His "new" status will last only as long as the celebrations for his return. For now, he is an object of curiosity; in the café or the *djema*, everyone wants to speak to him, they smile, they are polite and show interest in him. This is the way the latest arrivals are always received. Nonetheless, beneath all the pleasantries, courtesies, and discreet requests for information, the real question on everyone's mind shows through: did the émigré bring back any money? He is sounded out, measured, evaluated, while everyone waits to determine the degree of consideration that is due to him; people are affectionate and nice, in proportion to the size of the returnee's bankroll. The shrewdest stare determinedly; one need only observe the reactions the hard look provokes. They read their answer in the person's eyes. The manner in which a compliment is answered is an admission. If anyone responds softly or humbly, or seeks others out to greet them first, then it is believed that this man has brought nothing back. That much is certain. But when a man firmly accepts compliments, speaks loudly, and blandly answers the exaggerated expressions of interest, then this man warrants respect: he did not return empty-handed. Neither the suit he wears nor the amount of baggage is taken into account for someone returning from France; all that is meaningless. What matters are the banknotes hidden in dirty jackets and threadbare overalls. It must be said, however, that eventually everyone's curiosity will be satisfied. Those who live in France are never off by themselves; they live in the same neighborhood, never losing sight of each other. They all know, more or less precisely, what the others might earn or save. All it takes is for someone who precedes the returnee back home to tell the others what he knows, and after three or four days, everyone else knows too. Then, it's finished. The flashy clothes start to fade, cheeks lose their color, hands darken . . . the curiosity of others has been exhausted. A man takes his place among the important or the humble folk. One becomes a *fellah* again within a week, returning to the fields, hatchet at the ready, feet shod in moccasins, sometimes wearing a wristwatch with an illuminated dial, the last vestige of a dream that has ended. This, then, is the time to break out one's savings. One can buy a field, get married, give a party (a reason for one can always be found), or build if one is up to it. Amer-ou-Kaci senses all of this in the reception he gets from the people and the objects around him: this worm-eaten doorway, the mud wall crumbling down in the courtyard, the entire, old dwelling displays his immediate obligations. As for the rest: buying land, throwing a party, or any other display of wealth is less pressing.

In truth, Amer's present and past situation does not present any mystery. All of his fellow countrymen who went to Paris saw him living with this same woman in a third-class hotel in Barbès. They met her there, his wife, whom some believed to be the hotel owner's niece. Well, now, here they are together in Ighil-Nezman. It will certainly be different from Barbès. They must have their reasons. There is no doubt that they have also arrived with all of their belongings.

When he was in Paris and he happened to think about his

village from time to time, he imagined it as if it were a small, insignificant dot, far away, beyond more splendid horizons, a pocket of wilderness, dark and dirty, where pitiful people were hidden away. In his imagination, they grew uglier and more deformed until they were grotesque. Yet here he is back among them! Oddly enough, he feels good here. He isn't in a country of bad dreams. It is the other country, the one he has just left, that is imaginary; it crushed him by its very splendor. He now sees that over there, he was small and minuscule. Here, everything is as if made to measure for him, the men and the objects. He feels important, ready to act and to make a place for himself. Why did he forget his village? Why didn't he think about his fields, his house, his family? He forgot friends and enemies; he disappeared from others' memories. Other people buried his father, and his mother stopped waiting for him. He reproaches himself now for all this! But it will be a simple matter to redeem himself; it is enough to be there and to look around (he starts to be interested again in the lives of his relatives). All in all, he has recovered a sense of reality. In his own land, a Kabyle is inevitably a realist. All of the duties he freed himself from by leaving now wrap around him again, just as numerous, just as tightly, as if he had never shaken them off. He begins again to love and hate, to imitate and envy, to believe and act according to precise commands that are specific to his own family and *karouba*. He knows these commands intuitively, as if they have been transmitted by heredity, so much are they anchored in his deepest being.

Amer-ou-Kaci is suddenly aware of the conviction that others are jealous of him, a certain family wishes him ill, and another, even one close to him, is not above envying him. He recalls the historic duplicity of a certain *karouba* and the well-known courage of another—his own to be exact. It is no longer a matter of indifference to him that his neighbor, whom Amer never liked, now has a better house and that this fellow is more respected. The game of jockeying for position and status in Ighil-Nezman is going to be an interesting one, and Amer wants his own position to be honorable.

Land and Blood

A whole range of thoughts that lay dormant in him begin to jostle together in his head. He feels as if he is waking up to finish a task left incomplete. He is really waking up to start the task, because he has done nothing up to this point. It has been fifteen years since he left. My God, yes! Just like all the others. It had been a spring morning, perhaps it was March; he left Kamouma and Kaci with tears in his eyes because the parting words offered to him were so touching, all tenderness and hope. He was young and robust, he had been to school, and he did not shirk when faced with work. He could give up his thankless labor in Kabylia and go earn a lot of money in a factory. He could not be kept at home any longer. He was in a hurry to fly away. His parents had been eager to have their own "absent son," that is, their means of support. They were really disappointed, his parents. Finally, it became as if they had truly lost their only child. This entire awful time was not just a dream for Kamouma; it is hard for her to forget. Amer knows that she'll tell him about it in detail, she will forgive him, but she will always act as if she has not forgiven him at all. "It is never too late to make up for it," Amer tells himself. No doubt. This is a proverb that does not apply to the dead. What can the prodigal son do for his father, laid to rest in the small cemetery of Tazrout? Go and visit him this very morning? Moreover, this is his mother's idea. It is a duty to fulfill. Everyone would see him pass by. This also is important, since the living who think about their dead generally can't be thinking too much about themselves. The dead are at rest and lack nothing. Kamouma wants to see if her son is capable of such a self-conscious gesture, one that would put people on notice, show them that customs are recognized and will be respected. It would show people that they are determined to maintain their rank. No doubt she is also in a hurry to find out if he is rich.

To think that she believed he was lost to her, this son who has suddenly returned! Can Kamouma's thoughts be known? In her heart, there is perhaps nothing besides this sort of passive surprise that is not even astonishment, the feeling one has when faced with an unexpected but not very important event.

Land and Blood

For the time being, she has the plum role to play: to wait at home and to behave as she always does, to request nothing, to demand nothing, knowing that every change in her old and simple existence will be an improvement. That is why she remains unruffled and dignified.

III   Kamouma is a poor old lady, burdened by years and experience. She no longer knows where she is in her life. Married young to Kaci, she first lived under the authority of a harsh father-in-law and a tyrannical mother-in-law. She had sisters-in-law: her mother-in-law's daughters and the wives of her brothers-in-law. It was a big family, and life was difficult. She learned how to endure and to toil. She knew injustice and spitefulness, most often as the victim. But she was capable, on occasion, of paying back with an eye for an eye. She bore children, girls and boys. She knew suffering, unassisted childbirth, staying awake with sick children, years of privation and sorrow. She saw all of this big family scattered in the village and in the cemetery; her other children joined the relatives in the grave. Then one day she was alone.

The day when Kaci and Amer were all that was left to her, the situation was clear. It was quite simple really: Amer had to be raised quickly and made into a man who could take care of his old parents. Amer was cared for greatly, coddled not like an only child but like a precious source of future peace of mind, of senile and selfish happiness.

Kaci and Kamouma made several wrong moves during their lifetime, because the game of life demands trump cards that people like them just did not possess. Nevertheless, by dint of losing and continuing even so to live, a person usually ends up convinced of the silliness of the whole game. If one dies right at that moment of insight, then all is settled; but if someone holds out longer, then he no longer cares to hope, to love, or to desire; he just gives up. This is what happened to Amer's parents. When they understood that their last dream would be as pointless as all the others, they realized their hearts were broken. Their splendid vision of Amer lighting up their home in their old age like a glorious torch was just an illusion. It was better not to think anymore about the warm security that was supposed to surround them in their final years, about the affectionate son who promised to see them buried. Once in France, Amer took care of his own business. He did not honor the arrangement that stipulated all of his energies were to be for the benefit of his parents. They lost the game yet again, one last time. They were not angry with their son, but they lost interest in Amer just as one might turn away from something lost in a bet. Anyway, there was nothing left to wager.

Kamouma knew misery, but it would be wrong to dramatize or to get too sentimental about it, because well-off and good-hearted people feel compassion without even knowing why. When one knows misery, one quickly realizes that it is a harmless phantom that has almost no effect on those it encircles. Perhaps it was for this purpose that Jesus once suggested to the rich man that he conscientiously get rid of all that he possessed. But since that time, everyone is content to try to relieve the suffering of the wretched, but not to join their ranks. Mohammed, in order not to be outdone, imposed a prolonged fast on his followers so that they too can feel the torments of hunger. The result has not really been better. When all is said and done, a Muslim during Ramadan spends the day in expectation of what he is going to eat that evening, so the appetite is sharper, the sense of taste and smell are aroused, and one is happy to be hungry. This is why the rich man can never really know misery. Besides, the poor man is no hungrier than anyone else; his situation is not unique. It is simply a matter of degrees of hunger. You slip down an imperceptible slope, you descend and descend; if you start to give up, then you don't even notice. Ah, this slope! Who can be certain to never know this path?

When Kaci and Kamouma found themselves alone and abandoned, they wanted to make arrangements to be able to live out the rest of their lives in some comfort. Previously, they had decided to deprive themselves rather than sell their property, so that they could leave everything to little Amer. Now Amer was grown and had abandoned them. The implicit deal they had with their son had fallen through. No rancor. "We will soon be gone," the old man said. "We can't deprive ourselves." So he sold the fields, one after another.

The first plot to change hands was Tamazirt, a parcel coveted for a long time, located at the entry to the village, planted with fig trees and well exposed, suitable for building. When Kaci received the money, he felt as if he had won a small victory over himself. The old couple was as excited as a pair of children.

"Did he pay you in cash?" Kamouma asked.

"Yes, here it is."

"Well done. Now we will be all right. Our bread is assured."

"That is what I think, too. At our age, money is worth more than land. We can live off it right away. Tomorrow is Friday. I'll go to the market. Think about what we need to buy. We will have some meat," Kaci told her.

"You told him to keep the price a secret? We must not let people know we have some money."

"But there goes Tamazirt! The apple of my eye, the best-kept plot, the most envied! We really did like that one, wife."

"You can talk! The fig trees are dying out like us and don't produce anymore. The soil is worn away, and the rock is coming through. The hedge is no longer there, the shepherds and thieves scoff at you. No one respects our property line anymore. You are in no shape to plough and prune: it is a *mechmel* that you've sold. I am not complaining," she answered him.

"There was a time when I would have rather sold a piece of my heart. Let us not speak ill of Tamazirt; it is lucky for us that we had it to sell today to get the last profit from it," Kaci said.

"It will be of no use to us when we are six feet under. I was only afraid that we would not find a buyer at such a good price."

"You're right. We'll talk more about it again when we'll have to sell more land."

Kaci did not realize then how correct he was. They lived a certain time on that money.

On market day, his tall silhouette could be seen on the road. He left early that day with his careful step, a hood pulled over his head, carrying a walking stick and a lambskin pouch hidden under his *burnous*. Sometimes he had a companion like himself walking alongside him during the journey. They spoke casually about hard times, ungrateful young people, and the neglect of religious practices. But to himself, Kaci was only thinking of his shopping list: the piece of liver he mustn't forget to buy, the kilo of sugar his wife was expecting, as well as city-baked bread that would be for sale there. At the market, he made a tour of all the stalls, buying some treats from time to time that he stealthily slipped into the deep pocket of his *gandoura*. He didn't hurry, touching the foodstuffs on display with pleasure, but he didn't dare ask the prices. He slipped timidly from one merchant to another, fearful of being noticed. He managed to fill up his sheepskin pouch and then returned home early, without rushing, impassive, solitary, and silent, listening only to his inner joy stemming from an ephemeral peace of mind and a carefree attitude. It was the joy of being able to live well in spite of old age. Kamouma is just as discreet as him at these markets. They are quiet and they are as happy and selfish as the last days of September that finish off the small shrub weakened by the August heat with no regret. Their happiness is just as fragile as that shrub but they believe that they will not last much longer themselves.

They "ate" Tamazirt and thought about selling other fields. People saw that Kaci was cornered. They refused to buy or to offer suitable prices. The old couple no longer had any resources.

In all fairness, Kaci did not possess those beautiful plots of land that are always purchased for top prices and for which a great deal of malice and plotting are spent. These fields are well-known; their price is so expensive that the buyer is envied. Besides Tamazirt and Tighezrane—a smaller fig orchard—the other plots were not worth the enmity from the Aït-Larbi family that would result if someone tried to purchase them without their permission. Besides which, these Aït-Larbi were a big clan and had, of course, the right to buy them back. No outsider coveted Kaci's "bad" land anyway. His cousins got the plots for next to nothing.

The first cousin loaned him some money for a time and then one day demanded payment in full. Kaci had to give up a plot for the amount his creditor named. There was no escape from this affair; it had all been arranged by the cousins.

With the second, it was simpler: a *rahina* or mortgage, and Kaci kept the right to buy back his property one day. It was laughable and touching, but the buyer was not worried.

The third cousin came to the rescue of the old couple without any ulterior motive; he posed as a generous relative, and he seemed sincere. To spare Kaci the walk to the market, he offered to get him whatever he needed. He showed great tenderness toward Uncle Kaci and Aunt Kamouma. Often, he had them come over to his place, and his wife would fuss over them too. Sometimes he spoke of Amer, whom he had recently happened to see over there in France, and he only spoke ill of their son, but discreetly. The elderly couple bowed their heads and answered with blessings, blessings they wanted to give to their son.

"I only want their *baraka*," this fine cousin told everyone.

It was certainly commendable. But in addition to the benediction, it was not long before he got a hold of Tighezrane, the last plot of land. On this occasion, a hail of generosity and an exchange of affectionate words took place. Openly and publicly, the *cadi* was summoned, and a regular bill of sale was drawn up. No one thought anything of it. Only a few shrewd relatives understood that they had been duped, and they felt vexed. The only thing the old couple had left was their modest house, and no one would have been so cruel as to evict them from it.

Kaci soon died in the arms of this "adoptive" son, who was admirable right up to the end: he even paid for the funeral!

No one could have asked more of him. Kamouma was only the wife of his old cousin, or uncle, as he had called Kaci. Once Kaci was gone, there was no link between Kamouma and himself. He no longer looked after her. It happened without explanation or outburst. In the week following her husband's burial, Kamouma went to see her "son" on a Thursday, the day before market day, to ask him to do an errand.

"Tomorrow, my son, can you buy extra barley? I don't have any more."

"I am sorry, Aunt Kamouma. I am not going to the market tomorrow," he answered.

That was all. The following morning, Kamouma noticed him saddling up his donkey to go to the market.

She found herself totally on her own, since her own family,

which had only younger members left, abandoned her in their turn for reasons of "honor." (But more of that tale later.) Therefore, she found herself alone, and it occurred to her that she should have died before Kaci. Her eyes filled with tears, but she decided that this cousin really hadn't robbed them. The house was not completely empty. She began to do without many things. It was the beginning of the "gentle slope" mentioned earlier.

There were things to sell, small favors to render, gifts that could be skillfully extracted. It was more or less a question of struggling to survive: not a struggle of strength, but of small calculations, tactics against others, against herself, against her own instincts, wishes, and sensibilities. She had, once and for all, to acknowledge that she was unfortunate and accept her fate.

Kamouma was soon able to derive an advantage from her new situation. With Kaci's death, Kamouma's house became the only one in the neighborhood without men. While he was alive, the women could enter but couldn't hold their meetings there. From that point on, however, her home became a sort of refuge for all the women and young girls of the neighborhood. They were all free to go and meet there: a *djema*, of sorts. Husbands, brothers, and fathers felt no jealousy. Total security! Kamouma, for her part, put her home at everyone's disposal. She had nothing to hide.

Aunt Kamouma lived at the end of an alleyway. This neighborhood formed a *karouba*, like a big family. All the same, with time, family relationships grew vague, and there was not absolute confidence between them. There was no laxness; they lived as neighbors without too much familiarity. People do their outside chores among their own families. Once these are done, the women stay at home, and the men go to the *djema*. It is normal that any woman from the neighborhood would talk to her cousins: "Good day, good evening, welcome." She can receive a bit of news, be asked a favor, in passing, just once in a while. It is allowed. However, women talk among themselves, catch up on news, and meet up with each other just like men in the *djema* or the café. They don't just stand and talk at their doors. Time is evenly shared. The time of day when men are at home is known. When he goes out about his business, the wife also goes out on her own. She has to go see a neighbor to congratulate her on a birth, go and console another whose husband has just left for France, see the loom of a weaver, nose about here and there in search of some news, some information, join in if someone is having fun, or feel sorry if someone is weeping. She never wastes those moments of the day when her husband is absent. Just as much as a man, a woman has her double life: in a way both public and private.

The most amazing meeting place is the fountain. There, the women know neither God nor master. Young women feel at ease there and can relax a bit: blunt remarks, bold jokes, and songs. Sometimes, they really are unrestrained. Often, the water jug is just an excuse to get out, to be seen, and to spark rivalries or discuss a possible "match." The fountain occupies a considerable place in the heart of a young Kabyle woman. However, it must be said that it lacks intimacy, and women of a neighborhood like nothing better than to have a place to meet like Kamouma's house.

Kamouma has a hand-crank grain mill placed just across from her door. Everyone knows that the mill is available at any time of day. Grinding wheat or barley is a task usually assigned to the daughter-in-law or the oldest daughter. It is done after work in the fields, after the morning meal. This is when women are free since the men are out. For those ladies who do not have a mill, it became a habit to go and grind what they need at Aunt Kamouma's. Naturally, Kamouma is not going to request a handful of flour, but the daughter-in-law makes her take some with a meaningful wink since all the while she has been turning the handle, she has accompanied the monotonous rasping of the millstones with all sorts of gossip to which the old lady has listened attentively. The eldest daughter also has things to confide, and as it is necessary to show that she is nice and that she merits the praise that a girl needs in order to get married one day, she too invites Kamouma to take a bit of

Land and Blood

flour. This is not to say that it is a general rule and that one has to pay in order to use the mill. The elderly lady does not want to give that impression at all. But she is very indulgent, she accepts secrets, she knows how to console and how to erase a futile worry or unfounded sadness with just the right word.

For some neighbors, space is tight at home. They have only one room. When children are small, they all sleep on the same mat, one right next to the other, the youngest up against the mother, the father behind her. The others line up by age, with the eldest being farthest away from the parents. When the children are older, the eldest son leaves the house at night, and sooner or later he has his own small bedroom. The father's place is conspicuously apart; the mother has her own small corner where she settles in with the youngest children. It is most awkward for the daughters who are old enough to understand everything. When a secure refuge to spend the night presents itself to the young women, it is a blessing. This is the reason why Kamouma never sleeps alone. She always has one young woman or another who is in the way at home to lodge for the night. For many girls of the neighborhood, Kamouma's house has become a kind of prenuptial anteroom. To say that she derives a significant advantage from this situation would be an exaggeration. Nonetheless, when the young women live with Kamouma like this, they can see her destitution, and they speak of it afterward to their parents. Here, neighbors do not give alms to each other, but they do help each other. The elderly lady has a *burnous* to sell, the word spreads, and a neighbor offers to buy it. There is nothing special about this, since the buyer actually needs one. Moreover, he offers the price that suits him. All the same, it might be a favor since there is no shortage of *burnous* at the market, and Kamouma is not the type to propose a sale. She knows that she must not rely on anyone, but the small gestures of concern shown to her do her a world of good. Above all she benefits from the esteem of her neighbors; when they cross paths, men say "hello" to her first, the women all call her "*nana*," or "sister," and the young girls call her "*ima*," or "mother." She does not need to go the fountain: she receives her daily jug of water from one of the girls. When people return from the fields, from time to time they drop off an armload of dry wood for her hearth. Those who, by chance, are having a celebration do not forget her, and they bring her a plate of couscous with a small piece of meat. After all this, how could she want to lower herself by begging or calling attention to her hunger?

In this way, Kamouma was able to live modestly by selling or trading an item or a favor and doing without the nonessential. She got into the habit of not eating her fill. Hunger? An old acquaintance! The procedure is simple: you have to reduce little by little the ration of *belboul;* you mix a lot of bran with the flour and stock up on acorns when they're in season. There will always be a young girl to grind them. One can make a decent pancake with two-thirds acorn flour and barley for the rest. There are also fasts that one can increase as much as possible; they are pleasing to the Prophet, and they make a good impression on pious people. Those who are used to going without therefore know that one can easily manage to bear hunger: the appetite progressively diminishes, one is undernourished, but one doesn't suffer more than someone who overeats. It is merely a question of degree.

The most difficult days are the religious holidays. No matter what you do, the body just can't take it anymore: you have cravings, odors envelop you, you are so sad not to have anything. It is true that some charitable souls think a bit about the less fortunate. You end up tasting a little bit of everything being enjoyed all around you. But on these days, it is impossible not to cut a sorry figure and not to feel pitiful.

In the beginning, every public holiday was like a funeral for Kamouma. After that, she grew accustomed to other people's pity; her pride and her despair wore away bit by bit. She finally came to accept offerings with real pleasure; she even managed to put away a small reserve during these days of celebration. Then, all was as it should be. Her sensitivity lost its edge in the long run, because the poor man comes to understand that poverty is not a vice. It is not a vice, but a state of being that must be fulfilled like any other. It has its rules that must be accepted and its laws that must be obeyed in order not to be a bad poor man. Kamouma would never wish for that. A poor person is, above all, someone who knows how to wait. God is generous to those who know how to wait; that is why the neighbors prefer not to step in for Him, and they make do by shutting themselves away to eat their feast behind closed doors. How many times has Kamouma felt her empty stomach constrict at the smell of a spicy bouillon or at the slapping sound of dough being kneaded for a batch of doughnuts?

One icy winter morning, she couldn't help herself: she went over to the neighbor's and asked for some embers to start her fire. It was just a pretext. Her watery and lashless eyes saw the lady of the house throw a scarf over the large platter of fresh doughnuts. Then the woman jumped up to meet her at the door. The embarrassed tone with which she answered Kamouma's greeting, as well as the strong smell of hot oil, clearly revealed what the scarf was hiding. Ashamed, the elderly lady beat a hasty retreat. She returned home shivering and dropped the piece of pottery she used to carry embers next to the *kanoun*. Minutes later, the daughter of the other house brought her a ladle full of red-hot coals and a half-burned log that she placed in the middle of the hearth. Then she disappeared without a word. It was in order to return more quickly: this time she carried two golden doughnuts, dripping with oil, and a steaming cup of coffee. The girl walked carefully and smiled mischievously. She prepared the fire in the brazier using the embers and the log, and she waited to leave until the fire burned brightly.

Neighbors can figure things out. They know each other. It is not that someone is heartless, but you can't constantly put yourself in another's position. So one tends to just forget them. Living discreetly is the only thing to do. We call this decency, and in general, we Kabyles are decent. There is surely a lot of shame in being happy, not just within sight of others' misery, but when that happiness seems to taunt. This is a fault the Kabyles do not have. Out of a sense of propriety, the rich man hides to feast, and the poor man can be comfortable in his hunger. Unfortunately, there are some who are losing this sense of decency, and they are becoming unbearable and obnoxious.

It is the poor man, naturally, who becomes unbearable: people are fed up with always hearing his complaints and seeing him make a show of his misery, which he surely must be exaggerating. He ends up without a shred of dignity and sometimes even becomes dishonest.

The rich man is odious when he lacks discretion. We say that an insolent rich man always gets his punishment. If we say that, it is not from naïveté: we speak from experience. We are certain that every action down here on earth will be answered for. That is why, in our minds, the good poor man is the one who knows how to wait. Of course, the wait is not indefinite since, when someone dies in misery without having been rewarded, we are convinced that death itself is the reward. We say: death has freed him, and we accept His eternal wisdom.

As for Kamouma, the unexpected return of her son is simply a result of Divine will. Amer has come home to carry out heaven's plans, and his mother blesses her good *mektoub*.

IV The furniture arrived without too many difficulties, carried on the only truck in the village. It appeared strangely complicated, useless, and cumbersome. Kamouma first saw a kind of iron frame with a silver coating and with mesh and shining springs (she learned that this is a box spring), then a large bundle containing a mattress. Two varnished stools, a chair, and a table whose leaf flapped arrived separately on the porter's back.

The bed frame alone took up one-third of the available space in the house, but Kamouma was reassured when she saw that the mattress and all the blankets go on top. When the table and chairs were set up, there was just enough space left to turn around. The *kanoun* was dangerously close to one of the table legs, and the mill was hidden under a chair, while the goat casually wore the nicest of the stools as a hat. Amer made it clear that he wanted his mother to use that stool, but Kamouma was not too enthusiastic. All the same, she gave it a try. Her son gestured for her to get on as if he were in a hurry to teach her proper manners, and she, for her part, wanted to show that she knew how to conduct herself. When she was perched on her stool, all angular with her feet flat, glued to the floor, her hands under her long bony thighs, holding on to keep herself upright, she looked like she was standing at the edge of a cliff. She resembled a funny wooden sculpture of some African god. The demonstration seemed sufficient, and Kamouma was persuaded that one could indeed sit on a stool, and it would be relatively easy to get used to it if one were young enough. As for her, she admitted in all honesty that she only felt comfortable sitting on the ground, with her old carcass supported by the wall, next to the hearth. That was her place!

"But I brought it for you, Mother!"

"I'll pass, my son. It will be for the guests. Later, for your children."

"Children! I tell you that I am not hoping for any. I've already been married for three years."

"What do you mean, married?"

"Yes, if you like. We've been together for three years. It's the same thing."

"Ah . . . did you sign a paper?"

"Don't look at her like that. She already suspects we're talking about her."

"Me! But I like your wife, yes, yes, a lot, a whole lot. See, I'll kiss her."

The lady returned her kiss and asked what they had just been saying.

"Oh, you know. My mother is asking if I paid a lot the day we got married."

"That's it. I heard 'sign.' And . . . ?"

"So I told her that I got you for nothing. She is very happy about it. She says she loves you a whole lot."

"That nice old lady! Is it true that you buy your wives here?"

"You'll understand those things better later on."

Life became somewhat comical, full of small predicaments, funny incidents, and misunderstandings between the two women, while Amer acted as he pleased, "pulling the strings" like a child playing with puppets, laughing at their desperate charades, at their confusion, and translating exactly as he wanted. He was right to laugh, because deep down, he understood that his peace of mind depended upon this incomprehension.

In Kamouma's eyes, "Madame" could not be her son's wife. The one who really suited him was to be found here in Ighil-Nezman and nowhere else. It would be one of the young women she knew well. There were some who were nice, and their parents wouldn't refuse: some good matches, all in all. Although elderly, she still knew how to play her role: mistress of the house with a daughter-in-law, with allies, her in-laws would seek her out to flatter and cajole her . . . her, Kamouma! This is the role she has dreamed of playing, and she is still dreaming of it. May this *tharoumith* disappear!

On the other hand, everyone knows that Frenchwomen are "clingy." It is not easy to get rid of them. Ah, this signature business is a Kabyle woman's pet peeve. Anyone who signs is irreparably lost. Each time she asks about it, Amer manages not to answer a direct question: did he or didn't he sign something?

Land and Blood

That is not all: it is a well-known danger that when the lady runs out of arguments, she always ends up shooting her husband. If Madame kills Amer, what good would that do Kamouma? Might as well kill her too, which is what could happen if the lady is really angry: a total execution. After that, the criminal would go back to France, no problem, while the two bodies would be cruelly thrown to the dogs by orders of the officers. You can't fool her! Kamouma has figured all this out. She knows she can't boss Madame around. It hasn't escaped her attention that her son is nice to Madame, always saying "yes" to her. As the wise saying goes: "Kiss the hand you dare not bite."

Still, this way of seeing things is shared by all of the lady neighbors, in whose eyes Amer is just a victim. They are certain he signed away his freedom for whatever reason, and now nothing can be done about it. Might as well get on the good side of the lady, and Kamouma had better get along with her. This is how the *tharoumith* came to be accepted without hesitation by the ladies of the neighborhood, who think that Amer is indeed lost for the girls of Ighil-Nezman.

It's true that our women do not like women from the outside too much. There are even a few from neighboring villages who came to usurp households that they couldn't find back where they came from. For these women, acceptance only comes after a long initiation ordeal. The outsider must accept criticism regarding her dress, her behavior, and her language; she must be deaf to the mocking voices, buy the friendship of some ladies through gifts, flatter the others, show herself to be humble and reserved. Slowly she is integrated into a clan, but gains access, in short, through the back door. The woman who commits a blunder or makes a mistake had better watch out; she will be the object of ridicule for a long time. Neither her husband, her mother-in-law, nor her sisters-in-law—who are often the first to criticize her—will defend her.

Madame is not an outsider in the usual sense. She is from another, totally different world. First of all, she has an easy first name, Marie, one that suits her. She will never have any other. From now on, she will be Madame N'aït-Larbi, as her neighbor is Hemama N'aït-Ouamer, or Fatma or Dhabia. In addition, Madame outshines them all by her beauty: perhaps not by the regularity of her features or the harmony of their proportions, but by the purity of her complexion, the colors blooming on her face, the delicacy of her hands, the quality and cut of her dresses. Instead of being too jealous of her, the women decided to admire her. She is not one of them. She does not speak their language. They have nothing in common with this woman other than their gender. They admit the futility of comparisons. "Fine, let her think she is above us! That's her business, we won't tell her what we think of that."

What could have diminished her in their eyes would be to see her speak to men, to go out, to run wild, to provoke the Kabyle men, in short, to be indecent like they are in France. That is what they are waiting for. But Amer and Kamouma will keep watch. They are not so dumb! There is also Madame's material situation. They already know that she is French. She has a different way of life that sets her apart as much as her face and dress. Besides, everyone saw the bed, table, and large trunk pass by. It is a duty to go and see for oneself, to view Madame's belongings, to measure her importance, to try to know her or make oneself known to her.

Kamouma is happy to receive so many women visitors. She has her own way of interpreting whatever Madame says. Someone has to translate for the others, after all.

"Ask her if she has seen my brother over there," said a young woman mischievously, who was actually thinking of her husband.

"You know, it's a big place over there. It's not certain. Right? Madame, do you understand what she is asking, this poor girl? It isn't her brother, it's her husband, tall Ahmed. Do you know Ahmed? You've seen him? Yes? Good. Well, what do you know! She says she has seen him and he is well. Are you satisfied?" Kamouma replied.

"I'm satisfied, but she didn't say all that. She said 'yes,' and that's all."

"Listen to that, Madame! Maybe you weren't telling the truth? Talk to this stubborn girl."

This time Madame answered with a lengthy sentence that the elderly lady listens to with knitted brows. Then, without hesitating, Kamouma gives precise news of the man. The other woman listens and says thank you, but she is not very convinced.

Most of the lady visitors came with small gifts. They received more than one hundred eggs in one week. Madame did not know what to do with them or where to put them.

Truly, the dwelling is very small. The steamer trunk had to be put away in the loft which was already full of jars. The shelf that runs along the length of the wall, drab, darkened, and dusty, holds about a dozen plates, a stewpot, a portable stove, and all the dishes of their former Parisian household. This is what irresistibly attracts the admiring glances, as does the blue, leaf-patterned, satin bedspread.

It must be said that the women who called on Kamouma were not disappointed with all that they saw there, not counting Madame herself. Kamouma's hovel took on an unexpected, almost shocking appearance. The whole picture would have been out of sync, the contrasts too abrupt, and finally Madame herself would have been pitied if not for the undeniable signs of happiness that could be seen on Kamouma's face. The Frenchwoman's eyes expressed contentment as well. Once outside, the remarks went something like this:

"Kamouma is quite happy!"

"With good reason. Her son has returned to her. As long as she behaves, she will die in peace."

"Ima Kamouma is nice, but can we know for certain? She is an old lady, after all. We'll see when they really start to understand each other."

"With a Frenchwoman, you have to be meek as a lamb. They say she is the one who made Amer come back."

"She'll miss her country. They picked spring to return, there is still summer and winter. I'd just like to see her barefoot like us with a jug or a basket on her back."

"Oh, the poor thing! She is delicate. You've seen her skin! It would be a crime to put her to work like that. Our infernal sun will blacken her terribly."

"She'll only work when she wants. If you want my opinion, she won't be shut away like a rich man's wife. No, she'll be going out, to the *djema,* the café, the market, and the city. Just like a man! My husband explained all this to me. The women over there go out alone, buy what they want, and talk to everybody. Men and women work side by side. I can just imagine what kind of work . . . having fun more likely!"

"Is that why your husband has another wife over there, whom he goes back to every trip? Did he tell you that too?"

"He has several, not one, I'm sure. But I'm not worried about it. Those women are all alike. He still comes back to me each time."

"Don't worry, Frenchwomen don't even want them. In any case, Madame is very nice. I don't wish her any ill. I think she is a lot like us. You'll see: a real woman who won't need any lessons."

"Lessons? She could give us a few. They are experts and go about it better than us. But as soon as it is a serious matter or a question of honor, our husbands come running back to us."

"All the same, watch out! Madame will steal your husband from you. No need to go all the way to France now! . . ."

In general, as far as Madame was concerned, the youngest girls were more likely to criticize the customs and practices of Frenchwomen in order to try to tarnish Madame's beauty. But the old ladies were more understanding because they weren't even worried about whether or not she was Muslim or if she fasted. Those who thought about it told themselves that Ramadan was a long way off. On the whole, Madame received a lot of sympathy because a woman always feels pity for another woman. It seems that our women, more so than others, tend to feel compassion. For us, woman really is the weaker sex; she knows it and pities her fate. Women by nature are the sensitive ones, but life obliges them to become insensitive. Some women have to share their husband with a co-wife, others are condemned to an unmarried and chaste life, and a good many of them must accept a husband they did not choose, even if he's old, deformed, or nasty. They submit and squash their heart's desire; all that is left to them—along with limitless disappointment—is not so much a disgust that poisons their existence, but a kind of skepticism that helps them bear their fate and eliminates in advance any rebellious act one of them might attempt in order to free herself.

In theory, an honest woman does not keep company, or go to the fountain or fields, with a woman who is the object of gossip. This is because men might see them together. But if they meet up somewhere they won't be seen, there is no pretense and no afterthought for the honest woman. The other woman is equally at ease and is not embarrassed. Each of the women endures her existence without much ado. They understand each other, and they are sisters. There is no reason to see them as enemies.

As for Madame, nothing in her past is really of interest to them. They are certain from the start that now she will live a life that is much like their own; in all likelihood it will be as the most fortunate of them; Madame is French, after all.

Furthermore, any exaggerations about Kabyle women should be challenged. She lives closer to reality, which is her only source of knowledge, and in general, it is a reality that is less fortunate than many of her sisters face elsewhere. Every definitive judgment about peoples' lives is fixed like an axiom. Yet life is the very opposite of immobility. For this reason, individual cases and precise facts must be examined for the sake of reality; generalizations are difficult to make. The single most common character trait of Kabyle women appears to be the expansive indulgence by which they judge all weaknesses; this indulgence is colored by a kind of hasty and carefree fatalism that simply comes from living such a hard life.

As for the men of Ighil-Nezman, they do not have to adopt Amer. He returns to take his place. It is quite simple. As for his wife, the Frenchwoman, that is his business. For many, such situations are scandalous. The elderly men say as much to each other. But deep down, they are not angry with him. How times change. A *tharoumith,* the wife of a Kabyle; and a beautiful one at that! As a consolation, they are certain he is damned. As for the young men, they mostly think that a French wife is really very awkward for the man.

"None of us would have the nerve!"

"He thinks he is clever to have brought back a wife. Anyone could have done as much. He is so proud, and there really is not anything special about it, let's admit."

Indeed! Amer, back again with his own kind, recovered his aplomb and saw that he was considered a hero. Simply put, the young men were envious. He saw this; he had succeeded where others were all certain to fail.

However, when the most reasonable of the men criticized Amer, they knew how to go about it. It so happened that the *amin* made this young man stop and think. Kamouma's son was soundly provided the lesson he had vaguely sensed in the things and in the hearts of people since his return to Ighil-Nezman.

"I'm old, Amer, and in this I am closer to your father, Kaci, than to you. I am not criticizing your present situation because you have just arrived, and what you have done in the past, far away from us, is your concern. You are the son of your family; you carry a name from the village. It is a heritage that you have scorned for some time, but it is inalienable, and it awaits you here. Now that you have returned, you cannot discard it. I know that you will not tarnish your heritage. It is up to you to decide just how much you wish to call attention to yourself. It is not wise to meddle in other people's business; it may even be dangerous to do so. Know that here, everyone freely does as he pleases. But we always keep watch over one another, and we judge each other. However, we recognize worthiness and other qualities wherever we find them. You have spent several years in France without thinking of your parents. You were happy while they suffered. You find your mother in misery, and you show up in a nice suit, with furniture and a Frenchwoman accustomed to luxury. We are surprised and bothered by this. I imagine you thought long and hard before deciding to return

Land and Blood

because you know your country, its people, its possibilities. You have not fulfilled your duties toward your own kind. I do not reproach you, since God determines every man's conduct. Perhaps it was written that Kaci would be deprived of his child's attentions and that Kamouma would be neglected for a time. But know that, at present, you must carry on as we do, as a worthy son of Ighil-Nezman. May God put you on the right path!"

Amer understood this advice to be a reprimand. There are people who feel obliged to give advice. We listen to them out of courtesy, all the while thinking they would do better to follow it themselves . . .

V Amer realized that people back home held hostile and harsh opinions about him, but he would stand up to them and would finally be accepted. He knew that what really mattered was to be rich or to appear so. The wealthy can be excused many things, except selfishness, vanity, or stupidity. They are the ones who have no need of others. This is why there are always poor folk who flatter them, try to inspire their pity or to steal from them.

Amer's self-assuredness was taken to be a sign of his wealth. He soon had his admirers. His *karouba* was proud of its new couple. They were treated with respect right from the start, without any hesitation. Amer took advantage of this to buy back the last field his father had sold. This property meant more to him than all the others, and Hocine, the cousin who had acquired it, was precisely the one who had buried his father.

Hocine was, to sum it up, a nice man. He is still young and his face exudes good health. His regular and ordinary features make him think he is handsome; he is proud of his blue eyes and light complexion. He speaks in a pompous manner, dresses well, and likes to show off at the *djema* and the café. When anyone wishes to obtain something from him, the best way is to ask it of him in public: he cannot refuse someone when others are present.

Amer knew this about his cousin, since he has known him since childhood and had sometimes lived with him in France. He invited Hocine and some other cousins together to his home. At the end of the family meal, he asked for the field's return. Even though he was cornered like this, Hocine put a brave face on it. His eyes on Madame, he gave a flowery speech and spoke about family solidarity, honor, the intelligence and kindness of some of the young people of whom the village could be proud. He left that evening convinced that he had captivated the Frenchwoman. Amer was so happy that he tolerated Hocine's boastfulness. But Kamouma was not thrilled by this transaction and said as much to her son.

"Now that you are here, they all acknowledge you. I also think they believe that you are wealthy. They are afraid of you.

You would do better to keep your money, you will need it one day."

"I want to put them all to the test, Mother, so I know who my friends are."

"Have you not learned yet that a poor man never has friends? Your father had time enough to learn this and see them for what they are."

"And you too, Mother. God willed it."

It was always Madame who changed the subject when the discussions got too serious. As soon as she saw the son bristle and the mother lower her head, she asked what they were saying to each other. Amer told his wife that the old lady was unhappy:

"She claims that our hands are too soft to be farmers."

"Tell her that I would be happy to become a landowner. You promised me as much anyway."

"Yes, but she says that Hocine has robbed us."

"No! Why? Since he is only taking what he paid? He spoke very plainly just a while ago. On the contrary, I think he is nice. While you spoke to him in Kabyle, he answered in French. He is well mannered, you know! Isn't he the one who invited us out one day back in France? I remember it now."

"I am not arguing with that. Tomorrow, if you wish, we will go see the field. You will see the spot."

"I see! We will farm our little plot. Mother will be so happy."

Early the next morning, the new owners went down to their field. It was a beautiful day, and Kabylia is magnificent at that time of year. Our Parisian, who knew the gardens of the capital and had spent her childhood on the outskirts of the city, was acquainted with the charms of the season: birds, flowers, greenery, not to mention everything else one knows from childhood books. Nevertheless, for her, French birds all looked alike; her flowers were bright buds cultivated with love and artistically arranged. Her green spaces were geometric clumps, the vegetable plots were carefully tended, and the dense woods were accessible by paved paths. For the Frenchwoman, nature is embellished by artifice, stiff and elegant like a discreetly made-up woman in her evening gown.

To go to Tighezrane, they followed a winding, hemmed-in path that plunged relentlessly down to the bottom of the valley. From the top of the village, they could look out over a large part of Kabylia: to the north, the Aït-Djenad mountains that form an imposing barrier in front of the Mediterranean Sea. To the south, there were the Djurdjura, even more impenetrable, that seem to screen an imaginary world, very different from our own. It is a bare colossus, dark whitish gray on the crests, whose peaks often blend into the cumulus cloud cover. But in this month of April, the sky is blue, and the mountain peaks are still covered in blindingly white snow. The mountain inhabitants are treated to a grandiose spectacle of extreme strength and wild beauty. The minuscule villages that crouch down against the foot of the mountains or lie scattered along the smaller mountaintops look like fearful followers prostrating themselves before a harsh god. To the east and west, there are hills and mountains, deep and narrow valleys where rivers can barely be glimpsed before they join up with each other on the plain. This plain, moreover, is just a narrow corridor between the north and south mountain ranges. A real mountainous face!

Yet this face has its own unique features. Green is not the principal background color of this landscape. The olive tree dominates; the tall tortoise olive tree with a bluish-black color on the shiny side of the leaves and a light, almost white color on the underside. The appearance of the foliage changes with the sky, depending on the season or the time of day. The sunbeams and the play of light and shadow accentuate the relief and bring out this illusion of a face. Here, the landscape is all twinkling because the shiny leaves reflect the light. In other spots, the shadow is so thick and the leaf cover so dense that one could easily believe that the mountain inhabitants must always think it is dawn.

When the details of this landscape are examined, one sees it is not uniform. Around the villages, at the top of each ridge,

Land and Blood

the dark color of the olive trees disappears, replaced by a carpet of soft green barley shoots, in turn dwarfed by the plumed branches of oak, cherry, or fig trees. These are the Kabyle orchards, the ones for which they have kept the Latin name of *horti*. Tighezrane is precisely one such *horti*. The rough path to get there is bordered by exuberant brambles and perfumed broom trees full of small golden butterflies. Tiny flowers, white, blue, red, and yellow, grow on the embankments, covering the slabs of schist; warblers twitter and tease the passersby; women and children call out to each other in crystalline voices.

Madame cautiously follows Amer, who descends the path with a confident step. He turns around now and then to hold out his hand to her, and they chat.

Madame is wearing light-colored hose and low-heeled shoes. In her yellow crêpe dress printed with little red flowers, she looks like a kind fairy who has come to transform this rustic setting by her presence. She is slender, almost the same height as Amer. Her blond hair, silky and styled, falls to the nape of her neck. Her blue eyes are the color of pimpernels and her red lips are the color of poppies. Her face is graceful and open. It is wide more than long, with a smooth forehead, a short and centered nose, and thick and nicely arched brows. With a well-defined chin, Madame gives the impression of being strong-willed and sufficiently armed for life.

She finds Kabylia very beautiful and Tighezrane a lovely property—even though it really offers nothing to distinguish itself: three days of work, a half hectare, two triangle-shaped plots separated by a small stream used for irrigation in the summer. Madame wants to know the name of each tree: there are three orange trees at the edge of the stream; there are stocky fig trees with bare trunks and large leaves; two vines wrap around the ash trees like boas. There are also a few cherry trees and a pear tree; along the edges of the plot, outlining the triangles, runs a hedge of cactus that provides Barbary figs in the summer.

Madame is content. All in all, she is not disappointed. She expected less. They had to leave France at all costs. The miserable, poor life in Paris had lasted long enough. At least they now have a change of scenery. But other things have not really changed. She still has the same dishes, and Kamouma's shack is hardly better than the furnished hotel room they occupied. What has changed is an entire society: from a powerful and haughty humanity that did not like her, where she never mattered more than a castoff, treated like a servant or a slave. Now, she is a Cinderella, in short, who discovers a kingdom made to measure just for her, an ordinary, no-nonsense woman: the kingdom of Ighil-Nezman. All at once, she has found a world where she is raised to the highest rank, to first place. No more humiliations! Even her own self-perception has succumbed to the illusion. Now she sees herself as beautiful amid these peasant women, more beautiful than she had ever been. Her maid's dresses appear sumptuous to her; her furniture, seen in this light, is worthy of admiration. This gives her a certain confidence that inspires respect. She does not become vain from her new situation, but she is satisfied. She feels she has gained on the deal.

"I wonder if my mother isn't right," Amer says, seeing his wife lost in thought.

"Oh, she is old. She preferred to stay home. We can go back up right now if you'd like."

"It isn't that, you know. Yesterday evening she did not agree with us. Buying back the field did not appeal to her. What do you think about it?"

"But we have a beautiful garden here. It is a good deal. Besides, you are the expert. It's your country. As for me, you know I don't know anything about farming. But gardening can bring in money. Also, we are free; no more foreman or supervisor."

"No more paycheck either! Well, we can always resell it if we wish, one day."

"You know what? Since I've been here, I feel a bit like your women: they don't know much, but I know even less than them. Until I do understand, I am just along for the ride. If, one day or another, it doesn't work anymore, we'll go back to France. That's all."

"We came here with that very idea. Do you think I've forgotten?"

"It's not to remind you that I'm bringing it up. On the contrary, I've felt so happy for the past week! You know very well that I've gained a great deal by coming here with you."

"Good. At least you aren't too disappointed."

"Oh please! Put yourself in my place."

"The worst that could happen would be if we used up what we brought. Whatever happens, I hope you won't suffer here at Ighil-Nezman, not while I'm alive."

"It will be all right, you big silly. I am happy."

"In Paris, I needed to feel that I was liked. And I only had you. I know what it is like to be a foreigner. It is a pitiful state for a man."

"So! And for a woman?"

"For her as well, but perhaps less so. From the moment she has a man who looks after her, she is no longer a stranger. She becomes part of a family."

"My own family would not have rejected you . . ."

"Yes, of course not. But it is not the same thing. I cannot explain. You'll see for yourself. I just mean that here, the roles are reversed: it is up to me to love you and make you forget this exile. I will never fail in that."

"There isn't much that I miss. As for the rest, of course, I trusted you. If I didn't, it would have been better to stay in France. But don't think I am going to take advantage of the situation and become demanding. If you ask me, let's not get too many ideas in our heads. We will live simply, and we will be at peace here more so than anywhere else. So there! No more speeches! I see three ladies on the path, and I need to catch up to them. Let's go see what Mother is doing . . . How do you say it?"

"Ima."

"Yes, let's go see Ima."

VI It is less the fear of the future than a sort of disappointment that makes Amer speak this way.

He does not understand that his wife is so happy because, to him, everything seems old, abandoned, and ugly. Although he often pictured his village, its inhabitants, and lands in his mind in the least flattering light while in France, he realizes now that his imagination did not even go far enough to do the reality justice. Or is it that he sees things with new eyes? Does he see with a harsher gaze? Why, in this case, would the Frenchwoman see things differently? Logically, she should be woefully disappointed. The truth is, however, that this country has not changed. It is just that Amer's way of seeing is no longer that of a child. Now people and things no longer have that ideal glow that childhood gives them, like shiny cellophane wrappers around a gift: now he sees the roughness, the wrinkles, the cracks.

The path with all the scrub brush encroaching on it had become ridiculous. The big oak tree that he pictured as being colossal, that came to mind every time he encountered a large tree in France, did not really warrant any respect. It is still there, waiting for him for the past fifteen years with its dusty and sparse foliage, looking like a bony old man, with nothing majestic about it. The fig trees have aged but have not grown any larger. Here and there, a dry stump, twisted branches, and a sapling mutilated by animals. It is a field in distress. He senses all of this. Again, it is like a reproach. Yes, Madame is correct. It was better to leave. Well, no matter. He is stuck now. Neither contempt nor disappointment will help. He is a man back in the country that knew him as a child. There was no transition between childhood and adulthood. Like the full-grown olive tree that is ripped out of its plain to be transplanted in the stony earth of Ighil-Nezman, it will take time to recover and put down roots. All he can do is ruminate over memories. There is nothing like the recollection of the past to make the present bearable or to help it be palatable. On the other hand, one does not miss the past, because a person always feels completely changed. It is as if there had existed a separate person, one who had nothing in common with the person one is now. It is for this reason that the reproaches, stated or not, irritate Amer instead of troubling him. They are meant for another, and that is that.

What also proves that the past person has nothing in common with him now is the fact that he cannot even clearly see himself in the past. Amer searched his memories in vain; he cannot reconstitute his whole story without leaving gaps. He only has the sense that he has really been himself for the past several years. And from that point on, reasonably enough, he has nothing for which to reproach himself, although he does make excuses for the inexperienced boy he was when he left.

He will never forget this departure. It was in 1910, one morning at the end of winter. He sees himself at the edge of the village with three fellow countrymen who are now dead. Tearful relatives had accompanied the four there. He turned a desperate gaze toward his mother, and Kamouma grimaced, wringing her arms. Kamouma was still strong but her face was already etched with lines. He sees her there in his mind's eye, dressed in a *gandoura* with wide sleeves, and a woolen shawl she wove herself is pinned at her shoulders, covering her back as far down as her knees, gathered in the middle with a red flannel sash. It was the fashion at the time, peasant garb for women who slave away with their husbands, ignoring elegance, and the cold, true replicas of *fellahs*, who wore *djellabas* with wide leather belts.

Kaci was old too, but solid, holding himself straight and looking into his son's eyes, this son he was pushing toward adventure and the unknown without batting an eye. His voice remained calm. He wanted his son to depart like a man.

"Go, my son. Catch up with your friends. My blessings go with you. I have never done any wrong. The saints of our country will not abandon you."

Could he measure the void that his departure caused? He occupied all the space in the hearts of this old couple, but he was too young to know it. His anguish stemmed from the unknown he was about to face, from the sea he was about to cross, and from this society into which he headed with only the strength of his own two arms to live and to try to make something of himself. He was thinking that soon the meaning of his life would change. He imagined his future boss, the one he would have to obey, the foreman, the hard work, the pay at the end of the week, the schedule he would have to keep. Until now, he had lived so freely, and he was going to hire himself out, becoming a slave or a servant. He could not know. To make up for it, there would be entertainments, nice clothes, abundant and varied food, Sundays and holidays . . . The fellows he was leaving with had talked all about it.

It must be said that back in these pioneering days before the First World War, the Kabyles were just beginning to discover France. Until that point, they had been content to work on the large cork plantations in Philippeville or in Bône. Some went to work in the phosphate mines around Constantine or Gafsa, and most of them worked for twenty cents a day as hired hands for the French landowners around Mitidja. Only the bravest dared to cross the sea, believing they would confront great dangers and that they would be damned for having lived in a Christian land. On the other hand, they thought they would be welcomed, well paid, and respected. Upon their return, they brought back much more money than the others; they talked openly about all they had seen there, and they encouraged the others to accompany them to this new world. But generally, everyone else was skeptical and mistrustful. The idea of going to France only started to spread little by little. The most audacious were the younger men who had gone to school. Even then, they needed to find some initiate who was headed back there and who agreed to take them along. This is how Kaci had found someone to accompany his son. After all, the boy was headed for the unknown, and it took a lot of courage to let him leave like that. As for Amer, despite his impatience, he embarked on this adventure with a heavy heart.

Besides remembering his anguish at leaving, the rest is indistinct. Some insignificant details come to mind when he thinks about it: the arrival in Algiers, the public bath where he spent the night, a nighttime brawl because a man from the capital was caught stealthily feeling under the pillow of a man from the mountains; then he sees himself on the foredeck of the ship, surrounded by other Kabyles who fearfully huddled together, violently ill from seasickness. He made the crossing without getting sick. He has no precise recollection of Marseilles or of the countryside or cities that filed past beyond the train windows. Besides, he was too preoccupied by his own thoughts to think about enjoying himself. He had the impression that his traveling companions were growing distant from him, little by little, as they got closer to their destination. He waited, obstinately and with a heavy heart, for the moment when they would say to him: "We've arrived, now figure it out for yourself!" In reality, it was just his own edginess that made him think that way: he and his friends were fed up with traveling. Seated across from him, a lady wearing a lace bonnet was holding a little girl wrapped up in a brown coat. The little girl held out her tiny hands to him with a smile. Amer blushed from shyness and pleasure. The lady even began to speak to him. It seemed to him that his companions were jealous.

He can unfurl in this fashion an entire series of images, scenes, episodes. This is what constitutes his past. To understand it all, one would need to imagine an immense canvas covered with dark drawings or a gigantic roll containing several years' worth of sketches by a master using bad pencils: the whole thing is fuzzy and blurred. Here and there, a stroke stands out, having kept all its clarity and freshness—a stroke as black and neat as a recent scar, such as a specific face, harsh or smiling, a sad street with dark houses, a small and crowded room, immense, smoke-filled hangars, a barren and icy plain, endless forests . . . a painting by a true mad artist. Yet when he places himself into this picture, he really feels that it is someone else who is there. It is normal to forget.

In short, thanks to these phantoms that reappear more or less obediently, depending on the day, going along with whatever is asked, the principal outline of Amer's past, during those long years of absence, could be pieced together.

Land and Blood

As soon as he arrived at the Lyon station after a sleepless night on the train, he realized that his companions were not abandoning him. But he found himself lost in an unimaginable crush of people, in a purgatory of noise and sounds, lost in a teeming throng of a population waking up for the day. He had a hard time following the others and not losing his way. Finally, one of them took him by the hand, and all four made their way through the crowd, hesitantly, timidly, fearful, looking serious and humble. At the station exit, an incredible assortment of carriages, omnibuses, carts, wagons of all kinds, and even some automobiles! And then, the people! Children, men, and women all seemed to be hurrying to arrive at a precise destination. That was his first impression. Naturally, he saw many other things that astonished him and caught his attention, but there was no time. Only people who can understand these things can then appreciate them. He did not understand. He was filled with an instinctive fear, and he had a strong desire to get away from all of it, to go and rest in a tranquil corner, and to be alone with the people he had come with and for whom he now felt real affection.

They went down in the Metro and resurfaced again a few minutes later on a wide boulevard just as animated and just as tumultuous as the train station. Amer followed his companions, who seemed to share his unease and hesitation. They took a less crowded street and then went up a small street, turned at other intersections, and finally stopped in front of an old hotel that was tall and narrow. They went inside. The ground-floor room was also a café, and Amer saw some men from Ighil-Nezman whom he hesitated to greet at first, but it was them. His face lit up. The new arrivals were greeted with protective smiles. They sat down around a table and ordered something to drink and began to chat. Seeing himself surrounded by his own kind in this dark little room, hearing them laugh out loud and talking loudly in Kabyle, Amer felt a wave of well-being gently envelop him.

His stay in Paris was too short; his only memory is of this initial contact. He followed his companions to the mines in the north of France. There, he found an entire colony from Ighil-Nezman. All in all, everything was simple for Amer from the moment he joined up with the people from back home. The established ones did not seem to realize how much relief their welcome provided the newcomers. They knew how to put the others at ease. The only thing for the new arrival to do is to appear calm and wait for things to work out. There they were, in this small mining town, a dozen men, and Amer knew almost all of them, living together, working in the same place, sharing the same sleeping quarters, eating from the same dishes, and earning the same pay.

There were two types of Kabyle émigrés among them: the sedentary and the migratory. The sedentary ones postponed every reason to return to Kabylia. They were happy living in France and had secret reasons to spend their money. But the others always managed to uncover these secrets, because even if they refused to think of their families or to return home, they could not separate themselves from the Kabyle community and live totally apart while in France. No, they stayed with the others, lived exactly like them, and had only one additional vice. But it could be sensed that this vice was their reason for living. This group was the unchanging element of the community. Because they neglected their duty as fathers and men with family responsibilities, they made themselves helpful toward their novice countrymen. They welcomed them, supported them, advised them, and helped them get set up. They sometimes even derived a certain profit and a sense of pride from their role.

The migratory ones come and go, naturally. They get rich, buy fields, get married, and someday finally settle down back in Ighil-Nezman. They criticize the ones who remain in France. But the sedentary men do not care; they know their duty, and they do not fail at it. Let the ones who think they are so smart return to Ighil-Nezman! Others will replace them: men who are poor, young, or not too bright. How could they abandon these newcomers? Someday, other sedentary ones will be recruited from their ranks. It is a matter of destiny.

The principal character in the group was Rabah-ou-

Land and Blood

Hamouche, who had already spent ten years in France and was not thinking of returning home anytime soon. Rabah was in the prime of life. He was a hairy giant with a broad face, dark eyes, black hair, and a well-trimmed mustache. He impressed everyone with his booming voice, his powerful and easygoing appearance, and his neat dress. Rabah was the one who got the group the large room where they lived. He was the one who found them work in the mine and who served as a liaison among the offices, the police, and all the Kabyles who lived around there. He spoke French as badly as he spoke Flemish and the other northern dialects, but he made himself understood and knew how to sign his name with a capital H and R.

Rabah-ou-Hamouche was none other than Kamouma's first cousin, her paternal uncle's son. Rabah recognized Amer as his nephew, and Amer adopted this uncle without reserve, a man he had never met and had not expected to find there. Rabah became Amer's protector and mentor. He was proud to show off Amer as a young savage who knew French, but was bashful and naive. The younger man was happy to find someone he could deal with without fear or worries. After a few months, Amer changed. He forgot Kamouma, Kaci, and his village.

They lived at the end of a straight street bordered by identical brick houses, high, dark, and sad, but they appeared imposing to the young Kabyle. The men had a room on the second floor: a long room with a sooty ceiling, with one window on the gabled roof and another in the front. On the dirty, sticky wood floor, three beds were lined up. At the end of the room, there was an old armoire, a folded mattress, and all around on the floor there were bundles of laundry and blankets. Near the door there was a small table full of dishes, set next to a cast-iron stove. That is where they gathered together and took turns to wash, eat, and sleep every day after work. The image of this dormitory remains clear in Amer's memory. He spent four years there. The first year, he was not able to work in the mine. He was too young. In spite of Amer's insistence, the office refused to take him on. But the following year, his uncle got him "some papers." He changed his legal status and went down into the mine. Until that point, Amer was the cook for the group. He was paid enough, but felt humiliated doing the housework like a girl. He was afraid that his father back home would find out about it. It was bothersome for him, but Rabah told him many times that he would have to wait. The result was that during this year of relative inactivity, Amer grew, put on weight, and became a man. In one sense, he could think of himself as lucky and be grateful to the men he lived with. This was an advantage that did not go unnoticed, and they made remarks to him about it from time to time. Perhaps Amer should have been embarrassed about it. But now that he knew them all, he could stand his ground: it was a job like any other, and he had the right to respect, he told them. But still, Amer was happy when his uncle worked things out for him: yes, he would go to work in the mine; he would grow tough and strong, get dirty, and take risks like a man.

Amer often thinks of this distant period of his youth, and he is never happy about it. Besides the fact that some of his actions back then now seem ridiculous or reprehensible, there were also circumstances that evoked great bitterness and remorse in him. Whenever he thought like this, he would shrug and frown, as if to chase away a troubling idea. Those who learn about life all on their own necessarily come to resemble it. Once they are grown and have learned by experience, they are pitiless judges of themselves—not for what they are now, but for what they were. Besides, the younger he is, the more pitiless a judge a man is of his younger self. With age, everything wears away; the past falls away like dead skin, like hair and nails that break off. Finally, one becomes indulgent toward one's youth, and one forgets. Sometimes, however, a scar stubbornly remains and weighs you down under the weight of the past that it represents.

This is exactly what happened in Amer's case.

VII

Amer can never forget the emotion he felt at the first descents, the dark and gaping mouth of the shaft, the heart-rending alarm that signals the departure, the whistle of the machine, the cable that unwinds, the walls that ooze, the black holes of galleries, the heat that becomes more and more oppressive the deeper one descends. Down in the pit one feels like a man! Amer is proud: now he no longer cooks potatoes or gets the coffee ready.

However, thanks to his uncle, Amer does not start with the most difficult work. In the beginning, they had him sorting and dumping the coal into the skips alongside the weakest workers. Then he became a pit boy at the rear of a team run by a Flemish man. The stifling air, the sweat, the endless work done to the flickering light of the miners' lamps, the foreman who badgers you all the time, even all that did not make Amer miss his comfortable life of the past year. He felt like a real man; he got his pay like the others and did not take any advice from anyone. In addition to his countrymen, he came to know the people of the North; he shared their beer and food, adopted their way of speaking, and found them to be good-natured and sincere.

The men from Ighil-Nezman lodged with André, a miner whose wife ran a small café on the ground floor of the building. André was Polish; he spoke French as badly as Rabah-ou-Hamouche. They appeared to get along very well, even though they were nothing alike. Rabah was big and calm while André was lively. Amer still recalls his features: a short, stocky man with wide shoulders, built like a ram, with a thatch of red hair and a wide, ruddy face, a drooping mustache, and a wide mouth with thin lips. He got drunk every Sunday, but during the week, he only thought about work.

In the beginning, Amer mistook him for another tenant since he paid no attention to the Kabyles who lived there and brought in money for his wife's commerce. The real boss was Madame Yvonne! She was a heavyset blond with a loud laugh, but who knew how to get tough with miserly or unruly tenants. Later, Amer came to understand the situation in this house. His fellow countrymen whispered about certain things. Yvonne had been Rabah's sweetheart for a long time. It is just that Rabah was discreet. They both behaved in an irreproachable and reserved fashion when they were together in public, but with others, Madame Yvonne sometimes permitted a suggestive joke or gesture, or even a caress. When Amer came to live with his uncle, he noticed that he was very enterprising and that he spent his free time looking to meet women. He would leave the city on his bicycle and go to the outskirts. Sometimes he took the train and was gone for a day or more; he would go as far as Lille and spend his savings there. Rabah initiated Amer to the ways of "love," while the Pole taught him to drink, so much so that he took pleasure in his new life and forgot all about his old parents. At present, he does not bear a grudge against them for this. After all, he thinks, one cannot be a saint!

One day, Rabah admitted to him that he was Yvonne's lover.

"A lioness, Nephew! You can't even imagine. She would squash you. What can a runt like André do for her?"

"But isn't he your friend?"

"You're mistaken. I knew her a long time before him. We had separated."

"Ah, I see. She moved here before you did?"

"Yes. I followed her here when I found out. André became my friend. You know, it is thanks to me that they have customers. But she demands discretion; otherwise she would be capable of killing me."

In spite of this, some people knew. Some even said that little Marie was Rabah's daughter. It was just a guess. Marie did not resemble Yvonne, Rabah, or André, for that matter, with her innocent blue eyes, her blond curls, and her face as round and velvety as a peach. She was like a small fairy who brightened up the whole house, letting herself be carried around in the arms of those rough Kabyle men from the mountains, transplanted there, so far from their own dark and puny children.

Since Amer had started going down in the mine, he came to appreciate the physical strength of other men. Rabah and

Land and Blood

André were both fine specimens of vigorous men. They worked together. Amer admired them and dreamed of being on their team. No one was more impressive to Amer than a man who gladly took up his pick and got to work. How he wanted to be strong and tireless like that himself! He had already bested the weakest of the workers. Whether a job required speed or strength, it did not matter; he liked to try his hand at everything. Some who did not understand made fun of him or were annoyed by him. But he did not behave this way out of malice. Amer only wanted to prove to himself that he had the strength to do it. Besides which, he had never been so well fed in his life as he was in that period. He took to eating with the same passion he applied to his work, and he justified his being so selfish since the engineer had once told him that a good miner has to be a good eater. Amer did not have to skimp on food now. And whenever he happened to think about Kamouma, who might be grinding acorns for her flour, he quickly chased away that stray thought, dark as a bad storm cloud. Amer admired his biceps, drank beer to put on weight and to put some color in his cheeks.

It took Amer more than two years to get assigned to the team of Rabah and André. He managed to do so because André, who was fanatical about his work, understood that Amer wanted to prove himself by copying him. He recognized in Amer someone who could experience the same joy that the Polish man felt: the joy and pride of a man who scours the entrails of the earth, who refuses to rest, and whose fatigue is erased by successive victories. There were perhaps other reasons too. But Amer knew that André shared his enthusiasm. The older man had understood the younger one right from the start, and one day, not without some pride, Amer saw that the Pole had taken an interest in him. So they formed a trio. When he thinks about it now, Amer remembers himself as enthusiastic and naive, whereas André had surely premeditated his crime.

It happened in pit number thirteen. For the past week, Amer had worked with André at the end of a sloping gallery. The rest of the team was at the other end. André was tired but refused to rest. He accepted an easier task while he waited to recover his strength. The task was to send the heavily laden skips over to the coworkers at the other end, so the material could be unloaded and fill in the cavities. In return, the team sent back the carts loaded with coal. André was working the winch. Amer hooked and unhooked the wagon cars. An alarm bell signaled the working of the wagons, as well as the rest breaks. From the start, Amer busied himself with sending down the train. He knew how to operate the brakes, and the cars no longer jammed together under his watch. Nevertheless, this was actually André's job.

Amer still recalls all the details of that terrible day. They had finished their snack of buttered bread and coffee. André had stretched out, his head on his lunch bag, bare-chested and blackened, his big thighs spread out. He quickly began to snore, his mouth hanging open. Amer, with his back up against the rock wall and his feet against the wagon, his head resting in the palm of his hand, was dozing across from him. It was the moment of the day that Amer felt tired and sleepy, in spite of the coffee. Usually, a sort of sadness would come over him: he felt overwhelmed, and the same ideas returned to reproach his carefree attitude. He could not avoid it. He thought about his homeland. He saw again, on that particular day, Kamouma and Kaci far away, back there in Ighil-Nezman, cursing him, with good reason. Or at the very least, they had forgotten him, having given up waiting to receive a letter or a money order from him. He saw again the fields that he knew so well. He saw the faces of the young and old people from back there; then he saw the ones he knew who were there in France with him. He saw Si-Belkacem in the hospital, who had just had his leg amputated; Mohand-Saïd, who had a flock of kids back home and had gotten hired on under a fake name . . . He was the guy, just the night before, who had been turned in by an anonymous letter. Then he thought about this life they were living here, crowded into small rooms or shacks at the end of those narrow streets close to the mine. He had found that the Flemish had an esprit de corps, helped each other out, and hated the

Land and Blood

Kabyles. The Poles acted the same way. But as for them, the Kabyles, who, of all the groups, were paid the least, were the least educated, and needed to support each other, did nothing but fight with each other, envy each other, and denounce each other. There were more than a hundred of them. In France, they had found a way to revive their *çof* politics, showing their pride at belonging to one village or another. For those from the same village, it was pride at being from one clan and not another. Nothing had changed, in short. And under these circumstances, Amer should have been worthy of Kaci and imitated those who did not forget and kept his wallet shut tight, instead of showing off his muscles or his drinking prowess. This train of thought would usually lead him to resolve to straighten up and get back on track in his life. Sometimes he happened to doze off completely, or he stayed in a sort of half-conscious state that reminded him of having a nightmare. The alarm bell would catch him there. He would jump up, and André would tell him to release the next wagon, and he would finish waking up in the midst of the raucous sounds of the train heading off into the darkness.

This is how it occurred on that same day, except he did not hear the bell ring.

"You were sleeping," André reassured him.

"You fell asleep before me. I don't even think I really slept."

"I'm telling you that they already rang. Hurry up, they're waiting."

Then disaster hit. They listened in vain for the return signal. Under the bluish light of the lamps, Amer tried to meet the gaze of the Pole, but he was obstinate and stubbornly kept his head down.

"Well?" Amer asked.

"Okay. I'll go. Blocked probably," André muttered.

André was swallowed up by the tunnel. The small lamp he carried trembled and disappeared in the distance while Amer followed it with his gaze. As it became smaller and smaller, it became as unreal as a star, as a firefly, and then went out completely.

Amer did not have to wait long. The star reappeared, and André arrived disheveled and sweating.

"There's been an accident! I killed Rabah. He was sleeping on the tracks. His skull is crushed."

"Then they didn't ring? I was right!"

"Yes, but you're the one who worked the control. You killed him!"

"Oh, come on! You just admitted it! You tricked me!"

"No, I heard the signal. Maybe I just dreamed it. But why would I have sent off the wagon? Did I know Rabah was sleeping there? It's an accident, just an accident."

"You're a criminal!"

"I am not going to get angry," André yelled, "since you're young! After all, he is your uncle. But instead of wasting our time, listen to me: I will take responsibility for what has happened. You never touched the machine. Understood? Otherwise, it will not go well for you. Me, I can manage. You have to say that the signal rang. Yes, three times, as always. The others will manage. Your testimony will save us. Otherwise, I'll swear that I never touched the controls. You choose . . ."

From that moment on, Amer lost his mind. The same dark stain remains in his conscience and his memory to this very day. The only clear image is of Rabah's bloody skull, smashed to a pulp, with sticky strands of hair, a horrible face with a large blood clot on his mouth and nose, and his eyeball, shiny and white, stuck on his cheek. This is an image he has never been able to forget; it almost made him insane, although now, he can recall it without too much emotion. He remembers the anxious faces of the other Kabyles gathering around near the body, in the yellow light, waiting for him to explain what happened. And he did explain: he gave his statement to the investigators who questioned him.

Yes, he had heard the signal, and André had released the wagons. The Kabyles were astounded. It was the rest period. No one rang the bell. They were certain of it, just as they were certain of Amer: he was well liked by the victim. His testimony would be decisive. Would he let Kabyle blood be spilled in this cowardly fashion? His own blood, for that matter! Yet here he was, accusing his own kind and allowing his uncle to be assassinated!

In his panic, Amer had not thought about the indignation of the other Kabyles. He was accusing an entire team.

Amer spent a horrible week. He sank into a kind of stupor bordering on unconsciousness. He has no idea of what happened then. He only recalls that he was brought before the authorities (were they police? or judges?) with André. They reiterated their sworn statements. Since Amer had attached himself to the Pole, who was also afraid of the group from Ighil-Nezman, André had to get rid of the young man by sending him off to deliver a message to a friend in Arras. On the train, everyone spoke of war: it was August 2. Amer was indifferent to events. He arrived in Arras to a very crowded train station, and the same agitation reigned in the streets. People talked only of the "Krauts," the troops, and the deployment. He did not find anyone at the address André had given him. After that, Amer does not remember anything specific. How did his countrymen settle the matter? What happened at the funeral? What was going on at Madame Yvonne's? He did not even think about it. Since Madame Yvonne had returned his rent money to him, Amer had not stopped drinking.

One night, his compatriot Ramdane found him collapsed on a park bench, drunk and penniless. Ramdane was the oldest and most reasonable of the Kabyles living there. He led Amer home to the apartment as if he were a child and left him there to sleep. The following morning, Amer faced his countrymen for a proper interrogation.

This interview actually did him a great deal of good; it cleared things up for them and for Amer. He was able to pull himself together, and from then on, Amer dared to hold his head up again. His fellow Kabyles were most interested in understanding what had really happened and in learning whether or not Amer had betrayed his own blood. They also wanted to convince themselves that they really had no way of avenging the victim. That was all. As for shedding sincere tears for Rabah, he had too many faults to be truly missed. Even when they uttered the commonplace "We have lost one of our best men," it was said with a certain amount of mental reserve. Rabah was no angel!

"Yes," said Ramdane, "we have lost one of our best. We will let them know back in Ighil-Nezman. They will know that it was you, Amer, his nephew, who did not dare testify against this blood spilled in the mine. This blood cries out for vengeance. You are his closest relation here. We are duty bound to help you. But the honor of your name is in your own hands. You spoke against your uncle. Do you intend to kill André?"

"It is not about that," said another man. "Ramdane, you know the customs of our ancestors. But look at Amer now, and do not mock him. We are in France. He should have killed him right away down in the mine."

"We also could have killed him when André came over to see his victim."

"Well, there was nothing to be done back there in the mine. Just tell us, Amer, whether you heard the signal. As for me, I am certain that no one rang the bell. I was there. Speak frankly, now. Did you hear it?"

"No, I was asleep."

"You see? So, you were afraid of André?"

"No. I am the one who released the wagon."

"You!"

"I had already worked the controls other times. As on other days, André would yell over that the signal rang. I would get up, release the wagon, and we would wait. When the accident occurred and André came back to tell me, I lost my head. He threatened to denounce me if I said the signal had not sounded."

"He knew what was going to happen!"

"He told me the signal had sounded. How could he have known Rabah was asleep on the tracks?"

"I understand," Ramdane said. "Rabah always slept there

like that during siesta. The other day, in the café, someone even teased him about it in front of Madame Yvonne and André. Do any of you remember?"

So that was that. Several men recalled the remark now. Besides, during the break, André could have easily snuck over to make sure that Rabah was sleeping there as usual. André was the killer. He had it all planned. After having stewed in his jealousy for a long time, he had found a way to get rid of his rival for good.

If Amer had spoken differently, he would have been arrested. What weight would his testimony have had against that of André? They all knew well enough how things went for "Arabs." Just look at how the inquiry was carried out! Everybody wanted to close the matter. André had only one witness for his side, and poor Rabah had an entire team. But it made no difference; the matter was dropped, and André was acquitted.

"I am ready to tell them," Amer said. "Too bad if they send me to prison."

"It would be pointless, my boy," Ramdane explained. "You would be alone in this. They already told us in the office that Rabah must have wanted to kill himself. They cannot change their explanation now and say a nephew killed his uncle."

The men weighed the pros and cons; they understood that Amer had not had any other choice, and nothing could be done about it now. Kill André? That was one solution. But they had to keep in mind that they were not in their own country. They had come here for the sake of their families. They could not afford to cause trouble, poor and uneducated as they were, living in the midst of these powerful and educated people. It would be better to remain silent. Moreover, if Rabah had behaved himself, all this would not have happened. He had committed an unforgivable transgression, and the punishment was precisely this: death. André had actually acted just like a Kabyle. So why blame Amer now? God has placed a terrible burden on him, and so young too!

They spoke of fate, and they felt relieved. Amer felt a bit more at ease again in the midst of his countrymen. Each one had to put his best face forward. They would have to close ranks and not let anyone from the other villages back home know what really happened. Everyone must think it was just an accident. Besides, there was another problem worrying everyone: the war. Many of the Kabyle men were getting laid off, they were packing their bags and heading to Paris or to the south.

Soon, the newspapers broke the news of the German invasion of Belgium; people panicked and rushed out of their homes, clogging up the rail stations and the streets. Endless convoys of soldiers passed. It was a week of extraordinary confusion. Amer did not even have a chance to recover from his experience. None of the men from Ighil-Nezman were even thinking about him anymore. It was every man for himself. Some had already fled the area, but not without first taking the salary they were owed. As for Amer, he continued to wander around, caught in the middle of the noisy crowds as if in a strange world, only returning home to sleep.

One evening, he did not find anyone back at the apartment: the rest of his compatriots had fled, not even bothering to take their belongings. Down below, Madame Yvonne was alone with her daughter.

Amer has only a dim, confused memory of that last night spent at Madame Yvonne's. They were drinking quite a bit and speaking openly to each other. Little Marie was clearly irritated to see them so close to one another, seated at the same table in front of a bottle, with the door closed. She understood. She was twelve years old then. Finally, sulking, she left them alone. Amer recalls the scene like a hazy dream.

Yvonne acknowledged her relationship with Rabah, as well as André's jealousy. She had stood up to André about it. She was no longer afraid of him and would not let him come back home.

VIII

After the accident, Amer had many adventures, some difficult years, and some very bad moments. On several occasions, he came close to death, so close, in fact, that he no longer even feared it.

In early September, the Germans, who had already invaded France, found him in Douai. He was captured along with a few young Kabyle compatriots and sent to Germany as a prisoner of war. He came to know the forced labor and mistreatment of several camps. He spent five years in a cursed country, on a frozen and misty plain where he thought he would die. And yet, he did return!

Never in the course of this period did he find so much as a friend or anyone at all to show him kindness or take pity on him; not a single kind gesture or word that could have warmed his heart came his way. He was alone, in the midst of thousands of people who jostled each other, treated each other harshly, tricked each other, and only pretended to like each other. He learned, little by little, that human existence is "a constant kick from a horse," as the Kabyle proverb says.

With the end of the war, he returned to Paris, as did many others. He was happy to have survived. He thought he could start over again, be happy, as in his adolescence. He also tasted a bit of the general euphoria of a victorious people. With the war over, peace was at first like another type of madness, one of physical joy, just like nature is reborn after the winter snows finally melt. But Amer did not feel much like a victorious man. He could now only wrap himself up in caution and mistrust, like some worried people who see danger everywhere or like desperate people who have failed at their own suicide. He was a wrecked and pitiful man without spirit or direction. He needed to recuperate.

Many of his fellow countrymen, prisoners like him, returned home to their country to immerse themselves again in their milieu, to live the same life as their countrymen for a while, to rediscover a sense of purpose in their miserable existence and their periodic emigrations. They saw their relatives, their "friends," their "enemies," the *çofs,* and the land. They built a house or got married and then went back to France, this time with specific goals in mind. For the Kabyles, the years after the war were a period of unprecedented prosperity: everyone was hiring, they were not rejected, and salaries kept rising. Those who worked as street vendors or chose shady businesses quickly managed to acquire small fortunes that they would return back home to spend with great fanfare and haste so they could rush back to France. Amer did nothing. He was in no hurry to return to Ighil-Nezman. Still, whenever he thinks about the past, this period is still the one that leaves him the least bitter.

"Up until 1922," Amer says again and again, "I was not normal."

It is just that his position was not very stable. He found life to be absurd. The way of living for his compatriots, first of all, gathering together, here and there, always as an enclave, some fiercely saving their pay so as to later on buy up a neighbor's plot of land or a piece of his yard, wearing themselves out like beasts of burden, stingy, belligerent, petty, and then once back home, they became self-important and selfish. But some lived without worries or reserve, wasting their pay in a single shot, ending up wretched again and again, cursing their fate instead of blaming themselves.

After moving around four or five times, and having worked in about ten different places, Amer decided, in 1922 precisely, to settle down in Barbès, at 97 Myrha Street, at Madame Garet's. Was this a fortuitous encounter? Today, he believes it was: he sees this as his salvation!

Amer was looking for a room to rent, and Madame Garet ran a small hotel with twenty-four rooms. All of the rooms were let to North Africans, but no Kabyles. They were backward, dark-skinned, poorly dressed, coarse people, only speaking their guttural and hoarse Arabic. This was precisely what Amer needed: to feel a bit superior, to recover some of his self-esteem and confidence. If need be, he might pass himself off as a European and look down on these fellows, although, come to think of it, these men would have probably wondered why a real *roumi* would want to live there with them. In any case, he felt right at home from the start at Madame Garet's.

Land and Blood

It was on the evening of his payday that he happened, by chance, to stop by this café. It was a Saturday, naturally. He was wandering far from his lodging, as he often did. He would go from one bistro to the next, drink a glass of red wine, always just red wine, and then leave again with a worried look. That night, he had started at La Chapelle Square. Next, he came to Myrha Street and went into Madame Garet's establishment. Maybe it was just a coincidence, but fate does not choose.

"Good evening, Madame," Amer said at he went up to the bar. "A glass of red wine, please." After taking a drink from his glass, he asked: "You wouldn't happen to have a room for rent, would you?"

"No, sir. There is nothing left. Lucienne!" she called. "There's someone here looking for a place. There aren't any, right?"

Lucienne came out from the dark alcove that might have been the kitchen, ending just in front of the counter. She was a rather young woman, but homely as could be, brunette and as stocky as a man. She was a nice woman, nevertheless, with a mouth that was too big, a short nose, and a pink scar running across her chin like a single wrinkle. The boss was dressed all in black, short and chubby, but vivacious and attentive. She was the only one working the bar, serving the twenty or so noisy customers ordering drinks, playing dominos, banging on the tables, endlessly laughing, and arguing among themselves.

"But yes, Mama," Lucienne said. "Number four will be available after Monday. Joseph, the tall black man, is leaving."

"Oh, that's right. I had forgotten. Well, there you are: we will have a room on Tuesday. Will that work?"

"Thank you, Ma'am. That will be fine. It will give me time enough to move. I can pay you right away if you'd like. And I have my papers, too. You'll give me a little receipt, right?"

"Whatever you want. You see, I only have North African tenants. But I am not complaining, right, Lucienne? Besides, I've known them for a long time. But not like now. I used to just see them from a distance and I didn't like them much when I lived in C . . . ."

"Well, how about that! You were in C . . . ?"

"Yes, a little place in the north, right near Lens."

Land and Blood

"I know it too. When were you living there, if you don't mind my asking?"

"Before the war, of course."

"Do know the Moulin Café, by any chance?"

"I even knew Madame Yvonne."

"What a coincidence! Listen, Madame, we are old acquaintances. I don't recognize you now, but I must have seen you there back then. Allow me to offer you a 'pint,' as we used to say back there. Since you know Madame Yvonne, it must be the hand of God Himself that guided me to your place. It must be! I have looked everywhere for a room with no luck. I come in here, and I find a place. Ah! We are from the same village, then, Madame. I don't ever want to leave your place."

"Did you live there a long time, Sir?"

"Yes, a long time. That's where the Krauts grabbed me. But I didn't dare go back there again. The memory of all that is still fresh. Maybe that's why . . . Well, all the same, I'm glad to know you're from there."

"Me too. Now that I think about it," she said, "you do look a little familiar to me."

"You're sure you know her?

"Madame Yvonne? But of course! And many others from back there. We'll have time to talk later."

"Fine. Say no more, I see you have a lot of customers. Thanks for the room. Good night, Ma'am. Goodbye, Miss."

With that, Amer left hastily, overwhelmed by this meeting.

He moved into Madame Garet's hotel right away and did not leave it until he left to return to Kabylia for good. At her establishment, in a sense, he found himself again, little by little; he began to live a new life: a satisfactory but completely ordinary life.

From the very first day, during the meal (she had invited him), Madame Garet mentioned the people they knew. They spoke of André and even of Rabah-ou-Hamouche, whose tragic death she recalled. Her husband was a policeman. Amer thought that she must have seen him back then, so young and in shock at the police station. Madame Garet had not liked

André anyway, and she really believed that he had killed Rabah out of jealousy.

So Madame Garet knew Madame Yvonne! This, then, was a link between the past and the future. The war, the labor camps in Germany, added nothing to this fortunate string of events. Nothing, except for the accumulation of suffering that makes a man modest by obliging him to recognize his own weakness. He then learned that little Marie had suffered as much as he had. Amer is certain about it: Divine Providence had a hand in it all. Amer and Marie today can be grateful to the pleasant innkeeper, although in the beginning her attitude was a bit reticent. Amer recalls that for an entire month, she left him hanging. No doubt she wanted to examine him. Did she mistrust him? Was she afraid that he had some nefarious plans, especially once she learned that Rabah was his uncle? Yet each time, she was the one who got him talking about Yvonne and Marie. But everything was fine from the moment she discovered why he wanted to locate Marie and her mother. One night, he told her all about his past life, his sufferings and torments. She was moved to tears. On another night, in turn, she told him that she had seen the young girl again.

Since Rabah's death, Amer had been waiting for a miracle, some unlikely or unexpected chance that would let him make up for or repair some of the damage he had done. In his mind, little Marie was none other than the daughter of his victim; she was a Kabyle, a cousin, in fact!

They had been drinking together on that night. It had been his payday. Lucienne had left that morning. Madame Garet no longer held back what she knew about the other two women. She wanted nothing better than to help Marie and bring her over to her place. But Amer would have to take that responsibility himself, since the whole matter was rather delicate.

"Let's just say that she is with another man. He has a hold on her. I saw her again two years ago, right here, in fact. She was dressed very well; so was the fellow with her. She had left her mother's place. We chatted together, and she even spent the night here. They left the next day. Then I ran into her again, not too long ago. I almost did not recognize her! She tried to avoid me. She was in a pitiful state: thin and poorly dressed. The poor girl! She had had a child, I think. I wondered if the other man hadn't abandoned her. You know that she is not of age yet. Not for much longer, but she still is a minor. Myself alone, I can't do anything for her. I would have trouble with the police. Not to mention that I don't want any problems with her 'protector.' They live around here, but she doesn't go out often. I'll tell you where she lives. You could try to see her. You only need to go to Polonceau Street and hang around there, not far from the boulevard. There is a small café on the left. You'll surely see her there . . ."

In this way, Amer managed to see Marie again. While he was walking toward Polonceau Street, one Sunday morning in August, practically six years to the day after the accident in the mine, something told him he was on the brink of another existence. With every fiber of his being he hoped that this new stage of his life would be less tormented, more reasonable, more dignified. For the first time, perhaps, he had a goal, and he was not afraid; he was going to see Rabah's daughter with the certainty that his victim would have approved . . .

Amer-ou-Kaci could stop recalling his past right then and there. There would, of course, be an entire novel to write about what his life was like with Marie, back in France, after that moment, their happiness, their concerns, the difficult or harrowing moments, the struggle they had, both of them, to ensure their peace and happiness. Then, at the end of it all, how could he tell of the inexplicable nostalgia that made him leave France to answer the call of his native "land"? But what would be the point? From that moment on, nothing matters in his eyes except to return to Ighil-Nezman, to be among his own kind, and to take his place there. He is there with Marie, Yvonne's and, no doubt, Rabah's daughter. They have their whole future before them.

IX The Aït-Hamouche are proud of their past. Everyone knows that their ancestor cleared the first plot of land, plowed the first furrow, and built the first house on the hill of Ighil-Nezman. Now every year, after the first rainstorm of October, one of the Aït-Hamouche must get his oxen and plow a symbolic furrow. Only then can the *fellah* get to work. It is an homage freely given to the village founder, an old tradition that today's Aït-Hamouche do not even look upon with vanity. Nonetheless, once a year, everyone must be reminded that this clan is still important; the rich and powerful families of the village pay their respects on that day, as do all the others, to the Aït-Hamouche.

As for the rest, this is the only point of village history that everyone agrees upon: the Aït-Hamouche are the oldest family. After that, each *karouba* creates its own mythology, in which the best roles are reserved for clan members. The occasional narrator will always refer to the courage, virtue, strength, or diplomacy of his ancestors; if he does not speak ill of the others, it is simply out of discretion. The successive generations conscientiously transmit (adding something of their own) the imaginary tales of their past glory. The final result is that each group is proud of its name. But if someone tried to write the history of Ighil-Nezman according to people's oral histories, there would be as many versions as there are families. As we do not have any material remains or written documents, an impartial historian would have to give up on the idea, unless he could arrive at a sociological consensus based upon contemporary observations and conjecture. However, as far as the recent past is concerned, it is possible to sully it a bit, but not to completely deny it. In this way, an objective historian could learn, for example, just by asking anyone, who the Aït-Hamouche family had been until just recently. They were a good family, all in all, having the same weight as a *karouba* because they grew and branched out.

One of the branches of this family apparently had reached its height of glory at the end of the nineteenth century, when it had as its leaders three brothers, known to today's generation only through the stories told about them.

Slimane, the eldest, had five daughters and no male heir. He was a *fellah* who never made a mistake in his diagnostics. The others consulted him for any question related to sowing, planting a tree, or pruning. He had memorized the agricultural calendar and could calculate better than a *marabout*. He knew the wrong week for planting legumes, the three days that might rot trees, or the period during which pruning could damage a tree. He could predict snowfall and freezes. He knew all the proverbs that had the same weight as laws, and he could decipher all the changes in the weather. He knew how to observe birds, insects, and animals that could in turn teach him after their fashion. He was an accomplished farmer, and during his lifetime, it was easy to allow him to be the one to plow the first furrow of the season. It is said that he was very strong and hairy; he ate like an ox and worked like one too. His daughters were all married off young. None of them was very attractive, but they were all solid, sturdy, and hardworking. No doubt they would bear beautiful children.

The second brother was named Saïd. He lived in the shadow of his elder brother. He was a smaller, weaker copy of the eldest, perhaps a bit more alert and nervous. He was more fortunate than the elder as well: he was the father of a handsome son and had no daughters. The boy was named Rabah and resembled his uncle. Later, Saïd had another son, but meanwhile, Slimane died, and the child was given the name of his late uncle, whereas Rabah was the namesake of the grandfather.

The youngest of the three brothers was named Ali. He was spoiled as a child. Tall like Slimane, but with more delicate features, light skin, and blue eyes: he was the family's pride and joy. He was never refused beautiful clothes or spending money. All of his excesses were pardoned. He was one of the first Kabyles to go to France. He also made the pilgrimage to Mecca. He had friends in many Kabyle villages and was known to the colonial administrator, the justice of the peace, and the policemen. He often went to Algiers, where he claimed to know important people. He never worked the land, but no one even thought to reproach him for that. He was one of the leading men, not just of his village but of the whole tribe. His brother Slimane pampered him, and Saïd was proud of him. Ali did not expect to have any children. He was sterile, or maybe it was his wife. In any case, he was not concerned about it.

The family owned the most beautiful plots in Ihgil-Nezman. Moreover, thanks to his connections, Ali obtained a permit to open a Moorish-style café. It was the first one in the village. Ali built a large room for his café, located in a garden at the entry to the village, bordering the road. The building is still there, although it is falling into ruins. In the past, besides the large central room, the café boasted a straight roof, topped by a chimney (the first in the village), its façade impeccably whitewashed, with a green painted door set into a solid frame. There was a large, enclosed courtyard, shaped like a trapezoid because of the two paths that bordered it, which served as a terrace for the café. Today, weeds grow in the courtyard, and their stems dry out and die without even having been trampled. The stucco walls of the courtyard are cracked, and the roof has worn away; the whole place now appears small, bent, and shriveled up like an overbaked piece of pottery or a handsome face ravaged by wrinkles and wizened by age.

If that café could speak, it would sing the praises of the Aït-Hamouche! All the strangers passing through the village found a place to stay there. The Aït-Hamouche lodged the rich and poor alike: beggars, peddlers, friends, friends of friends. They never refused a guest. The courtyard could tell of all the couscous eaten and spilled there and of all the coffee that was drunk there. In the past, strangers who, for one reason or another, stopped to spend the night in Ighil-Nezman had to beg door to door for a bowl of soup and had to spend the night sleeping on the cold floor of the *djema*. Then there was the café. Each night before closing, Saïd, who was the manager, or later his son Rabah, or after that Slimane, counted the strangers staying the night and would bring them a large plate of couscous, and then they would be allowed to sleep in the café's main room, under the watchful eye of one of the waiters, after the till had been emptied for the night. The café became an inn that was free of charge, like a providential refuge. It was spoken of very highly for twenty kilometers around, and Ali, the real boss, had friends everywhere.

Only God is eternal! What remains today of the Aït-Hamouche and their prosperity? Slimane, the eldest, died first, a long time before the others. Then it was Saïd's turn, leaving his sons Rabah and little Slimane, the namesake of the first one. Ali still represented the family with dignity, running the café, assisted by Rabah, and maintaining his network of connections. By then, he was rather old, but still one of village's dignitaries. One fine day, Rabah left for France and never returned. It was an inexplicable departure that foreshadowed the family's decline. That left the young nephew and the old uncle, full of wisdom and experience. When Rabah died in the mine, *by Amer-ou-Kaci's own hand,* Ali's consternation was great: Kamouma was the eldest of his late brother's five daughters.

Kamouma was not much younger than her uncle Ali, the youngest of his family. During her father's lifetime, she was never abandoned by the Aït-Hamouche. But afterward, when the others had numerous nieces and nephews, they were not able to look after all of their relatives. As often happens with women who are married and have children of their own, Kamouma grew distant from her own family. She became an Aït-Larbi because her husband was an Aït-Larbi. When she was alone and abandoned, it was the Aït-Larbi who failed in their duty to her. The Aït-Hamouche were not blamed.

The village learned of Rabah's death in early September 1914, when the miners from Lens returned home to the village. Ali called together a family council: his nephew Slimane, Rabah's brother, as well as the numerous Aït-Hamouche cousins all attended. The circumstances of the death were carefully analyzed in order to decide upon the correct course of action to best preserve their sense of honor. It was not possible to condemn young Amer. No vengeance could be hoped for. They would have to be reasonable about the matter, and Ali, in spite of his cleverness, had to agree that a nephew of the family could not be killed. But it was no longer possible to continue to think of him as a member of the family: Kamouma and Amer were publicly disowned. The old woman was deeply affected by this, even though the Aït-Hamouche had already abandoned her a long time ago. She had just lost her husband, and her son, who should have supported her in her old age, had only brought her disgrace. It was too unjust. Her pride rebelled and enabled her to shrug off the family that had become so unrelenting toward her.

Ali and Slimane wished that the criminal had died in the war, that he would never come back to the village, and that all would be forgotten. But a few years later, ill and feeling that his end was near, Ali spoke to his nephew Slimane and explained to him what his duty should be. He said that the Aït-Hamouche had never been cowards. Old Ali extracted a promise of vengeance from Slimane, in secret, before God. This eased his last few moments in this world, but would come to weigh heavily upon Slimane's remaining years.

Slimane witnessed the end of a wealthy and respected family. He saw the demise of his father, his brother, and then his uncle, who took with them the best properties. He found himself alone, a feeble heir to an enviable past, but the future only promised him suffering and poverty. Ali had lived quite well. He died at just the right time, leaving many debts but never himself having known hardship. The café was closed, although it remained in Slimane's possession, along with the attached garden and the village house. He was also able to save a few small plots located at a distance from the village.

Like his uncle, Slimane had no children. People said it was a curse, that the family was destined to die out, since in earlier times, they had taken advantage of their strength and that this warranted punishment. It is also widely known that all those who have controlled the fate of the village, who have been rich and powerful, always come to a bad end and that the good they may have done can never outweigh the abuse and wrong-doing. The newly powerful people watch this decline with barely concealed smugness, and the poor folk merely observe the reversal of fortunes with calm indifference.

Besides, Slimane did not care for the hypocritical compassion of people. The only person he was responsible for was his wife. He resigned himself to living like the poor, having only the memory of past wealth that would allow him to hold his head up and scoff at the rich. He was the malicious gossip of the village, criticizing the upstarts, slandering those whom others praised, claiming to know the faults, weaknesses, defects, and origins of every family, and he placed everyone else's family at a lower rank than his own. People knew he was belligerent and mean. They preferred to avoid him. It had become very awkward for anyone to talk with him. He was left to his own devices. With him, other people were afraid to compromise themselves. Slimane did not care if he provoked or injured people since he was used to fights. It was not difficult to get the upper hand with him. But even when he was knocked down, he continued to hurl insults. He was often compared to a toad, a nasty creature that gets you dirty if you touch it and that bothers you even if you do not. He was a small, thickset man with a square, bony face from which small red eyes glared out. He had an unpleasant face that looked stubborn and stupid. His whole head expressed aggressiveness, but it was not that frightening since it sat atop an ordinary, smaller man with gnarled and stunted limbs: he looked more like a tadpole than a toad!

His Aït-Hamouche cousins could not stand him, since he did not treat them kindly. He knew it was useless to expect anything from anyone, so he decided he had no need of anyone else and he allowed himself to be perfectly frank. In fact, he went beyond frankness, and for this reason, Slimane was despised.

Slimane was much younger than his brother, Rabah; when he left for France, Slimane was still a child. Nevertheless, he had known his older brother well, and his death left an empty space in his heart. Oh! If only Rabah were still alive, then there would still be a chance to revive the family. How could he ever forgive fate for killing him? How could he bear Amer-ou-Kaci, a nephew who had been fate's tool? The proverb was indeed accurate: "Whoever raises a nephew raises a serpent for his own neck."

Amer's return surprised everyone. He was thought to be lost for good. Slimane, however, was not surprised. He became ill over this turn of events. He had hoped to nurse a pointless hatred toward his nephew. He had hoped never to have to see him there right in front of him again and be obliged to act or, on the contrary, to do nothing and let others think that he had no honor. When it was just a matter of snubbing Kamouma, he had carried it off magnificently: the snake's mother! It had been easy to reject her. All of the Aït-Hamouche went along with it. It suited everyone in that fashion, anyway. But now, it was different. He knew that his cousins would not follow him and that they would leave him to seek vengeance on his own. They would find plenty of excuses: Amer had not purposely killed him, etc. He knew their arguments. They had already spoken this way in the past. Even old Ali himself had been hypocritical like this when he had to find a reason that would save face. But afterward, Slimane had spoken about it with his uncle in private, and the older man had been uncompromising: "Amer cannot be forgiven for his testimony. In this affair, it is not just a matter of what the Polish man did. The real adversary is Amer." The matter had been given a great deal of thought. Ali, before his death, obtained the promise he sought. But perhaps neither one of them seriously thought the day would come when this promise would have to be carried out!

Naturally, from the very first day, Slimane declared himself the young man's enemy. The cousins all welcomed the return of Kamouma's son, either when they chanced upon him in public or at his home. To avoid suspicion, the smartest ones went directly to Kamouma's and reconciled with her at the same time. Kamouma received them with an exaggerated politeness, with a hint of irony. But not Slimane. He stayed at home, avoided the café and the *djema* for two or three days. It was known that he had not forgotten anything, and from that day on, Amer had an enemy. Public opinion watched and waited, analyzed, and guessed at what Slimane's intentions would be. This in turn both flattered and frightened the man since he felt that, for once, people were taking him seriously, seeing him as a real Aït-Hamouche! On the other hand, he recognized that public opinion was backing him up against a wall. He would have to act. That is what frightened him! Curse him? Sure. But meet his enemy face to face, cut him down, and acquit himself with honor, thereby taking a risk? That was another matter. He had never thought it through. The truth is that everyone knew Slimane was capable of showing his hatred; it was in his nature to find reasons not to like anyone. But everyone knew he was incapable of following through.

Everyone thought Amer would not be in danger from such a man. He had been informed about the situation before he returned home. Kamouma talked of Rabah's death on Amer's first day back home, admitting it was a question of *mektoub*, and reminded him that the family had coldly disowned him: "Just an excuse, they are bluffing." Kamouma spoke to Amer about Slimane with a great deal of scorn.

"Don't worry about that man. His insides are rotten from spitefulness. He is a chicken-livered man who cannot act. God did well not to give the ass horns like the bull," said Kamouma.

X In short, the whole affair was old. Amer understood that he need not worry too much about it now. In the past, he had suffered greatly because of it, until the day he was reunited with Marie, his cousin. Since then, he has had no reason to reproach himself: he is paying his debt. Marie, however, never wanted to take this cousin business seriously. Now, neither one of them cares about it anymore. Still, it would be best not to speak of it here in Ighil-Nezman. Who could recognize Marie as the chubby little doll, the landlady Yvonne's daughter, after so many years? There are only two of them now, men who had lived in C . . . back then, two old men, naturally. One is blind, but the other, Ramdane, is the one who brought Amer back home that night and got him to relate the whole story of what happened in the mine. Ramdane is now Slimane's father-in-law, but back then, he had no ties to the Aït-Hamouche. He alone would be able to recognize Marie, if she had not changed so much.

Ramdane is very worried about Amer's return. He knows how touchy his son-in-law can be. He sees how Slimane's cousins have abandoned him, a bit out of fear but also just because they despise him. They want to show him that they think he is incapable of doing anything. But by this behavior, they are driving Slimane to do something rash. Ramdane's role is clear: to calm his son-in-law and prove to him that he has no reason to resent Kamouma's son. If he can achieve this, then many people will be disappointed to see Amer and Slimane renew their blood ties and accept what has happened, and then they can return to a normal uncle-nephew relationship.

First, Ramdane explained to Slimane in detail what had unfolded that day in the mine. He downplayed the importance of Amer's testimony and reassured him that the real culprit had been the Polish man and that, as far as he knew, André must be dead by now. Ramdane emphasized to Slimane that he and Amer, Kamouma's son and the grandson of the great Slimane, were the only remaining Aït-Hamouche. They were not going to lay traps for each other, after all!

At each occasion, Ramdane presented his arguments in a

different light. He did not do this out of malice, but rather he was so determined to avoid any incidents between the two men that he became Amer's defense attorney, and he sincerely believed in his innocence. For three days he did not leave Slimane's side. By the end of that time, his daughter was able to repeat her father's words to her husband. Together, they succeeded in soothing Slimane.

Of course, Slimane understood all this. The explanation was reasonable. But he would have preferred not to have to convince himself of the reasons, not to find himself in this situation. Since Amer's return, he had lost his haughtiness. Act as if nothing had happened? Deep down, his father-in-law annoyed him by talking about it so much. He saw himself as helpless to act. Ramdane was holding out a lifeline to him, and he had no choice but to grab it.

Slimane had nightmares and confusing, unclear dreams. One morning, he told his wife about the dream that had just awoken him with a start: he found himself in the café courtyard; it was full of customers like in the old days. He was a customer himself, seated on a mat. A young man in a black *burnous* was walking among the guests, serving them drinks. He knew it was his brother, Rabah. He could not see his face, which was hidden by the hood of his *burnous*. Suddenly he found himself alone on the mat. The café was empty. Someone held out a serving platter, it was Amer. The man in the *burnous* had disappeared. When Slimane reached for the cup, he saw the face of his uncle Ali draw close to his own and grimace in anger, blocking everything else. That is when he woke up, terrified. Chabha-ou-Ramdane, his wife, reassured him that it was just a dream and a good one at that. Slimane was hardly convinced. He thought about the promise he had made to his uncle. Was not this dream a reminder and a sinister warning? His whole existence from now on would be poisoned because the mere sight of Amer would remind him of his brother, his uncle, and his promise. It was no longer a question of what other people thought. He did not care at all about that. He knew his fellow countrymen, and, if need be, no one would gain anything by criticizing him since each one had his own weakness. But would he be able to appease these dead men, to quiet the voice in his head that rebuked him? Only on this condition could he accept being a coward.

Since the meaning of his dreams was not clear, he decided to consult a dervish. He spoke to Ramdane about it. Fearing the outcome, Ramdane tried unsuccessfully to discourage his son-in-law from taking this step. They left together one morning, first going to the cemetery, as custom dictated. Slimane walked fourteen times (one generally walks seven times in one direction and seven times in the opposite direction) around Ali's grave with an egg in his hand; he spoke out loudly to his uncle's spirit and called upon him to be present at his meeting with the dervish, and then they left. It was a good distance away. Ramdane had to drag himself along, as old as he was, behind Slimane because he wanted to know the pronouncement and, if need be, interpret it in such a way as to avoid any conflicts.

They walked for about two hours across a mule track that led them to the river, zigzagging between boulders and oak trees; next, they started the climb up the other slope of the deep valley, taking a straight path that led between the olive trees. They arrived at the village of Si-Mahfoud, a picturesque village perched at the top of an enormous outcropping of rock upon which, as if by a miracle, a prodigious patch of prickly pear cactus held on, giving the whole picture a slightly strange, greenish tint. It was a very small village inhabited only by *marabouts*, men of religion and *baraka* who are quite at home here in this unchanging landscape of gray rock and sickly greenery.

This is where all sorts of amulets, exorcisms, and invocations to the dead are made. In the small mosque, situated in the middle of the cemetery at the entry to the village, the ill and infirm come and stretch out on the mats to pray for a cure. This is also where the *cadi* and the magistrate come to take the oath of defendants each time there is a case without enough proof or witnesses to issue a judgment. In all, it is a village whose renown and reputation are known for leagues around.

When they arrived at the village, Ramdane and Slimane

stopped a moment at the mosque to kiss a corner of the wall. Next, they were brought before Si-Mahfoud. They were fortunate to find him available on this April morning when work in the fields keeps everyone busy. He received them without delay, in a simple fashion, in his home. Si-Mahfoud disliked pretentiousness. He appeared confident and sincere. His ancestors all had this gift of second sight, and apparently the family had been greatly esteemed in their own village. When one realizes the extent to which selfishness, jealousy, and malice can be present in some *marabout* villages, one is forced to admit that the esteem granted to Si-Mahfoud is well deserved. It must also be said that Si-Mahfoud never dabbled in amulets (each one has his specialty, after all) and that no one in his village could rival him except through the use of trickery.

He was in the habit of sitting upon a stone bench, behind the courtyard entrance, facing his house. When he judged that the villagers were important, he invited them to sit down upon the same mat as himself, and he engaged them in small talk while his wife prepared coffee. Naturally, this favor was only granted to men. Women visitors were never invited to sit with the *marabout*. Squatting on the ground, they humbly listened to the holy man's message, then rose, slipped their *ouada* under his mat, and leaned over the venerable head of Si-Mahfoud, who, impassive, let them leave.

After the holy man indicated where they should sit and called for coffee, Ramdane and Slimane understood that they were welcomed. This gave them confidence. Si-Mahfoud was an imposing man: he was tall, dressed all in white, seated austerely with his back against a large cushion stuffed with wool. The hood of his *burnous* was pulled up slightly over his turban, revealing a tanned face, regular features, impressive with his gray beard, dark eyes with a deep and stern gaze. His legs were crossed under his *gandoura,* and he held a chaplet with shiny beads on his knee. All that would be required to make a person feel lost, condemned, and ready to beg his pardon would be for him to put a bit more severity in his unwavering gaze and make a bad-tempered gesture. But when he received you well, he immediately exuded serenity, and you could leave relieved of your burden.

After a moment discussing pleasantries, the meeting itself could take place. Si-Mahfoud took the egg in his hands and studied it at length. One must not speak anymore, only listen attentively; no interruptions or questions were permitted; no attempt to solve the riddle of the obscure words he was about to utter would be made. The visitors were aware of this. The *marabout*'s lips moved rapidly; his eyes plunged into the egg as if he saw some fascinating spectacle in it. He ran the prayer beads between the tapering fingers of the hand that held it. A strange presence seemed to slip into their midst, brushing against them softly like the touch of a silent wing. They were ready to believe in a miracle.

Then Si-Mahfoud began to speak: "We are old and worn out. Why did you weary us by wandering in the ravines? Our knees ache, it was hard to follow you here. We need to rest . . ." It was true. The two pilgrims had gotten lost around the riverbank; they had found the route very difficult; they too had thought about the effort they imposed upon the dead man. They were expecting this reproach. ". . . Whom do I see here now? A venerable old man, with a white beard and red cheeks, wearing a yellow turban with white flowers, and a camel-hair *burnous*. Yes, sit down there on the mat, right in the middle. What is that you say? We cannot hear your murmurs; you are sad but not wrathful. But you are not alone anymore. Who is the other who followed you? What does he want? Yes, he is your elder, wearing moccasins, with his hands and feet dirty from God's blessed soil. He is a *fellah*. What does he want? He prevents you from speaking . . . He covers your mouth? Wait! Let him speak, then. Do not leave! Listen . . ." Si-Mahfoud remained motionless, his head down, straining to listen. Then he suddenly sat straight up in surprise: "It is finished," he said. "Did you understand? They have left. Someone came with him who wanted to prevent him from speaking. Sometimes it happens that way. You must know the reason why."

Yes, Slimane knew very well what the reason was. He

anticipated that Ali would not speak, that his uncle Slimane, Kamouma's father, would hamper him, in order to protect his grandson. So everything happened as Slimane had foreseen. He had not invited his other uncle's soul along for the journey, but since their graves were right next to each other, he must have made the fourteen turns around both of them. The unspoken invitation had still been valid. He had suspected as much since this morning. As for the rest, it could be said that the *marabout* had read Slimane's thoughts like an open book. He had described his uncles exactly as he imagined them himself at the very moment Si-Mahfoud spoke; their behavior did not surprise him: he was even expecting it. There was nothing to say. Si-Mahfoud was a great *marabout*, and his *baraka* was great. He knew what people held in their hearts!

His sternness was also widely known by all. It was well-known that for some supplicants whose consciences were indeed burdened, he reserved a terrible reception that appeared to them to be a foretaste of what awaited them after their deaths. On the contrary, with Slimane and Ramdane, he had been pleasant and wanted to make Slimane happy by predicting his future: "I see you are troubled, my son," he said. "I know what causes your worries, but you will be granted a great joy a year hence. A white lamb bleats behind you; he bleats with joy because you offer him all of your love."

Ramdane and Slimane exchanged a look of satisfaction. They were to be rewarded for their efforts. Then, feeling more at ease, the father-in-law explained to Si-Mahfoud the reasons for their visit, the ties that linked Slimane to the criminal, and the promise made to Ali. The *marabout* beamed. Once again, he had triumphed; he had not spoken without cause.

"Everything you say we already know. Why bother with the details? Is our oracle by any chance unclear? You have understood, have you not? Why the invited soul could not speak? It is quite clear," the *marabout* said.

"Yes, our master. Only, what should Slimane do? Is he released from his oath? Must he keep it?"

Land and Blood

"And you come to ask Si-Mahfoud's counsel, you wicked man!"

"Oh, pardon me," Ramdane begged, now regretting his audacity.

"You should have my curse! The young man is wiser, keeping his gaze lowered, not daring to speak."

"For a week I have sought only to make him forget and forgive."

"Quiet. He has no need of your advice. Listen, my son! Once there was a wise and learned sheikh (there is no one more wise or learned than God). This saintly man lived in poverty and shared with the young the knowledge that God had permitted him to acquire through his brilliant intelligence. He was loved and admired. The sultan became jealous of him. One day, he summoned the teacher and told him: 'You are a renowned master, an expert teacher. I am going to entrust you with a student. I give you three years to teach him.' And he presented the teacher with a young camel, a beautiful beast like all of the ones in his herd. 'Here is your future student,' the sultan told him. 'Think it over until tomorrow. If you deem this task too difficult, you can refuse. But in that case, I have prepared for you a deep dungeon that will be your prison and your tomb.' The sheikh went away sadly, cursing his knowledge and his wisdom, ready to rebel against his creator. He met a dervish like myself, a simple and unsophisticated man, dressed in rags, living on plants and roots with only wild animals for company, as he preferred them to humans. He asked the dervish's advice.

"'Oh, learned man,' he responded, 'your knowledge makes you blind, narrow minded, and fearful. Can you claim to know the plans of the Almighty? Only He can inspire fear, not the sultan, a mere mortal. Go! Accept the student he offers you. Three years from now, you might die. You would then be in the hands of the Most Merciful. The camel could die. Then, you will not have to prove your cleverness. If the magnificent sultan's last hour arrives, you will inherit the camel and be better

Land and Blood

off than you are now.' This is indeed what happened. The sultan died, and no one thought to reclaim the camel.

"This, my son, is an anecdote that can teach a lesson to everyone who is impatient, worried, and seeks to know God's plan, instead of letting himself live and trust in God. I do not know if it applies to you: I refuse to discuss your case. But torment yourself no more, and do not harass the dead."

XI   One could easily imagine Marie's predicament in Ighil-Nezman, in the midst of Kabyles. If, on the one hand, she could make herself understood by the men, there was nothing to be gained from the women. Yet it was the women who interested her. She realized right from the start that she would have to live like the other women and not stand out. Amer could not be of any help. He offered to take her to the café to cheer her up a bit. She followed him but found she was the only woman there, so she was bored. She went to the market and caused a stir. She also noticed that men were always uncomfortable in her presence, barely speaking, not daring to look at her, turning to Amer even if the question concerned her. And yet she had seen many of these men in France, acting as boldly as any others. So she remained silent, just listening to the discussions around her, sometimes without even understanding a word, since people spoke in Kabyle, even if she was present. Marie even went to the nearby city. She paid a visit to the colonial administrator of the district, a pointless gesture (Amer too was fooling himself). Disgusted, she returned home. For a moment, she felt as if she were back in that hostile society that had rejected her. She walked the streets, went into stores, the café, and the restaurant. She did not feel at ease anywhere, not with the French or with the Kabyles. It seemed to her that she and Amer formed a strange, ridiculous couple—that with her, he had lost his Kabyle character, and she no longer felt entirely like a Frenchwoman. As a result, they seemed diminished and awkward, because Amer's attitude mirrored her own, and their thoughts were surely identical. Of course the administrator received them, but it was pointless. They had nothing to ask of him. They were given a cold reception. He displayed an ironic politeness that revealed how indecent he felt their union to be.* So Marie stopped going out in public with Amer.

For company, she had to settle for Kamouma and the women

*Note that this scene takes place in 1925.

neighbors who came to call. Little by little, she began to like her new society; she lived intensely with these women who obliged her to understand, to make herself understood, and to discuss things. She had recourse to gestures and amusing charades that ended in outbursts of laughter from all the ladies present. Marie was no longer bored. It was a total immersion in the language. Words began to impose themselves, imprinting themselves in her mind as it gradually began to accept them. First, it was the words needed for everyday life, as indispensable as the air we breathe: here! give me, good, bad, yes, no . . . Then she learned the words needed to be courteous, the words that express beauty and admiration. She learned others too, rude words the others made her repeat out of spite or to shock Kamouma. Marie said everything with equal candor, and more than once she let slip a swear word in front of the son and his mother. Amer explained to her the requirements of Kabyle prudishness: everything that concerns sex is taboo and never said among relatives. Sometimes she made them laugh by repeating faults and defects; she had been taught to say by some neighbor: "I am black as coal," or "I am as dumb as a donkey." When Amer asked her what she thought she was saying, she answered: "I am as beautiful as the moon," and "I am as intelligent as a goddess." All the same, she was making rapid progress and soon knew how to defend herself. In the beginning, she thought she would never master this muddle of rough and sharp sounds that is the Kabyle language, always spoken too fast for her liking. She knitted her brows, squinted her eyes, and tried to comprehend something, but could not even succeed in repeating it. Then there were the impossible sounds. Her tongue found it difficult to imitate the very subtle but essential nuances. She noticed right away that in Kabyle, there were many more than the twenty-five different sounds of the French language. She decided to make others laugh so that she could learn more. She was no longer impatient with herself when she had to resort to gestures. She became like a small child: she could eventually understand everything that Kamouma or the others said to her before she knew how to answer. As she slowly learned more and more, she came to see life in Ighil-Nezman in a new light.

Marie was a poor girl, without any arrogance. She had no prejudice against the people with whom she now lived. However, in the beginning, this society seemed to her to be absurd, incredible, and backwards, to say the least: the women were excluded and ignored, confined to the role of unseen housekeepers or perhaps even slaves. The women themselves seemed so insignificant to her that they could not possibly be treated otherwise. She had to change her mind about that. First of all, the women were not that foolish. Marie realized as much from the way they talked with her. They were polite, reserved, discreet, and knew how to be helpful. They were the ones who would give her advice on how to run her household in the Kabyle fashion. They taught her to make couscous and pancakes, how to light the wood fire in the hearth, sweep the courtyard without raising too much dust, and operate the hand mill. She noticed that underneath their casual appearance, all of the women were meticulously clean; they never touched flour without first carefully washing their hands. They waited for the end of their menstrual cycle in order to begin preparing meals again, and their personal hygiene was done with the utmost care. In general, they did not need lessons on these matters from anyone.

The married woman whose husband was around could allow herself some coquetry, but widows and wives whose husbands were away dressed without any special care to avoid drawing attention to themselves. Young women who hoped to marry could dress to seek some attention. Thus, everything was in order. What shocked and surprised her in the beginning became oddly logical. She knew that a Kabyle woman must be serious and modest because men, for their part, are serious. Everything happened as if each couple had to be content with each other; there was no question of extramarital affairs. Afterward, of course, she learned that there were some exceptions to the rule, but they were rare. The austerity of morals was the result of necessity and habit more than from any exceptional virtue.

Land and Blood

What mattered the most was not romantic love, but life itself. That was the sole issue. Everything else depended on it. That is why pleasure was relegated to the background. The act of love-making was for the night. During the day, each spouse worked separately to manage the home. Even then, Marie noticed, women had their specific roles. Wives who carry out their duties efficiently make the men's tasks that much easier. All things considered, the woman is not eclipsed in the home. She fills it with her presence, perhaps even more so than the man, who is often the head of the household in name only. After a while, Marie no longer thought of things as strange or unusual with the people of Kabylia. She simply needed to understand and then adjust her thinking to find that men and women here are just like the ones she knew before in France.

Like Amer, she knew that this setting suited her as a woman from a modest background. She had no reason to envy the peasant women who fussed over her. She was content and comfortable. She felt that she was beautiful, well dressed, and had a suitable home and husband. She knew that the fact she was French made her respected, yet she did not take advantage of it. Sometimes it seemed as if she was on vacation here, and the day would come when she would return to France; then she would dream of having a real existence back there. She would forget this tiny village and its inhabitants, working like ants, huddled against each other, being satisfied with so little and accepting their fate as if they did not even suspect that a better one were possible. When she began to think like that, she was almost sorry to be there. It was a no-win situation. She became sad, gloomy, and irritable for no reason. Ima Kamouma would notice and avoid talking to her. Amer would be extra nice, and some young neighbor girls would come over to cheer her up, eventually making her laugh.

At other times, on the contrary, Marie saw things in a different light. She was a cherished queen. Amer took care of everything outside of the home. She had no more worries. Why not bear this existence like her women neighbors did? She belonged to the village, had friends there, and occupied a certain position; why not give up thinking about the past? She became ambitious; she imagined Amer among the village's most important residents and herself as the first among the women. She made many plans and would discuss them with Amer, who was pleased to notice that she was settling in and starting to become like a Kabyle.

She also wanted to have children. At first, it was a distant, vague desire. Then the women, especially Kamouma, succeeded in giving her a taste for that possibility, so much so that her desire became a kind of ideal to which she aspired with her whole being. Like a real Kabyle woman!

It must also be said that Kamouma's feelings toward Marie quickly began to change. She soon came to admit that the young woman had many qualities and did not have a mean bone in her body. This nastiness is what so often poisons the relationship between a daughter-in-law and her mother-in-law. In the wrong hands, this nastiness could become a dangerous weapon. But no, Kamouma could feel at ease: her Amer would never change. But are old women ever satisfied? It is not just meanness that they possess. They are driven by a demon! And everybody knows what demon drives an old woman. However, since it was part of Kamouma's plan to have her daughter-in-law like her new life in Kabylia, she worked at making life pleasant for her in all sincerity. Marie began to grow fond of her new existence . . .

XII

Marie had lived three years with Amer at Madame Garet's. When they made up their minds to leave Paris and move to Ighil-Nezman, it was not because of a sudden impulse, or any illusions, or even out of a desire for adventure. They were simply tired of a certain type of life that maybe in the future could still promise some excitement for them, whereas another life, the one Amer often spoke of, offered itself to them free of charge, without too much risk.

Once she was settled in Kabylia, Marie in turn reviewed in her mind the events of her past. What did she have to regret after all? Her life could have unfolded otherwise, only fate had stepped in! For her as well, everything had depended on a twist of fate. Her mother had moved in with an older man who had a shack on the outskirts of the city, in Pantin. His name was Joseph Mitard. For five years she had to call him "papa." No one ever spoke of André again.

Marie did not know how her mother had met this man, but she has enough precise memories of this period. She can clearly recall Papa Mitard; she has not forgotten either his habits or his preferences, nor his faults or defects. She never liked him. As for him, he never bothered about her until about the time when she left for good, because of him, as a matter of fact.

Was it not, in fact, strange that one Sunday she found herself alone with him, with Papa Joseph, who watched her stealthily with his large, fishlike eyes? He began to talk to her about her mother, pouring out all the bad things he really thought about her, claiming that anyway, he was beyond all that with her mother now, and that was how life was, and that sleeping with one man or another did not really matter. Marie saw where he was going with all this. It was enough to make her vomit. Ugh! This flabby old guy she had called "papa"! Now, he made her want to strike him.

There you have it! It was no longer possible for her to live in that house. Besides, it was not the first time she had thought about leaving. She had already begun to vaguely consider that eventual possibility. Suddenly, this idea hit her, and it was

Land and Blood

actually the only unexpected event in her life, like a bolt out of the blue. All the rest followed in a most ordinary fashion, to say the least.

She was a minor, living under assumed names, risking prison for having had an abortion; her lovers no longer cared about her and began to exploit her; the last one even talked of placing her in a "house." No trace of her mother, or of Joseph, since she had spent a year traveling before landing back in Paris. She had made her "tour of France" and had stayed in different cities: Chartres, Nantes, Bordeaux, and finally Lyon. It was after her return from Lyon that she ran into Madame Garet. She was wearing the last of her dresses, and her prospects were not looking very good. Her lover had rented her a small room in a hotel on Polonceau Street. The hotel owner, who was a "friend," housed them without asking any questions and only registered the man's name since he had already "worked" with him. Marie was pregnant again.

Misfortune was quick to show up again as her lover was arrested for theft. She found herself alone at this man's place, and the owner threatened to throw her out every chance he got, but he allowed her to work there as little more than a slave. She spent several months like this, washing the sheets and laundry, polishing the floor, drying the glasses and dishes in the midst of drunks and pimps, as her belly grew big, making her ugly.

Marie has kept these memories intact, just for herself. In her heart, she is rather proud to have lived through all this. It is this same pride that can be glimpsed in her gaze whenever she happens to admit vaguely and in a general fashion that she too has known misery and hunger. What she does not like to evoke, now in Kabylia, are her days of "wild living," of unhealthy pleasure. This is her biggest regret. She would like to forget. But she feels that the memory of her past suffering allows her to live with remorse. That is the price of error, but this is true only to a certain extent.

All things considered, she is not sorry to have followed Amer, first to Madame Garet's and then to Kabylia. She met him again at a particularly low point in her life: she had just gotten out of the hospital alone (her child died at birth) and was drained of strength and courage. She was in need of support. Oh! In the beginning, she was not fooling herself. Amer was amusing with his ideas about Rabah-ou-Hamouche and Yvonne. He wanted so much to be her cousin. She did not think the matter to be very important. She told herself that things would not go that far. However, his poor dream took shape, and little by little it came to be, quite naturally, to say the least. Since that time, there it is, they stayed together: back there, here, or elsewhere, it made no difference. The past is dead, and the future is not at all frightening.

XIII

While Marie was getting accustomed to her new life, Amer set about studying his relatives. To say that he was just getting to know them would be an exaggeration. He had known them since childhood. During his long absence, he had never really been able to cut himself off from them since his memories of them continued to live in him. Then again, news of them would reach him from time to time. But he never felt himself concerned by what went on back at home. The cheating, the nastiness, the hypocrisy, the misfortunes seen from afar—these were only children's games of no importance. Now, he found himself mixed up in all these games. He felt as if he were being pulled into a dance, sometimes exciting and pleasant, sometimes funny or distressing. However, this world in which he had his own place suited him—where, even if it were possible to change, no one could just be the sum of his actions. A total change, thereby putting others off the scent and making them forget the past, was not possible. It was a world where a person was so and so, the son of so and so, and nothing more.

A series of tight circles imprisoned people within the family, next within the *karouba,* and then it made the entire village a teeming cage where people ceaselessly rubbed shoulders with each other and measured each other. In France, in larger villages or in cities that are the same size as Ighil-Nezman, in the industrial cities at least, families can come and go. People who are total strangers can meet, live side by side, and then separate. There is a kind of freedom of thought and speech, a kind of independence, a kind of selfishness that makes life a fair fight that each one must undertake alone. Ordinarily, people can go about their lives as they please, only taking others into account to the extent that one needs to win them over. One can extend or narrow one's relations; one creates one's own constraints. In a Kabyle village, the situation is different. The *karouba* is both a social and a geographic unit. Cousins live on the same street; families are established for eternity in their neighborhoods. If, for example, one of the families moves to Algiers, it is rarely accepted that a family from outside the village would come to live there. They form a whole, they know each other, they have judged each other for generations. They do not throw their judgments in the face of someone, but each one knows very well what they must think of the others. They are there to greet each other every day, to say hello, to do a favor, to help each other, and also to keep an eye on each other, to envy or to hate each other. And every single one of them is obliged to keep up appearances. Seen from the outside, village life seems hard to bear. One would be afraid of suffocating there. But in reality, one would be just as free there as anywhere else; people laugh and joke. If desired, one can misbehave too: defying the censors or just behaving well. It is simply a matter of not condemning oneself, since, once one knows who the censors are and that they have made up their minds about one, one no longer fears them, and their opinions become meaningless. All the more so, since they never speak out openly anyway!

The bond among the present, past, and future is an illusion. It comforts the simpleminded and does not weigh too heavily on anyone as long as only the good side of the past is remembered and no one thinks about future sanctions. Here, like elsewhere, a keen observer could notice that, despite a few superficial and obvious aspects, the Kabyles are men like everyone else. Nevertheless, they are men condemned to a bitter struggle in order to survive. In this unequal struggle, we are obliged to neglect our fine principles a bit, all the while giving the appearance of holding to them dearly. This is perhaps a great quality—the only quality. We have a very rigorous sense of honor, courage, and virtue. We really would like to be generous and selfless. We are full of noble intentions. Everyone strives to keep up appearances, but the reality is oftentimes revealed, in spite of our desire to hide it.

Here are a few random details about some of the families living in Ighil-Nezman that everybody knows and shares with each other. These are neither the best nor the worst families of the village. They simply live in the same neighborhood as the Aït-Larbi.

Land and Blood

There are only two Aït-Rabah left, Hassen and Saïd. They are poor and have many children who are always disturbing the neighbors. As their wives do not get along, their existence is a continuous quarrel. Their children bite and scratch each other, the wives spitefully spy on each other, and the two men are envious of each other like real enemies. But on occasion, they remember that they are brothers: it so happened that one time, a neighbor, taking advantage of this situation, wanted to beat up Hassen, who was the weaker of the two. The two brothers together gave the man an unexpected lesson that cured his desire to get the upper hand over a divided family.

Saïd's daughters will certainly never marry due to their own insolence and their father's poverty. If one were to believe everything the girls said, their two mothers have many faults, as do the fathers. But people are likely to say anything in the course of an argument.

Hassen and Saïd had an elderly mother. When they divided up the single orchard of fig trees and set up a partition made from reeds in the middle of the old shack they inherited from their father, Hassen said to Saïd:

"We still have one more thing to divide up."

"What?"

"The old lady."

"I'll look after her if she is too much for you."

"You just want to be the only one to benefit from her *baraka*. No! I will have my share."

It was decided that they would each keep the mother for a month, alternating turns. So she had to move from one side of the reed partition to the other, dragging her pillow stuffed with old rags, her small mat and faded rug. She derived an immeasurable advantage from this monthly move, because she was always treated very well on the day she arrived and the day before she left for the other side. So she had four good days out of every sixty, whereas before, if she were not always the cause of the arguments, she still had to put up with their results. Her new way of life brought her a measure of peace: she merely

Land and Blood

had to take the side of whoever housed her at the time. But she made the wise decision to change her mind about whatever it was every month.

While waiting to receive her *baraka,* Saïd got the idea to send the old woman to rich people at harvest time: a camouflaged begging. Hassen was not happy about this. Since his brother refused to share the charity she received, she also began to beg at Hassen's bidding. One day she died unexpectedly, like an insect as winter draws near. It is obvious that she did not leave her *baraka* to either of the two brothers. They were not counting on it too much anyway.

The Aït-Tahar's gate is across from the Aït-Rabah. Behind this gate there is a group of six or eight houses, one across from the other. Each member lives in one of them with his wife and children. An open gutter crosses the courtyard, and each dwelling has a channel draining into it. It is not very peaceful at their place either. They are obliged to see each other morning and night, and they despise each other deeply. When they fight over the condition of the gutter, they take precautions to close the outer gate of their compound. They are disciplined and have a sense of honor. Even when the disputes become pitched battles, they keep all others out. They settle matters among themselves. Loud outbursts are forbidden. They insult each other in low voices; they whack each other hard enough to break the skin, but know the secret of striking each other without making a sound. Behind the closed gate, on the day of the battle, one only hears a long murmur of muffled voices, a dull, prolonged echo of deadened blows, sometimes the heavy thud of a body falling or the strident cry of a child interrupted by two expert fingers that plug the throat of the child. When the gate opens back up, calm has been restored. Old Bachir, the eldest of the Aït-Tahar, comes out with a smile on his face. He utters a few lofty words to satisfy the curious: "Our children are real devils. I cannot stand them anymore. I am going to the *djema.*"

The Aït-Tahar pride themselves on the exploits of an ancestor who in the past belonged to a group of thieves. They are very attached to this proof of their nobility. They know that they are envied for this status and that they have many enemies because of it. This is why they are so reserved and hypocritical. They like to tell others that they still have a lot of connections all over Kabylia, and for this, they should be feared and respected.

Old Bachir's daughter is married to a rather simple man who lives at the end of the village. He is rich and only has some cousins for family. He spends the entire day out in the fields. His mother-in-law is always at his home and extorts things from him shamelessly: oil, figs, grain, everything is scrupulously shared. He does not notice a thing. His father-in-law has proven many times to him that he could not find better allies than the Aït-Tahar. They watch over him without his knowing: one dark night, the son-in-law is brutally awakened from a deep sleep by a crash on his roof. He listens: someone is throwing rocks at his house. Without a doubt, an unknown enemy wants him to come out and show himself so he can then become a target. He spends a difficult night. The next day, Bachir arrives, full of noble indignation.

"Son-in-law, I know that your home was stoned last night. It's no use denying it. Do you have any suspicions?"

"No."

"You are naive. You think that you are respected in this neighborhood where, in fact, there are only jealous people. Let me take care of it. From now on, you can sleep soundly. We will keep watch."

Indeed, Bachir did keep watch, until the day that a nasty story threatened his daughter. That was when, in an unexpected way, the unknown enemies showed the son-in-law their desire to get revenge. Even more than before, he felt the need to rely upon a solid family, and then Bachir's daughter could assert her position in her husband's home even more.

The Aït-Abbas live next door to the Aït-Tahar. They are farmers and *khaounis*. Their piety is known to all the sheikhs and *talebs* who pass through and do not hesitate to stop by to enjoy their hospitality. Picture an Aït-Abbas of the older generation dressed in a plain, sleeveless, coarse fabric *gandoura*, with

Land and Blood

a wide neckline, belted in the middle with a studded leather strap, holding the *gandoura* up high, revealing dry knees and shiny calves. On his head would be a worn-out *chéchia*, grimy on the edges, with a stained turban; on his feet would be slippers revealing a large toe and a flattened, cracked, wide heel. His face would be wrinkled, dried out, and as inscrutable as a mask. Only the eyes would show some liveliness, and to see them sparkle, one might wonder what had charmed them enough to keep them attached to this face.

The Aït-Abbas are extremely devout. They pray regularly, adhere to strict fasting, and despise nonbelievers. They transgress God's law a bit in the matter of charity, but they believe this to be insignificant. The good reputation of the Aït-Abbas is presently undergoing a difficult test. Satan leads their children astray. They go to France, drink wine, probably go out with Frenchwomen, and return wearing trousers and jackets. Some of them do not even return. If only they at least would send some money back!

The houses of the Aït-Marouf border alongside the large village square. They like to stress the fact that they occupy the center of Ighil-Nezman and that, consequently, everything revolves around them. As bleak as they may be, circumstances cannot take away their legitimate pride and absolute disdain for other families. They have furnished the village with two of its *amin*. They really are the "leaders." We all knew Arab, the last *amin* from this family. He was a friend of Mohand Amezian, the moneylender. His wife was very beautiful and, coincidently, was named Yamina.* She liked to show that she was the wife of the *amin*! The women of the neighborhood put up with her like a soldier puts up with an arrogant officer. Each time she found a reason to fight with one of the neighbors, the naughty lads knew that she would get around to showing off her lovely thighs to the spectators, so they knew to take up positions to get the best view. This was her own way of showing how superior she thought she was.

*The name Yamina can be the feminine form of "Amin."

"You all see why she does not like me! I am not crazy like her . . ."

Arab, who inspires fear outside of his home, is a lamb at home. Besides, he gets along well with the moneylender. Their tyranny over the village lasted about ten years. They amused themselves at making and unmaking the *çofs*. Mohand pitilessly destroyed those who owed him money and were not very forthcoming about it. The procedure was simple: a court summons, a deadline that passed, a public auction, a seizure of goods presided over by the notary judge, and thus, the enemy became a beggar. All methods were used to accomplish this: lying witnesses, fake promissory notes, threats, intimidation; the debtor's gullibility was exploited to the limit, as well as his carelessness or bad luck. Mohand could not lose a trial. All of the *fellahs* trembled at the thought of falling into his clutches, even those who did not owe him anything. He knew all the tricks of the trade for legal proceedings and paid a lawyer a monthly salary. He was as implacable as fate. The wealthy ones who thought they were his rivals dealt with the *amin,* who was on the best of terms with the *caïd.* There was no option but to accept this state of affairs: the two friends were at the height of their power.

They did not hesitate to exclude certain families from the collective life of the village. It was a stringent blacklisting. Under the threat of being fined, it was forbidden to speak to the members of these families, to do them any favors, to work in their fields, to attend their celebrations, or to bury their dead. The annals of the village recount the story of an unfortunate pariah who had to summon help from a neighboring village in order to bury his son. No one in Ighil-Nezman could avoid this cowardice.

Then came the day when the friends had a falling-out. The *amin* was ruined, and the moneylender was himself blacklisted. It was indeed their turn. Today, the Aït-Marouf have no fortune and no influence, but they are still insufferable and nasty.

One could easily blame us for our naive fatalism; it is just that the weak always console themselves by dreaming that an all-powerful being will punish wrongdoers. It is, of course, easy to make fun of our simplicity. However, we who live in our mountains on the edges of civilized society, we know full well that the only justice that strikes down the wicked without fail is not man's justice. But fate only strikes; it does not put things right. It is always that way: the blows never come at the right time, and everyone believes he is an innocent victim of the gods . . .

XIV

They more or less expected this meeting. They had both been preparing for it for a week. Yet it was as if they were caught unexpectedly. It did not come to pass in the manner that each one had been imagining.

It took place outside the village. Amer was on his way to the new café. Slimane was returning from there. They found themselves face to face at the turn in the path that hides the café from sight. One, tall and strong, in good health and clean in his blue silk *gandoura;* the other small and dry, gray all over in his old clothes the color of earth. Amer never knew exactly what happened within him. His eyes grew wide. He did not have the strength to smile, but suddenly his face lit up and took on an indefinable expression of deep sadness tinged with sweetness and goodness. He had never had a feeling like that. It was as if all that was noble and intangible in him could leave his body to envelop this man that stood before him, pitiful and weak. He also felt a certain pleasure in humiliating and lowering himself, as he felt his position to be too advantageous in comparison to this wretched man. He drew near to Slimane and kissed his head, blushing a bit.

"Good day, Uncle," he said to him.

"Welcome, Nephew," Slimane said, and he then took Amer's plump, soft hand in his bony and darkened hands. He brought it to his mouth, eagerly kissed it, and then quickly left, disappearing around the corner. Slimane's head buzzed with contradictory thoughts. His answer and gesture had been spontaneous. He had prepared himself for enmity or hatred. As soon as he saw his nephew, he began to frown and lowered his large, unpleasant head in a belligerent and stubborn manner, like a bull that encounters another. He had taken the upper path and had begun to keep to the embankment. He was quite surprised! All of the hatred he had managed to summon inside himself abruptly left him as soon as he raised his eyes to that wide, good-natured face that made itself sweet, almost humble. At that moment, the same current of affinity united uncle and nephew. In the space of a second, Slimane was truly moved. He

Land and Blood

felt sorry for himself, and he saw himself there, facing the man whom fate had turned into his enemy. He knew he would be an insignificant adversary, certain to be beaten if he dared attack or certain to feel shame if he fled the confrontation. But when he looked upon Amer's face, when he saw the compassion and friendship written there, it was like a soothing balm. The reaction was instantaneous; his own heart responded to the goodness of Amer's heart.

They both understood that they could never have prevented this language of the heart. Slimane would have had to keep his eyes lowered, for example, and stay closed up in his hatred. There, once again he had betrayed himself. Even while hurrying home, he was annoyed at his own weakness; he ran without looking back, as if to hide his shame. "What have I done?" he silently asked himself several times. "No one saw me. I still have time to think: we shall see, we shall see."

For his part, Amer knew he was guilty and needed to be forgiven. In truth, it was really the memory of the deceased man that made him weaken. Slimane, who had remained in his country, leading a quiet life, could not imagine either the true circumstances of the accident or Amer's remorse. Amer told himself that after all, he really did not have to justify anything, since there was already God and his conscience. Let Slimane accept his fate as a good believer, let him no longer disown his nephew; Amer was even ready to take the first steps. Otherwise, it would be as his uncle wished: "I will not attack him but I will defend myself." He felt that having gone to Slimane first, kissing his head was neither baseness nor hypocrisy, but that he was obliged to make that gesture. He would even have done it in full view of the café, even at the *djema* in front of everyone. He was sure that people would have approved of him.

But Amer was also happy that this first meeting took place in this way, without witnesses. Slimane's touchiness might have been triggered.

"I just ran into him. He bent to kiss my head," Slimane told his wife, Chabha-ou-Ramdane. His face was a bit flushed, his mouth turned down, and his eyes glittered, with joy or anger, one could not say.

Land and Blood

"You see!" she told him.

"See what? Is that all you have to say?"

"No. I am pleased! He is your nephew, after all. Blood ties won out. You could not have prevented it."

"But he is the one who took the first step!" Slimane said angrily, surprised to learn that his wife had read his thoughts.

"Exactly. He is not dumb. Do you think he does not know the meaning of family?"

"In his place, I would have acted more honorably . . . I would have tried to avoid the meeting, or I would have turned my head away . . ."

"Oh! You would have been pleased at that. You would have taken his actions to be a challenge, admitting to a crime that he never committed. I am sure that his conscience is clear. That is why he did not hesitate . . ."

"So now you are defending him?"

"You are foolish, Husband. What are you still worrying about, even after you have spoken to the dervish? Do you not see that your stubbornness will delight the others? Don't you see that your cousins, the Aït-Hamouche, have dropped you and are all sweetness with Amer? Listen to your blood, Husband; do not choose the wrong path. I am happy about this meeting. Tell me frankly, did you not feel your heart stir when you saw him, like his own must have done?"

"You'd think so! I was confused, that's all. He resembles my older brother, Rabah, as I remember him. Furthermore, according to your father, he looks like my uncle Slimane, his grandfather. That is even sadder. How can I forget since he carries with him the image of his crime?"

"But that's it! You see that he is closer to you than all the others. You cannot deny him. And as for him, he can be devoted to you, since on his side, there is no one who cares about him. We know how they are, these Aït-Larbi. Did any of them look after Kamouma when you had all abandoned her? There was only that hypocrite Hocine! And he managed to get the two best fields. You can be proud of Amer: he already bought back Tighezrane! It seems Madame went there with him. Have you seen Madame? It is true that you have spent a crazy week, hiding yourself, off brooding like you have to change the world. No, these people are our allies, our relations: Amer, Madame, and Kamouma. That cannot be bought for any sum, but enemies can be had by the dozen. You do not have anything to say? Think about it, Husband. You always come to see things my way, which is merely my father's way of seeing things too. But he can explain things better! Since Amer is kind, I am not worried; we will manage."

"On the one hand, it is better this way," Slimane said. "We can talk to each other. You are right. Amer is my nephew. Only God knows the future. Like the dervish said, the sultan could die. I hope the sultan will be the one to die! We shall see," he concluded.

But things did not stop there. That evening at the *djema*, Amer found old Ramdane seated off by himself. He seemed to be waiting. Amer greeted him, hesitated for a second, then went over to a group seated on a stone bench. From a distance, the elderly man returned his greeting with a nod of his head, accompanied by an insistent stare that Amer noticed. Then he saw him leave. Several moments later, a boy came to tell Amer that someone wanted to speak to him.

"Who is it?"

"Follow me. I'll take you to him."

Amer followed the child. They took the main street, where Ramdane was waiting at the other end.

"Good evening, Ramdane. You wanted to speak to me?"

"Only for a few moments. Would you like to walk a bit . . . to the cemetery? Thank you, child," he said to the boy, and he scampered off.

"Let's go!" Amer answered.

Located at the end of the village, the cemetery is a public place, like the *djema*. It occupies a flat plot of land, at the foot of the hill that dominates the houses of Ighil-Nezman. The last houses are side by side with the first tombs. Four of the paths that climb up from the valley end at the cemetery and form a wide path that becomes the main street of the village; then, at the end of the village, it becomes a paved road right in front of the new café. The walk from the café to the cemetery is rather pleasant on spring and summer evenings. It is the liveliest route. One can often see people seated on a tomb, discussing their business off by themselves. The space is large but entirely filled up by the rectangular slabs flat against the ground or slightly elevated to mark the graves. The whole place looks like a ghost village, a flat, two-dimensional village, drained of substance and full of sadness and mystery. There is no fence and no border. Spindly grass grows between the slabs. Sheep pass through there, stopping to graze.

It is not that we do not respect the dead! They have known us. They knew all along that they would be trampled on. We will be too when it is our turn. It is the best way to be remembered. The dead are always there, at our door, witnesses to our gestures, our words, and our secrets. There is no need for a wall. When we sit down on a tomb for a chat, it is simply that we think it is a good spot. Often, there is no other reason for doing so; we are not even thinking about the person who is buried underneath. We feel at home there, that is all.

While people returning from the fields passed by, greeting them or pretending not to see them, Amer and Ramdane sat talking peacefully.

Amer knew that at first they would only discuss unimportant subjects. The serious conversation would only come later, after a logical transition that the older man would manage at the correct time. To give him time to get there, Amer spoke to him about the cemetery. He was familiar with the general layout. Only there had been some changes over time. All of those from the village who had died were there, but he did not know where, exactly. Three times he had now passed through the cemetery: the day after his return, when he went down to Tigherzane with Madame, and now this evening. This would be a good chance for Amer to find out about it since old Ramdane knew where everyone was buried.

"Our cemetery has changed," Amer said.

"It was bound to happen. It has gotten larger, just like the village. The graves are changing. You see? All of the newer ones

Land and Blood

are higher. Some are covered in cement. There are even inscriptions . . . in French. Some names, their age as well perhaps. I do not know how to read."

"You know all of them, I bet."

"That's to be expected, at my age! The older graves give us some trouble, but there are still enough of us to recognize almost all of them. In the future, it may be different. You and your children will have some difficulty locating them."

"It is not so tricky. I just need a few details. Listen, Uncle Ramdane, here are the *marabout* tombs, easy to recognize since they are grouped around the tomb of Sheikh Elhocine, the highest one of them all, the one we are sitting on right now. On the left side of the path, those are the Aït-Belkacem; next to them are the Issoulah, and then the Aït-Larbi."

"Yes, with your father Kaci's grave. You have already seen it, right?"

"Across from there is the other section. Of course I recognize them. But I cannot tell them all apart. As for the Aït-Larbi, it has been engraved in my memory from childhood."

"You see, Amer, here it is like the village, right? More or less the same layout by *karouba* and by family. The cemetery is a faithful reflection of Ighil-Nezman. But in reality, the opposite is true. The real village is not the one that rises proudly from the top of the ridge. It is this one, frozen in our earth, immobile and eternal, but not really frightening in my opinion, because we, the living, know it well. We all get accustomed to our place, and we are not afraid to come here. You see, I am old. My spot is there, just a few steps away. Sometimes, I happen to imagine myself under the slab, surrounded by the ancient ones and feeling the youth still alive. Amer, our land is not wicked. We come from it, and we will return to it. It is very simple. The land loves her children. When they neglect her too much, she calls them back to her. You know this too, right?"

"You are right, Uncle Ramdane," Amer said humbly, already guessing what the other man was getting at. He lowered his head, moved to the depths of his heart because night was falling, and in this place words seemed to him to take on a serious tone that they might not have had elsewhere or in the light of day.

"Yes, you can see why the dead, if they are foreigners, are to be pitied, laid to rest in a land where they will find nothing and where none of their own kind will pass by their graves. Say, do you see over there, where the two roads intersect? That is the grave of a stranger: a beggar who died by chance one winter night in the *djema*. He was buried at the crossroads. No one knows where he came from or what his name was. Now people swear by his grave. When they want to convince someone that what they say is true, they say: 'May God grant me a grave like the stranger's.' It is a sad fate, for certain. I know, my poor boy, that it was not your fault. It was written: Rabah's grave was to be in France, not here. The voice of our land was not strong enough. I do not remind you of these things to anger you. When I found you one day, half crazy on a bench in the town square, I could see your distress. You were still young. Slimane was not my ally. We understood everything about the matter back there. When we returned home to our land, we spoke to the Aït-Hamouche. They accepted it all. They are not too upset with you. But the blood! Their blood was spilled! The debt exists. There is a victim coming between you. That is why they abandoned Kamouma."

"Uncle Ramdane, I am not calling them to account for anything. Did they send you to ask me about this? It is my return that makes you all uncomfortable. Would you like me to offer myself as a target for your son-in-law, or that I just go away? Is that it? Rabah's death has haunted me for a long time. Do you think I have forgotten or that I need your reminders? I know that I am not guilty. I am not afraid of Slimane or of anyone else!"

"You are losing your temper, Son. Let me explain."

"All right, I am listening. What exactly do you want?"

"God knows that since your return, I have not slept well. My daughter either! We only want what is best for you and for Slimane as well. There is no point in smiling; you are not a child anymore: I speak in all frankness. I am looking for calm and understanding. It is in my interest, in Slimane's interest, and in your own as well. Do you see?"

"I understand."

"The time when entire families killed each other has passed, since the advent of policemen and jails. Thank God people think carefully now! This is what I explained to Slimane. Today, how many cowardly acts, retreats, and arrangements tarnishing both parties do we see? As for your case, nothing irreparable has happened. It was a bad twist of fate; that is all. But you share the same blood, so much so that Slimane thought he saw his own brother when he met you this morning."

"Ah, did he tell you that? Me too, my heart stirred, by God, I can tell you."

"Amer, if you only knew how unhappy he is! He is sensitive, abandoned by his cousins, hated by so many people because your uncles were powerful, and they want to make him pay for that. But he is not a coward, he knows how to defend himself. He lashes out. But afterward, he always feels badly about it. He has a big heart, and it is always overflowing. Only my daughter knows how sensitive he really is. She says that one day his heart will burst. It is also killing him not to have any children. We have tried everything to no avail: *marabouts,* old wives' remedies, *koubas,* nothing helped."

"What about doctors? You should try to see one."

"Yes, we will see about that. Besides, now we have a bit of hope. Let me explain about his situation. I am not talking about his material situation because there, everyone has his share of difficulties. Now you know why I am worried: public opinion is going to brandish the rules about honor for your benefit. They will whisper that Slimane is seeking revenge for his brother by killing his cousin's son. You must pay no attention to these rumors. Just accept that my son-in-law is not angry with you. They will go and tell him that you say you are not afraid of him or maybe that you are threatening him."

"Well then, I agree. I will not listen to what other people tell me. And you will do the same, on your side."

"Do you think it will be enough?"

Land and Blood

"I don't know. Tell me what is on your mind."

"What is needed is to prevent this rumor from even start-ing, to signal to everyone that your business does not concern anyone else. I can only see one way out: renew your family ties, show that the past has been forgotten and that you are still family."

"I could not ask for more. And Slimane, what does he think?"

"Ah, you see! Let me embrace you! This will not be a prob-lem for you; I was afraid you might be touchy about it."

"I don't see why!" Amer said, a bit confused and suspicious.

"Let me arrange it. You trust me, don't you?"

"Yes, Ramdane. As long as you do not attempt to make me look like a coward in other people's eyes, one who tries to get in his enemies' good graces. Because, you see, neither my father nor anyone in my family has ever lived that way. As for myself, I could not accept . . ."

"There you go again being suspicious. This is what I was afraid of. But I will trust in the blood that unites you both. It has already been spilled once, and that is enough. You would not refuse to come and eat in my home, with my son-in law, if I invited you both someday?"

"All things considered, I accept," Amer said, after a mo-ment's hesitation.

"That is all I ask. May God keep us. Let's get up and return home now, Amer."

"Has Slimane been your son-in-law for a long time, Ramdane?"

"For ten years. He asked for my daughter some time after my return from France. Ali, your uncle was still alive, but your father was already dead, I believe."

"And no children?"

"No, as I was telling you, we have tried everything. But lately, we have consulted a dervish, about whom much good is said. He gave us some hope. He told Slimane that he saw him with a small lamb following behind him. If God grants us such

Land and Blood

a favor, we will again take pleasure in life, him, my old wife, my daughter, and I. It means something, right? We have promised a real sheep to Si-Mahfoud if this comes to pass."

"It is always good to hope. Me too, I would really like to have a child. But in my opinion, those things are in God's hands. Dervishes cannot help."

"This is another reason to unite you and Slimane: you have envious cousins. You are both childless, and you are of the same blood."

"May God keep us, as you just said. My heart is as honest as my tongue. You can reassure Slimane; tell him that I am his cousin's son and that I cried for Rabah like no one has ever cried for him."

XV We like to say that there are two types of friends: those who first hold each other by the shoulders, then draw apart imperceptibly from each other until they are no longer touching except by their fingertips, then let go and turn their backs to each other. The others start by touching fingers, then hold each other more and more closely until they embrace, then never let go and remain inseparable. These are the rarer sort of friends, naturally. They are more like an ideal category, spoken of each time that two tired friends have just gone their separate ways.

Be that as it may, thanks to Ramdane, and especially thanks to his daughter Chabha, the uncle and the nephew became friends, the kind who hold on tightly to each other's shoulders. Nevertheless, Slimane's attitude remained reserved, as expected. His lack of enthusiasm could have been attributed to shyness, his unpleasant nature, his inferiority complex, or his selfish stubbornness, or even a diabolical intuition. But in any case, it was accepted that no one should be bothered anymore about his ways since Chabha made every effort to make him appear in a positive light.

Chabha had gotten it into her head that she had to conquer the Parisians. It would have been nearly impossible to discourage her. All of her advances would have had to be rejected. You could not but be touched by her delicate attentions, by her kindness that was free of ulterior motives or, in short, her devotion.

Chabha is a young woman the same age as Amer; she is older than Marie but hardly appears so. She has never had a child, has never suffered too much, although she has lived the difficult life of village women in our land. She is the only child of Ramdane and Smina, who continue to protect her, after having spoiled her as one spoils a boy. At the age of twenty-eight, she still has the appearance of a sturdy young girl, well proportioned, with smooth, olive skin, a warm supple body, an animated face brightened by large, dark eyes, an expressive mouth with sweet lips and a ready smile; she can pout with the exquisite grace of an unhappy child.

She had no trouble making herself loved. She began with Kamouma, whom she called Nana.

"Nana, you are going to leave these young people in peace."

"Oh!"

"Yes, you will come to our house. You are not afraid of me, are you?"

"You, my girl, are more difficult than one would think."

"That is what we shall see. You do not have enough space here. You will use our little room that is always empty. You can sleep there every night. It is not far. Your son can bring you over, if need be, or your cousin can do it."

"Oh, he never really liked me, that one."

"Even better, then it will annoy him. You Aït-Hamouche, you are all so stubborn. You can fight it out, and I will watch."

"Well, all right. I will ask my son about it. You know, so far I have not bothered them, there in my loft. I sleep like a log. I do not trouble them. They are at liberty to speak; I do not understand a thing. As for the rest . . ."

"Ah!" said Madame, now on her guard from the "understand nothing" that she understood precisely.

"As for her, I will explain it to her," Chabha said. "It's like this, Madame: Nana Kamouma sleeps at Chabha's house."

"Oh really! Today?"

"What?"

"For how many days? *Achhal?*"

And Madame held up her fingers.

"Forever, Madame, forever."

Laughing, Chabha took Madame by the hand and led her toward the bed. Then, her gestures finished the explication.

"You there and Amer here. Two of you, like two fingers crossed." Chabha winked. "Nana and I . . ." She took Kamouma by the hand and made as if to leave.

"Is that all right?" Chabha asked. "*Ilha?*"

"Yes, *ilha*," Madame responded.

"Then it's settled. We will leave you with your big silly goose. Besides, you deserve him. Right, Nana? She is beautiful, your daughter-in-law."

"I am not saying no. But you know what is really in my heart. But what's to be done?"

"Do not trouble yourself. It is in God's hands. You can see that I too, I am waiting, waiting. Everything is in His hands. Amer will have his share, one day."

"What are you saying?" Madame asked.

"Oh! This will not be easy to explain to you," Chabha said. "Try to understand: you see? Me, nothing here." She indicated her belly. "You neither, nothing. Do you understand? Nothing to cradle, like this. But there is someone up high. Right?"

"Yes, Chabha, I understand."

In this way, Chabha grew accustomed to going there almost every day to visit Kamouma and Madame. At first, Kamouma was suspicious, but finally decided that her cousin's wife was not malicious, but she simply wanted to make up for the past. She agreed without too much trouble to visit once again her father's home and to call her cousin "my brother, Slimane." But Kamouma persisted in thinking that Slimane indeed had a black heart and could be contemplating some treachery, by using, if need be, Chabha's hypocritical attentiveness. In her elderly mind, which had already witnessed so many trivial things, anything was possible, so while her silly son went along with this, she would remain vigilant.

Time passed. Madame learned to express herself better and better. Ties with the Aït-Hamouche became closer. Chabha spoke to Amer with familiarity; she called him "our Amer." Often, there were exchanges of good couscous, and sometimes a meal was shared together at one or the other's house. Ramdane was always invited; Ima Smina met with Kamouma, and they chatted together frequently. It must also be said that Slimane, even if he remained a bit reserved in his dealings with Amer, took a liking to Madame. It was an affection that was somewhat hidden, it is true, but the others did notice since he accompanied each one of his timid and awkward attentions with complicit smiles.

One could no doubt see in this unexpected reconciliation the call of blood ties, if one accepted, as Amer did, that Marie was actually Slimane's niece. In truth, Slimane probably knew the whole story. By this point, Ramdane had already had several conversations with Amer. One day, he learned that Marie was Yvonne's daughter, the child he had so often taken into his gnarled and swarthy miner's arms when he was in France. Of course she had changed to the point of being unrecognizable to his weak eyes, but he almost choked with emotion.

"It really is a miracle what you are telling me, Amer!"

"Yes, our reunion was a miracle. From that day, I understood that my uncle forgave me."

"But you did not need to hide this! This will simplify things!"

"She does not have her real father's name! And, well, as for Yvonne, you know . . ."

"I only have to look at her now to see it. There is a family resemblance. I saw her the other day wearing Chabha's dress; she reminded me of your mother when she was young."

"Let's not exaggerate anything. It is pointless to dwell on it. We are not anxious for her to pass as a Kabyle. Neither she nor I want that. I prefer that you keep it a secret. You promise, right, Uncle Ramdane?"

"All right, since it is your wish, but I do not see why . . . and Slimane? Can we tell him?"

"I would prefer that he not know."

"All right! I am happy about all this anyway. If the call of blood ties really exists, Slimane will really like her. Just think how much your families are intertwined. God's plans are mysterious; we can only follow the path He chooses for us. Now I am not afraid for you. Rabah's blood returns in his daughter. Yes, he has returned to our land. Land and blood! The two essential elements in every person's destiny. We are but insignificant playthings in the hands of the Almighty."

Seeing the importance that the older man attached to this revelation, Amer understood that Slimane would quickly be informed, but that the blood tie would never be openly proclaimed. He understood that it would be better this way since the touchy Slimane was liable to misunderstand everything. He would not go around telling everyone that his brother's assassin had taken his victim's daughter for a wife. It would henceforth be a shared secret for the families, an additional link. No, Slimane was not the kind to yell from the rooftops that Madame was his niece.

In the depths of his heart, Slimane forgave Amer a great deal of things when he learned of the existence of this new relationship. He pardoned him for having found and collected this blood relation, and he began to love Marie in secret. It was not that he was ashamed to recognize her publicly as a relative, but he was afraid that he would not be taken seriously by a woman who was so different from the others!

"Let her be who she is, father-in-law," he said to Ramdane. "What would I do with such a niece?"

"Yes, she is your niece, there is no doubt. But you would do well to ignore it. In this way, you are not responsible for anything. His actions do not concern you, and in the eyes of other people, you do not owe him anything. A niece, though, one looks after her."

"I am planning on looking after her. She is my brother's daughter, after all. This concerns me too."

"And the inheritance?"

"I tell you she is like a daughter. I have no children. If I do not want it known, it is not so I can get out of my duty. I do not need any advice. Only you know about it. If my mother-in-law and wife learn of it, it will not be secret anymore. Then, I will recognize her openly, and I will give Madame everything the law allows me to grant. It will be that much less for your own daughter."

"And for yourself," Ramdane said. "You can keep your threats and bad mood to yourself. I am sorry I spoke, because I did promise Amer to keep silent."

"I am happy to know about this, and I am grateful to you. You are the one pushing me to tell the truth. So be it. I will talk to my wife about it. Only Ma Smina worries me. She is too much of a chatterbox to keep something quiet."

"You are right about that. I never tell her anything either. But as for my daughter, that is different!"

Land and Blood

Since this revelation, Slimane's attitude had changed a bit. It was a change that was hardly noticeable. Chabha saw that he was not as tormented, that he accepted this rapprochement of the two families without too much grumbling. At the same time, he became less communicative with her and grew silent whenever it was a question of Amer or Marie, as if he had run out of arguments. He may have felt that Chabha was abandoning him, going over to the other side. The young woman did not delve too deeply into all this; the important thing was to not openly annoy her husband. This is how a gnawing hostility came to exist between them, one that they refused to acknowledge since it took on the appearance of a kind of weariness.

All in all, if they were both just as tired of each other, the couple had become accustomed to living together without expecting anything beyond this shared existence. They had finally accepted that it was their fate to be together. It was not a matter of mutual understanding or disagreement, or of love and happiness. They were together, that is all. And then, at the moment Slimane thought he could do without love, he began to see that inexplicable, pouting expression that suited Chabha's lips so well and that had pleased him so whenever Chabha was defending him against his cousins. But now, she directed her little expression against him, and he hated it all the more. He did not understand it, and he said nothing about it; as for himself, he started to sulk. But then again, he wanted her to see that he was annoyed, all the while giving himself the appearance of a man that nothing could bother. Chabha figured out his game but pretended not to understand. This exasperated him even more. Sometimes, they had brief moments of frankness: a look, a nod of the head, a word spoken carelessly that revealed the depth of their thoughts. But then everything would be hidden behind a curtain that they quickly pulled between them. In short, each one of them ended up having a strange feeling that refused all compromise, like a small bubble full of resentment, like a cyst in an otherwise healthy body. It was like a tumor that would have to be removed someday so that it would not poison the entire body, or it would have to be ignored while waiting for worse to come.

This tumor (Chabha noticed it by now) she had always had, from the start of their marriage. This husband had been imposed upon her! In her dreams, as a young girl, she had wanted something other than Slimane. She had been a flower full of tart sap, not too showy of a flower, but one with enough perfume to intoxicate. She herself had been tipsy with youth and desire . . . and it was Slimane who showed up. Slimane was thirty years old then. She was fifteen! It was a good match for Ramdane and Smina: a big house, an enviable past, a man who was going to put their daughter in charge of his house right away since he did not have any sisters and his mother was gone. He was welcomed with open arms. Chabha was persuaded that she was lucky. She forgot her naive dreams, adopted the stance of a reasonable woman, mistress of the house, and considered herself fortunate. Only one small part of her refused this easy happiness: maybe it was a little, wispy voice inside her, or maybe it was that small bubble deep in her heart. Most of the time, she did not think of it or feel it. But then again, sometimes, she felt she was suffocating. In reality, what could she say to Slimane? It was true that lately she often had this feeling, but she did not even understand it herself. Maybe it was simply fatigue, after all.

She did not have anything specific to reproach him for. What had he not done for her? Slimane was only a *fellah*. He had never been to France because his parents had not dared advise him to go after his older brother's unfortunate departure. Slimane had never gone to school either: he had been too old when it was built. Nonetheless, having lived all of the time in his village, seeing the generations come and go, he had acquired a natural self-assurance, and his initial shyness was now taken for arrogance. In the end, he only managed to make himself despised, and in turn, he hated everybody else. People thought he was mean-spirited. But his heart was a clean slate. Without even being aware of it, Chabha conquered him with her impish, childish ways, and they spent ten peaceful years together. No doubt there was passion on Slimane's side, but he was so much in the habit of hiding his desires that Chabha managed not to understand too much, that is, enough to rebuff the impulsive gestures he sometimes attempted. While she believed herself to be reasonable and took pride in her wisdom, she actually exasperated the poor fellow, who turned away in anger and became more timid than ever. He quickly felt himself to be the guilty party, and he would return to her, calmer and more docile. In this manner, even in their caresses, they followed a set of restrictive rules issued by Chabha's sensible mind, since she naively believed that a woman and a man from good families should not stray from certain limits. For example, suffice it to say that when one of them got dressed in the other's presence, it would be total darkness, or the other one would turn away . . .

Yes, they were a sensible couple. This is why neither one of them was completely satisfied. Chabha sensed there was more to life, but she carefully hid her turmoil. When she would hear some of the neighbor women openly discuss some "games" that they seemed to enjoy, she felt a sincere disgust. But she would hear these remarks in broad daylight like an unexpected parenthesis in the middle of normal conversations. At night, when she began to dream, with Slimane lying asleep next to her, she saw things differently. She envied the audacity of these women.

Slimane knew. Maybe he even knew too much. He had married late. He was an old bachelor with many adventures under his belt that he could not really discuss. When he became angry he missed all of that a bit, even to the point of wishing he had one of those easy women, ready for anything. But once he calmed down, he would not have wanted Chabha to change for anything in the world, and he was pleased with her modest, girlish ways. So he loved her in all his selfishness and made do with the occasional caress.

XVI   In the scope of everyday life, they got along quite well. She obeyed him without difficulty, knew to go along with his ideas, recognizing his experience in matters. She always took his side, which greatly comforted Slimane. Each of them was sure of the other's affection: they trusted each other.

If this had not been the case, then they would not have stayed together after ten years of waiting. For they spent their lives waiting! Their dream was to have a lot of children, especially boys. When, in the beginning of their marriage, someone wished them seven sons (seven is the usual number in this type of wish), the wish was accepted with a beaming smile: it was right on the mark. They began to worry right after the end of their first year of marriage. Was it a spell or a curse? They had to take the necessary precautions: seek forgiveness from relatives—forgotten until then, pay a visit to family graves, distribute food on their graves to seek their protection, go to see the renowned *koubas,* leaving offerings there and promising even greater ones. Each one of these rituals was carried out with great humility. For the entire month, Slimane said his prayers, Chabha purified herself in the evening and in the morning, and their lovemaking went on with as much vigor as hopefulness (in the dark, of course). On the morning of the twenty-ninth day, the young woman inevitably felt a warm trickle between her thighs. She would run behind the eaves where the small reed hut was located and pull up her *gandoura* to contemplate her shame: her disappointment manifested itself in a flood of curses that were addressed to nothing or nobody in particular: the hen scratching in a furrow, the chipped jug she had carelessly knocked over, a door panel that did not want to remain open. Slimane guessed right away. He got up without a word and left for the café.

The first day was as morose as his heart. The house became as ugly as sin, the streets hideous with dirt; the early swarming of children with their unwashed faces filled him with disgust, as did the housewives sweeping away the night's refuse from their doorways. Some of them still had puffy eyes with sticky lashes, the bottom of their *gandouras* wrinkled from their sleep. The large pile of trash on the edge of the road to the café was a perfect symbol. Good! We are nothing but garbage. What is beautiful around here, anyway? This blue sky with its pale splotches, sometimes sticky and heavy, sometimes over-heated by the sun, or biting and icy but always poisoned with the stench of refuse and carrion? These hills sticking up like the back of a skinny, mangy donkey? These miserable villages with their whitish houses sinking into the red clay soil like snail shells in clumps of silt? At the café, people seemed stupid or ridiculous to him. They all had the same sallow face. They spoke, laughed, played, and gestured. No, they swarmed like their offspring. There was nothing else. Vermin, all of them, born from the dirt, and they would return to the dirt . . .

Then, slowly, he calmed down, woke up, enjoyed his ciga-rette and cup of coffee. Then, inevitably, he would join in. Sli-mane became sociable. He played with gusto, making everyone laugh at the expense of someone who was not there. He would return home late, ravenous, tipsy from chatting and pretending to be carefree, his eyes burning, his mouth in a grimace. He greeted his wife with one of those meaningless aphorisms that transmit an eternal truth and supposedly soothe misfortune. He would say, for example: "Do not be sad, Wife, we cannot change our fate. The Creator only owes us life, and He has given it to us. We cannot demand anything else of Him."

Each time, Chabha knew that his eyes glistened with sad-ness, an elated sadness, almost joyful. Maybe it was a peculiar joy brought on by a bout of helpless sadness. She was sorry for it and answered: "Your life and my own are my children. I do not desire any others."

She would then become cheerful as well. It was, at first, a forced cheerfulness, and then it became irresistible. They ended up in the same frame of mind. Their unhappiness made them closer. They bore it well together—so much so that they ended up having new hope the day she was purified from her men-struation. He would always learn, at that precise moment, of an unknown remedy to try, a ritual they had not yet performed, or a drug they needed to obtain. The two spouses submitted themselves to a new experiment and then waited for the result with the same trust that ten years of disappointment had not succeeded in destroying.

As for childless couples, there were enough in the village to make childlessness, after all, a tolerable fate. They all hoped for children someday and envied the families blessed with children. For their common consolation, there were some poor mothers who only bore daughters: three, four, five, one right after the other. These were the women to be pitied, and indeed they were. But everyone knew, coming from the "barren" women, it was never sincere.

"Good. You want children? Have some girls, and then some more. That's great. This reassures us. You can envy us in the long run."

But it was just spite. One day, Slimane said to Chabha:

"At least have a girl! Even if she is born and then dies on the same day, I wouldn't care. At least no one will say anymore that we cannot have any."

"But that is the truth, Husband. It is either you or I, but which of us, I do not know."

"Then it is you. I am certain of my abilities. I can procreate."

"I am not privy to God's plans. Only He knows. He has a plan for everyone."

"We can never win this discussion. You can wait until the end of your life. All right then, let's wait."

The truth is that there is a way out if one wishes. They both think about it but avoid going too far, stopping at the edge of the real explanation, skirting the truth. A solution exists. They both know it. There are examples to follow; there are others who have gotten out of this predicament. One day, Chabha believes, they will doubtless have to resign themselves to it, after they have exhausted all other options. Slimane will never be cornered into it, she knows him that well. But his desire is so strong that he will not refuse to put a price on it one day, if she wishes it.

Land and Blood

The acceptable solution is for the man to take another wife. The boldest always end up doing just that and usually send away the first wife. Besides, it is not a question of courage, but of brutality and selfishness, and it requires, in all evidence, that one have no real attachment in order to agree to send her away. There are many other factors too numerous to list or to imagine. Sometimes, one suddenly just decides to no longer keep the unfortunate wife around anymore. Without even wondering why, the man repudiates her, even if it means missing her when it is too late.

Old Ramdane and Ma Smina were afraid that Slimane, one day, might arrive at the same decision, and they urged their daughter to be submissive and sensible. Chabha made light of their concern. Her reasonable little head controlled the situation with great confidence—until the day when Hocine's example came to light, troubling their calm and challenging Slimane's resignation.

Hocine-ou-Larbi had gotten married at the same time as Slimane. As he thought of himself as someone very important, he was very exacting in the choice of his wife. Chabha knew his wife very well. She was one of her childhood friends, several years older and more beautiful as well. After five years of marriage, she had no children either. Hemama, Hocine's wife, tired of waiting, took, unceremoniously, from among her uncles, the ugliest and most insignificant of her cousins and offered her to Hocine, who got her with child right off the bat. The people of the neighborhood knew exactly what was going on. But outside, Hemama could pass for a heroine, sacrificing herself for her husband, obliging him to accept this sacrifice, and finally succeeding in providing him with the longed-for heir that seemed to come down from on high as a reward for her generous spirit. The reality was very simple. Slimane finally had the chance to see for himself. All the same, on the day of the child's birth, he appeared sadder, as if it had happened to someone else. Chabha had to explain it to him since she had all the details.

"Don't look so sad. Hemama is not as extraordinary as one might think."

Land and Blood

"Maybe you're just jealous."

"Yes, that must be it. I pity her, poor Fetta. That ninny Hocine thinks only of strutting around. Hemama is the master!"

"She married him to Fetta for her own pleasure, no doubt?"

"I am telling you that Fetta does not matter. I have the truth of the matter from both of them! She gave him to Fetta for the first week. That's all. Hemama waited until the end of the month. She had planned it from the start. Either she would send Fetta back, or she would keep her to produce a child."

"She is just bragging. She wants to appear important."

"If this wasn't the case, then why would Hocine have accepted a woman like poor Fetta? Don't you see that it was planned that way in order to turn him away from other women, so that he could see with his own eyes the difference between beautiful Hemama and another, so that he could appreciate his happiness? She thinks she is so clever, Hemama, but it is as plain as day. It is all right for the men. But we women realize it right away. I don't need her confidences to understand her."

"You are a bit like her. Except that you don't have the courage to try."

"No, I am not going to try. Get married if you wish, I can handle it. But you are not a bit like Hocine. He is too stupid and too handsome. Hemama told me that during this generous week she granted them, she was sleeping in the loft. They were down below, indulging in their quasi-clandestine game, smothered and timid, and several times Hemama, full of rage and hate, wanted to climb down and strangle them in their bed. It was all done in the dark. At the slightest noise, she would cough and growl in anger so that they would stop their embrace for a moment while she, Hemama, enjoyed their discomfort. In the morning, when she came down from the loft, Hocine would sneak away like a thief, and poor Fetta had to endure the shame of her beautiful cousin's sarcasms. You think I do not have the courage for it? Yes, that must be it. We are not that mean. Fetta told me she thought that week would never end. And then, no more husband for Fetta. Hemama heated some water, closed the door, and they were alone in the house.

"'Scrub my back,' she told Fetta.

Land and Blood

"She undressed, strutted around, and brazenly showed off her well-shaped legs, her full thighs, her shoulders and arms. After her bath, she took out her two best dresses, her silk sash, her new scarf, then combed her hair and perfumed herself. She forbade Fetta to get changed. After making her puny rival admire her beauty, Hemama welcomed Hocine home with all her seductive powers.

"She carried on with her coquettish scheme the whole day, demanding that he embrace her in broad daylight, in front of Fetta. Then she became angry and sent him to sleep in the loft by himself. But from that day on, she returned to him, and Fetta was the one to climb up to sleep in the loft, with an old mat and the most worn-out blankets. She set up her bed between the jars of provisions and other old utensils."

"But Chabha, you must admit that she deserves credit. She must really love Hocine. To be obliged to share him, even with a cousin, must have been hard for her. What she did afterward is just childish revenge. Fetta should not be angry with her for it."

"It's possible after all," Chaba answered.

"I'm certain of it. Hemama is an honest woman, right? There is nothing to reproach her for; she has never been unfaithful."

"No, she has too much self-respect for that. But she could have spared herself this fuss. It's just that she wanted to show him . . ."

"What do you expect? With you women, one always has to be careful. Besides, you all know each other, and you are all so judgmental toward each other. You are all so malicious that even for the best of you on Judgment Day, the Prophet will turn his back on you."

"That's what men say (may God forgive me). He loved women, he had four of them."

"Yes, obviously. But to get back to Hemama, I think she was very reasonable, after all."

"Too reasonable! If, at the end of the first month there had been no sign of a child having been conceived, she would simply have sent Fetta back to her parents. Hocine would have been cured of his desire to remarry."

"And his land would have fallen prey to his cousins. In his old age he would risk being cheated out of it like he cheated Kaci, his own uncle. But then, look how fate works! Kaci did have a son, and it did not prevent his land from being taken; Hocine almost didn't have a son, and now he does have one. It must be that he never did act maliciously against Kaci."

"It's different. Selling one's land, 'eating' it during one's lifetime, that's bad enough. But to die without an heir . . ."

"Like me, Chabha!"

"Then get married, my friend, since you keep bringing this up."

"You're the one who brings it up."

"Let me finish! Hocine is attached to his land, Hemama to her peace of mind. She did not know which of them was cursed, so she tried an experiment to prove it, one way or the other. When she understood that Fetta was expecting, her position became clear. She would no longer have to give up Hocine; the only thing being asked of the girl was to carry his seed. Fetta kept her precious deposit without asking for anything more. She was treated like an old jar filled with oil. That's all. And now, God rewards Hemama's generous spirit in giving Hocine an heir. In the village, everyone credits Hemama. You said as much yourself. Hocine praises her to the skies. Only God knows how she is going to settle things with Fetta afterward."

Indeed, everyone was talking about this event. In general, people congratulated Hocine on finally receiving his just reward, and people insisted on saying kind words to Hemama, who received the praise with a gracious modesty. Hocine was content, of course. But his joy at having this offspring was tempered by tenderness toward the woman who should have been the one to give it to him, so much so that he quite forgot about the other woman who was there, lying on her soiled mat, stunned from pain and surprise. Fetta was, indeed, overwhelmed with happiness. She had never dreamed that she would be the one to grant such a longed-for wish. She had thought that she would have a daughter who would not be welcomed and would become a second underdog for one of those superb husbands to whom she found it normal to defer.

The idea of "raising her head a little higher" or according herself some importance did not occur to her. She merely thought she might be granted a bit more kindness with the little bundle of wailing pink flesh she held out each time. She humbled herself to soften up her cousin, admitting to her that she did not know anything about babies, effacing herself at every turn in order to be forgiven for her good luck and to try to enter just a little bit into the conjugal intimacy.

It became evident to all three of them that Fetta's role was over or almost over. Hemama changed the diapers. Hemama discussed things with the elderly woman who had brought the child into the world. Fetta was not capable of retaining any advice about the baby, nor could she respond to congratulations, nor was she able to protect the little treasure from the evil eye of ill-intentioned visitors. Hemama was sure of herself. Her confidence reassured Hocine and astounded Fetta.

Time passed. Naturally, it is not possible to relay all the details of the daily life of this "ménage à trois," the pitiful existence of Fetta, her self-abnegation, her misery. Everyone lives his own life, after all. But in the long term, very little remains hidden. There are no secrets among us. Even when one is discreet, distant, and reserved, mysterious antennae inform the entire village, which then begins to whisper, then snicker, and finally to criticize with a wink. Fetta did not have a mother to defend her. She only had a stepmother. Her father wanted there to be peace above all, and he too obsequiously praised his niece Hemama. Out of cowardice, he even encouraged her to be stricter with his daughter.

"I brought her up badly. I am counting on you, Hemama, to straighten her out."

And how! So then, the child grew up as Hemama's spoiled son. Fetta's story is a sad one. At present, everybody knows the details. Whenever anyone tells the story, they even cite examples of sly cruelty that are perhaps pure invention, because when it comes to criticism, we have infinite resources, and it does not cost a thing. There are people who take great pleasure in this. What is unfortunate, however, is that public censure often arrives too late to right the wrong that has been done. One can imagine and relate anything one wishes; in this particular case, it is pointless: Fetta died leaving her child of two years. The orphan was not really to be pitied since his real mother was Hemama, while the other woman was referred to in his first babblings as Tata, which sounded a lot like Fetta. That was it. He said "mama and papa" to the two spouses. As for the intruder, she was Fetta for him as well. She must have suffered, of course, seeing her son taken from her and being pushed aside, but it would be an exaggeration, perhaps, to accuse Hemama of killing her by all sorts of humiliations.

There is a punishment for spiteful gossip mongers. We know that those who speak ill of others run the risk of having the sins of their victims placed upon their own shoulders. That is the punishment. Usually, when someone finishes maligning a person, he concludes with an odd saying: "May he keep his own sins!" This wise precaution amounts to saying: "If my gossip is justified, then I am not to blame. But I cannot guarantee anything. It would not be fair to burden me with the sins of another. Let him sort it out with the Good Lord; I am not swearing to anything." And there you have it! Given such a phrase, one is permitted to embellish. This is why each time someone tells you about Fetta with hypocritical sadness, he inevitably ends with this neutral phrase based on caution and cowardice: "Yes, well, Hemama is like that. May she keep her own sins."

For whatever reason, Chabha was right to want to squash Slimane's enthusiasm, since he could not praise Hemama enough when Hocine remarried. Like everyone else, he finally knew the truth, and it made his blood run cold. He bluntly declared that he was not foolish enough to let one woman torment another one just for his sake. He stopped thinking of "remarriage." They once again took up the old wives' remedies and made the rounds of shrines in the region with the same touching regularity. This is where they stood when Marie and Amer came home to Ighil-Nezman.

XVII

It is whispered here and there that some people have "made arrangements" that are even more radical. When the men are enjoying themselves, and they are the kind of men who do not anger easily, one of them might say to Slimane: "Say, old friend, just look at that strapping young man; one night with your wife, and you would have an heir." Slimane replies as best he can. These are obviously crude remarks. But they are honest. The men laugh and then change the subject. In any case, that is a solution; it is there right within reach. Just like suicide. A person can obtain a son like one can end one's own life.

Old Kamouma is not one to spend her time gossiping, and neither is Aunt Smina. However, they do know each other's thoughts. They know each other thoroughly and accept each other's faults since they like to get together and chat. They are friends, in other words. Whenever Madame sees them squatting in the sun, seated in front of the threshold, blocking the way with their brown legs stretched out in front of them—Kamouma's dry and sticklike and Smina's heavy and puffy around the ankles—she thinks of good old Madame Garet, rambling on at her counter with some nice, old gray-haired client. She knows that the image is not the same, but the impression of triviality is identical. Madame takes care of her housework and lets them chat; if she were interested, she could understand their conversation. Sometimes she goes out into the small courtyard to get some wood or to empty a pot. She steps over them both, coming and going, recognizing that she really has other things to do than to listen.

They have a lot to say to each other, these old women. Both of them are worried: one about her daughter, the other about her son.

"It will be as God wills it, Kamouma. My daughter is a simple and honest woman. You know me well enough: she is just like me. We just have to be patient and wait."

"Yes, there are those who can. Others, well, we usually reproach them, but really, are they to be blamed? These days, everything is allowed if you are wealthy."

"The Issoulah? They knew how to go about it. I admire them for it. A woman like Tassadit, well, there aren't any more like her these days. What do you think, Kamouma?"

"We all know that she could go the *djema* and teach the men there a thing or two. I will not speak ill of her for what she did, but I know that during Kaci's lifetime I could never have acted that way with my son. Kaci was the master, do you remember? He was a stubborn one."

"That's how it was for me. Right from the beginning, Ramdane made all the decisions. He knows what he wants and intends to get his own way. And then again, our temperament, you and I, we don't mind being obedient. We are naive and loyal. My daughter is like that too."

"I believe it. But then again, Tassadit, she took the upper hand right from the start. Her husband was a widow's son. What can you do? He was easy to dominate. Even more so since she had brothers and he needed allies."

"He wasn't poor, no, just forlorn. His cousins didn't like him, and he feared them. They wanted to get his lands."

"He managed to keep his land, the best in the village. Now, he is the richest man."

"He was able to keep it thanks to Tassadit and her brothers. Do you remember, they gave him their *fellah*. For thirty years, Salem cleared, worked, and planted Hamid Issoulah's land. It's more than enough to go and retire among the French. He left wearing his *gandoura,* worn out like an old plow. Do you remember? He was a strong one. As solid and black as the trunk of an oak tree and as ugly as could be. However, more than one woman, secretly, would have had him. He was a real man. Good thing he has four sons to support him in his old age, four sons and no daughters."

"You mean eight sons, don't you? She had four sons too, Tassadit, and they looked just like Salem's. How we gossiped about it back then! Hamid is blond with blue eyes . . . but that's all forgotten now."

"After giving the father some heirs, now he gives some to the son. Tassadit is a capable woman; I can't bring myself to blame her. She is protecting her eldest from the greed of his brothers. He deserves it, Mohand-ou-Hamid. He has worked hard, helping Salem here, going to France as a young man, advising his brethren abroad, replacing his father little by little in the meetings at the *djema*. He has a special place in Tassadit's heart. She married him to one of his cousins when he was quite young in order for him to have children. She has been waiting for fifteen years."

"Well, she did the right thing. She knew how to set up her family. I like people who know what they want."

"Me too."

Mohand-ou-Hamid had just had a son. It was wonderful. Everyone was talking about it. And, well, since he was well-liked in the village, it seemed to be to everyone's relief. At the *djema*, at the café, on the road to the cemetery, one could hear people commenting upon the event, saying, for example: "When one sows well, one harvests well," or, "He who waits for God is never disappointed." They all hastened to congratulate the Issoulah family.

The Issoulah are wealthy and very charitable. Their reputation in the village is great. All the poor know their house and its goodness. It is even a bit showy since, as they say, it has happened that Hamid and Tassadit deprive their own daughters-in-law in order to give alms or that they go to some lengths to avoid having passersby seeking hospitality anywhere else. Since the Aït-Hamouche have "fallen," as we say, it is the Issoulah who claim to uphold the village's honor. They answer for its fame: "In Ighil-Nezman, they say, no traveler has to spend the night outside or without eating." This is all well and good and warms our hearts; each and every one of us, in our hearts, is always welcoming. If it were not for our avarice or our poverty, we would all like to be more hospitable. It must be said that it is Tassadit herself who oversees the behavior of the family in this way, to the extent that sometimes her children and Hamid are furious to see her so generous with others, while she does not allow them any generosity. For her, it is a matter of principle, maybe even a little obsession. We do not reproach her for it, since we all benefit from it, more or less. As she insists upon her reputation as a remarkable woman, we say that she is a saint, and her two biggest sins take on—in our eyes at least—the appearance of a judicious action that is above the reproaches of petty people.

In our minds, Tassadit is a great woman, just as a man can be great. This is not a small thing to say for a Kabyle. People suspect her of having gotten her four sons from her laborer Salem. But aside from these suspicions, who in the village can reproach her anything? No one. She is elderly now, with no enemies . . . a wise woman! Not only has she been forgiven, but it was understood that Hamid was incapable of doing what Salem did. Why not simply imagine that he was not virile at all, and Tassadit, saddled with such a husband, had for a long time stoically put up with her disgrace, never breathing a word of it, only taking Salem to found a family and to save the land, thus giving heirs to the solitary, puny widow's son, despised even by his own family.

The same reasoning led her, no doubt, to use Salem once again for her son's wife, her own niece Ourdia. Ourdia was a great beauty. She outshone all of her sisters-in-law: light skin, black hair, and wide, smoldering eyes. When Tassadit accompanied her to the fields, she let her walk in front, dressed in her yellow silk dress with fringe on the shoulders and chest, Tassadit would gaze longingly at her as if she were a treasure and recall that she had been like that too as a young woman, filling out her traditional-style, white satin *gandoura* in the same way, with her full, firm, and rounded curves. She admitted that her complexion had been darker and she had not been as graceful, but above all she dwelt on the likelihood that poor Ourdia's womb was destined to remain empty. No doubt she slowly brought her around to the idea of accepting Salem. She must have exploited Ourdia's heartache, her jealousy in seeing her sisters-in-law give birth, one right after the other. One might assume as well that the notion of sleeping with another man did not repulse her. Her Mohand was not handsome. And then again, they knew each other too well: they were cousins, after all, who had practically always lived together, sharing the same bowl of couscous. They had been together since childhood. Marriage had not changed that. Ourdia had perhaps thought that an unknown man would be a revelation for her, a brief moment of paradise. But she knew her dream would be impossible. In all likelihood, her aunt's suggestion must have been poorly received; after all, Salem was now only a darkened, old stump of an oak tree. It was difficult to picture Ourdia in his arms. Ourdia would have preferred anyone else, that much was certain, but not Salem. No doubt, Tassadit had to reason with her niece: Salem was the only one at hand. They could trust him completely. He would not be able to say a word about it. His silence on family secrets had already lasted for thirty years, in spite of the reasons to be angry she had given him by dismissing him. Even if he said anything, no one would believe him. Ourdia, so young, so beautiful, with this old monster? Not possible! Another argument: his great age. They would have to hurry and take advantage of his presence; in a year or six months he might no longer be around.

The women who were familiar with this matter suspected that it had been arranged in this way. The younger ones—the sauciest ones—said among themselves that after all, it would not be so bad, since he was blind anyway. She just had to shut her eyes too and imagine that some other young man was taking her in his arms. As for passion, you could count on the "old, darkened oak tree." Age probably made no difference. For him to once again feel a smooth, firm body in his dried-out arms, it would be enough to revive his past vigor long enough and be like a foretaste of heaven. It was not that bad for Ourdia either.

As for the rest, these types of questions did not even occur to elderly women like Kamouma and Smina. They were too old for that.

"I think all this fuss is scandalous. Fine, Mohand has his heir, but Tassadit should be more discreet. Even if she has kept up appearances, she knows she hasn't fooled anyone."

"No, Kamouma. It's important to her. Her eldest was desperate. He and Ourdia were to be pitied. They are correct to do things in a big way. They are wealthy, that's normal."

"They promised three oxen to three different *koubas*. We will have what we need for Achoura; the best kind of charity begins at home, they say. We will have our bit of meat."

"You'll see that everyone will be firing off their rifles in their honor. We will hear the ululations all week long, and on the pretext of inviting the riflemen, the whole village will eat meat and couscous next Friday."

"Indeed. But I am telling you that this is all too showy. You have to agree that there are some things best forgotten. There is a tacit understanding with the Issoulah: their generosity makes up for all the rest. Will they have the courage to keep the blind man, Salem, for a few days? If only to receive his *baraka*?"

"Or to flout it. It would be too noticeable if they forgot him. Even if, in all innocence, someone there would draw attention to the fact that the old man is present, they won't be able to forget."

"No one will be surprised to see him there. It has been more than a year since he started going back to their home. His sons neglect him a bit. One of his granddaughters acts as his guide and walks him around everywhere to receive alms. But for a year now, he has been seen crossing the *djema*, going to the other neighborhood, to Tassadit's house. And now, it's definite, isn't it? She was enticing him there. It must have happened one day when all the other daughters-in-law were in the olive grove. On days when everyone goes out, it is always Ourdia and her aunt who take care of the house, while the three other women go out with their husbands. Mohand goes to market, while old Hamid, well, anywhere is fine for him as long as he finds someone to listen to his incessant chatter . . ."

But for these elderly ladies, no, this was not chitchat, everything they were saying to each other. Madame would indeed be naive to think their conversation was trivial.

Ima Smina stood up stiffly with a groan. Her heavy and glistening forehead was creased with worry; her jowls drooped on either side of her chin, marked by two deep wrinkles that joined together below her chin like two elastic bands. Then she absentmindedly dusted off her backside while looking at her friend. Kamouma drew her pointy knees up to her chest, clearing the way across the threshold, but did not stir more than that: this was her home. Her blurry eyes did not blink under the placid gaze of Smina.

"May God forgive us and them as well. I am leaving. Peace be with you. Good day, Madame."

"Go in peace. Are you busy?"

"Yes, I am going over to Chabha's. She should be back from the fields. Slimane has gone to the market."

"Do not worry too much about her. I love her like my own daughter, especially since I spend my nights at their place. She spoils me, you know."

"She is very fond of you as well. May God keep and bless your son."

Kamouma smiled. It is precisely this blessing that worries Smina. Oh, she had understood her well enough. She answered as expected. The allusions were the same from all sides. We understand each other completely, thought Kamouma with a smile. It is not some Salem that Chabha needs. But what would she think about Amer, for example? She is naive and does not suspect a thing. But here is Smina, trying to change the course of things. It is too obvious as well. Slimane is more and more sullen. He is a dangerous one; he must not come to understand. Chabha should be on guard. She is too open about her feelings. Amer is smarter. He must have learned things back in France. He has understood, but he hesitates. However, everything is ready: her safety depends upon it. Chabha has Slimane wrapped around her little finger. She must make friends of these two men. Slimane will no longer brood over his revenge. I will die at peace, and I will have my revenge over them all. If only this plan could take shape! The Aït-Hamouche would not die out, thanks to the blood of a woman they abandoned. Amer will bear the remorse of betraying the brother of the man he has killed, and maybe he would regret not having married a Kabyle (cheating me out of the fate that all elderly women

Land and Blood

experience), after having forgotten and abandoned me in his fashion. At least, I will have helped him avoid an implacable animosity with his vicious cousin. He is my son, after all. As for this stranger, she would know that she can't keep her man, even as white as she is, with her fine manners. It is not that I dislike her, but after all, it is her or women like her who ruined it for him and for Rabah, the one who caused my own and Kaci's misfortune. This is my score to settle with Frenchwomen; God himself will have to step in to help me. Smina is worried, but she is in agreement. She cannot convince Chabha to discreetly try just anyone. She must have already suggested other men! Chabha is an honest woman, after all, but the temptation is more than she can bear. She loves my son. Smina is hopeful. Tassadit's example is there to follow. But what worries her is that there are no guarantees: Amer has no children, and neither does Chabha. Four people are involved. Which two are the right ones? If she ignores this, she risks having her daughter make a mistake. Too bad about her. I will not go that far. But all the same, if only Madame could get with child! That would gratify us, and it would remove any doubts from Smina. It would surely embolden Chabha. Madame must, therefore, take care of herself!

XVIII

Madame does not like Hemama very much. She knows that Hocine is their cousin, but she does not care for this woman. With her way of saying "Madaame," of openly admiring herself in the mirror above the bed, she has the look of a young and arrogant female boss. Marie has always disliked young, female bosses. She knows all about her now. Chabha has told her about Fetta; she sees the image of Fetta in their sickly offspring, refusing all care, growing up with difficulty, pale and pitiful, in the suffocating shadow of that couple.

"He is not very handsome," Chabha tells her one day. "He looks like his mother."

"I might have known. But he is very nice. He must remind them of the dead woman."

"Oh! They feel sorry for her now. They cannot say her name without adding 'May God forgive her.' She never even bothered them."

"No remorse? Doesn't Hemama reproach herself for anything?"

"She does not have any worries. Remorse is for those who fail at something, or maybe at the very end, just before one dies. But when that happens, there is no remorse or anything else. One loses consciousness and goes to meet one's maker."

"You might be right. I can't find the right words to explain. I don't know Kabyle well enough. But you see, all the same, they know she suffered and cried in secret. What do they think about that now?"

"But they don't think about it anymore! They watch over their child. What makes you think of that? It's obvious that you, you're educated."

Chabha burst out laughing, as did Madame. Then they spoke of other matters. Madame knows just about everybody in the neighborhood, but she is only fond of Chabha. Chabha is lively, frank, and strong. She is dark haired, and Marie thinks she is beautiful. She is full of common sense and seems intelligent. She has shown herself to be affectionate and talkative, tells her about everyone, and sparks her interest in all the stories, all the gossip, and their discussions always end in laughter and slaps on the back. She likes her for her simplicity and her carefree attitude. They are inseparable.

Marie does not go out, naturally. She maintains her rank. Just like the wife of the *amin,* or those of the *marabouts* in the village. Besides, there are other Kabyle women who stay inside. It was that way when Ali was alive, and during the height of their opulent era, the Aït-Hamouche took pride in the fact that only the old women or the very young girls were allowed out. Kamouma recalls these good old days. She likes to remind people when they forget. Still, there were others who, thanks to a more or less enduring wealth, knew the privilege of remaining indoors and not being seen by men who, all the same, knew you already. For us, this is a source of pride. This is possible at very little cost, yes, at very little cost, so much so that it became ridiculous in the eyes of wealthy *fellah* families who always stayed at home. The Issoulah, for example, or the Aït-Abbès never cloistered their women in spite of their own wishes, since they wanted to prove to others how devoted to them their families were. But the Issoulah and the Aït-Abbès are reasonable people who do not follow trends. They feel that they do not have to imitate anybody.

People understood that Amer would want to keep his wife at home since the lady could be of little use outside. Would she be carrying a basket or a water jug on her back? Impossible! Better to leave her to her dishes than to see her wandering around empty handed on the narrow paths that tumble down both sides of the village, toward the north and the south. But there are some who have no sense of the absurd. They are the targets of numerous epigrams and short poems that they know as well as anyone else, but that they only call to mind when they apply them to others.

Everybody knows the short poem that goes:

> When he was in France
> She went about the paths
> Now she is surrounded by four walls
> He pays a maid to fetch the water . . .

Land and Blood

It is true that some people have no self-restraint. Indeed, when they were in France, they forgot everything, their wives were free. But upon their return, they shamelessly change their ways: fancy clothes, wastefulness, pretentiousness, and their wives under lock and key. They crush others by their wealth, pull themselves up to a position of power, realize an old dream they had, and refuse to remember the times when they were wretched. If this attitude lasts a long time, the others end up taking them seriously; otherwise, they fall back again and find themselves once more "sitting in the dirt," snickering in turn to see the ones who are "rising." This is why sensible people prefer to neither "rise" nor "fall." They are, one might say, our bourgeois. We have grand and small ones like this.

Slimane and Chabha are "petit bourgeois." Chabha has never been tempted to shut herself inside the home. There is work to be done in the fields (Slimane cannot do everything). As for the rest, her temperament would never put up with being locked away indoors. She has no children to raise and no neighbors to entertain her. The entire little street is inhabited by the Aït-Hamouche. The cousins are not nice to each other; their wives spend their free time quarreling among themselves. The men rarely come to blows, but many do not speak to each other, and they scowl when they pass each other by. They hate Slimane, who responds in kind, and Chabha reserves her most disdainful pout for them. Now that she has gotten in the habit of going to see Kamouma as soon as she has the time, she has forgotten all about them. The Aït-Hamouche and the Aït-Larbi are not from the same neighborhood, and crossing through the *djema* each time to pay a visit is not very practical because it would openly display a new friendship, supported only by somewhat tenuous kinship bonds, the very bonds that until just now, Slimane had tried to sever.

But there was a more discreet path: Slimane lived in the last house of the neighborhood; Kamouma's home was located at the end of the Aït-Larbi alley, so it was possible to get from one house to the other by crossing through the small garden plots that each family kept behind the house. Kamouma and Chabha preferred this path, but when Slimane and Amer paid a visit, they crossed the streets and the *djema;* the hidden path was only suitable for the women.

Marie went out less and less, either with her husband or with Kamouma to pay a visit. She was quite highly regarded, so others came to see her. Everyone appreciated the fact that Kamouma did not become "stuck up," thus proving that she had not forgotten her past destitution. In the past, women went to her home to enjoy themselves as if they were in a public place. Now it was different: they were dealing with someone worthy of consideration, someone worthy of respect. All the same, they knew Amer was not easygoing: he liked peace and quiet and did not care for these women (the proof was that he did not want a Kabyle for a wife). In short, things had changed, and Kamouma never failed to emphasize it. No one was annoyed with her for that, but a few impertinent individuals understood her attitude and declared that God had taken an interest in the old woman to the extent that she no longer needed anybody. But she could not, in good conscience, close her door.

Madame did not complain too much about all these visitors. In her view, having visitors file in and out all day could not really be a suitable way to live. But it was her only distraction. In the end, she noticed how costly it could be: a cup of coffee for one, a crust of bread for another, a worn-out piece of clothing for an old woman or a sweet for a child. It was so nice to make the others happy. But in the long run, some of the women became unbearable, those who came just to lament their fate: "Ah, Madame, you must know . . ." as if Madame, once she "knew," could do anything to change someone's bad luck or misfortune. Others, on the contrary, came to boast and to show off riches they did not really possess in order to compare themselves to Marie. These women above all found themselves rebuffed by the old woman.

Then Kamouma would regret having openly taken the side of the Frenchwoman and would berate herself for it. In this way, Marie discovered much pettiness, meanness, and slyness mixed together with stupidity, true sensitivity, kindness, and hypocrisy. On the whole, it was amusing. She was a spectator and lost herself a bit in her observations. She even forgot that what she was witnessing there in Kabylia she could have also seen almost anywhere else. But in that earlier life, she had never found the time to have fun; she had been too preoccupied with trying to get by.

She rapidly learned Kabyle, and at the end of a year's time, she was able to chat and joke with her friends. She only spoke French with Amer and with the neighborhood children, who, in order to demonstrate their learning to her, would call "Bonjour" or "Bonsoir, Madame" through the cracks of the old front gate, without being overly concerned about which phrase was appropriate for the time of day. Many of the young girls in the neighborhood sought her friendship. In the beginning, she liked them all because they all seemed the same to her. Then when she got to know them better, she adjusted her attitude, with each one taking on the correct tone or appropriate demeanor, and in this way she became initiated into life among us. She came to understand that this kind of "mask" or adopted demeanor was necessary the day she, in turn, discovered it on all the other faces. If Madame only truly became fond of Chabha, it was because Chabha came to her, or so it seemed, with an open heart, and this enabled Marie to be sincere in turn.

Of course, for her part, Chabha felt herself to be a bit hypocritical since in the beginning, she was the one making all the overtures. But she had to make up for Slimane's gloomy attitude. Indeed, Slimane was afraid. But he forgave nothing, and she knew it. It was fortunate that Amer was astute enough to act as if he had not noticed anything and to be the one who took the first step toward his uncle. But he might grow weary of it. Then again, she also wanted to prove that she was capable of generosity. In short, she managed to attract attention to herself, away from Slimane, so that he would be forgotten and no one would pay attention to his own attitude. She succeeded in making herself loved by the whole family. In the end, Amer took the same liberties with her as he would with a sister.

It was not long before they were joking and laughing together openly.

"Are you the one who taught Madame how to roll the large couscous grains? Well it's a fine sight, this couscous. Like goat droppings. I cannot congratulate you on it."

"She did not let me do it," Chabha answered. "She only asked for advice. Right, Madame, you're the one . . ."

"Oh, it isn't that bad," Marie responded.

"That's right. It's too good for Amer. What's gotten into him to be so demanding? He should just ask for French dishes."

"Is that how you defend me, Chabha? Maybe you would like to marry him yourself too?" said Marie.

"If you agree, yes. Then he could have all the foods that he wants."

"What do you think, Amer? Would you like a new cook? Would you like one like Chabha?"

"We can arrange for that," Amer answered. "Let's begin by marrying off my uncle."

"Age before beauty!"

"Well said! Well, what do you say about it, Chabha?"

"Wait, let's ask Aunt Kamouma."

Kamouma looked at them impassively, and her wrinkled face was immobile.

"You know, children, my days are numbered. If my son had lived a normal life, he would be married like everyone else. But I cannot know God's intentions. Madame, you are my daughter like he is my son. I have no wishes other than your own."

"Come on, Mother, we are just kidding around. It's because of the coarse couscous," Marie said.

When she returned home, Chabha took a large platter, chose her flour, and began to shape some coarse couscous. That night when Slimane came back from the fields, she told him it was time to go and bring Kamouma and to lead her by the hand since it was dark out. She held out the plate covered with a new yellow scarf.

"Here, take this over to them."

"What is it?"

"Oh, nothing really. Madame tried to make coarse cous-cous, and it did not work out. Amer told me it was more like goat droppings. I understood what he meant. It is not that they don't have enough to eat, but this will please them. What do you say? See, I put three hard-boiled eggs on top."

Chabha lifted the scarf off the platter to show him.

"That's fine, just give it to me then," Slimane grumbled.

He grabbed the platter brusquely and left without saying anything else. He brought Kamouma back for the night. She ate her share of the couscous with them before going to sleep in the small room they had set aside for her. For her part, Ka-mouma showed no surprise at the dish . . . she had her own ideas about it. Everything was becoming confused in Slimane's mind. After all, he could not reproach Chabha for the dish of couscous. Each time he had thought to give something or make a small gesture, Chabha beat him to it. He had a weakness for Madame. But Chabha was not obliged to have the same feel-ings for her. She no doubt liked her well enough, but this affec-tion for Madame was not without some self-interest. She had spoken about it to her husband. She said that since he did not seem willing to let go of his closed and insolent attitude, she would take charge of making friends with them. But that alone did not explain all Chabha's actions. Even though she blamed it on a necessary hypocrisy, Slimane was suspicious: hypoc-risy was not this spontaneous. Chabha was naturally good, he knew this. With Kamouma and her family she had always been kind; there was no question about it. His discovery troubled him because he could not say anything about it. He felt that Chabha was growing distant. He was shrewd enough to under-stand, but he was certain that she did not understand it herself. If this path was the wrong one, would it not be wiser to warn her about it? But this would, he sensed, be the surest way to make her rush headlong into it. Besides, how could he put it into words? For some time now, they no longer understood each other, even in simple matters. There could be no question of discussing it. It was all too vague anyway. In all fairness, he had to admit that Chabha had not waited for Amer's arrival to "awaken" and give him cause for concern. That's what it was: an "awakening," no doubt about it. But now Slimane feared that his nephew might be the cause of this awakening. In the beginning, he trusted her. Hypocrisy? Perhaps, but maybe she was caught in her own game?

Sometimes, he saw things differently. His suspicions were really too serious. He knew his Chabha well. She knew how much she owed him. Together they formed a united front. It would be unthinkable for her to . . . No. He had to trust her.

Besides, this Amer, a man he could not bring himself to dislike, was he a threat? Would he dare to flout him after having killed another uncle whose daughter he then married without anyone knowing exactly why? Marie was prettier and younger than Chabha. Amer was happy here. It had been a year since they had returned to Kabylia. He was well liked. He knew how to behave. The Kabyle women did not seem to interest him. He had already been judged to this effect. He was not the kind of man to stand at a crossroads and stare at the girls who passed by or to wait in hiding for a chance to pounce on their "prey." The "hunters" of this sort were well-known and despised; no one trusted them. All the young women speak to him and say hello. Everyone finds him charming and cheerful. His glance is not deceitful. When his glance lands on a woman, he looks at her naturally, whereas other men have that telltale tick that everyone knows well: they quickly turn their head away as if they eyes had been burned; then, no longer able to resist, they glance again furtively at the woman as if to better retain the desired image. Astute people find this amusing. They know what it means. With young men, people are generally forgiving. If they blush, then it was not done maliciously. But the "regulars," the "habitués," do not blush. When they cast their hungry gaze, they assume the others have not noticed since they are quick to turn their head away. But we see them, and we hate them.

Amer is precisely not one of these men. Whoever passes by, he looks or does not look; it is all the same to him. Everyone says he is a man of wisdom who lived a long time in France; he knows what life is about, and he married well. He is respected, and the Aït-Larbi are proud of him. Slimane had best not get any ideas about him. He clearly feels at ease with Chabha: he jokes and laughs with her. He has no ulterior motives. Amer is always respectful even though there is not a large age difference between them. What should he believe?

XIX Slimane and Chabha cultivated Tighezrane and gathered the figs. This arrangement was made at the start of the first season, when Amer realized that he could no longer swing a pickaxe or work the fields. Slimane was a good *fellah*, like his father before him. Amer's property could not have fallen into better hands. Chabha assisted him well, to the point that even Kamouma admitted that she had not done any better in her youth.

One day, Amer and Madame surprised the two *fellahs*. They went to find them at Tighezrane on a perfect day for plowing. The field looked completely different. The earth had just been turned up for the second time that season. It was beautiful to behold. The two patches of the property, divided by a small stream, were shining like a heart saturated with blood. This heart was decorated with vigorous cacti growing in a tight line around the perimeter. There was a small path through the hedge that led to the edge of the stream and then followed along the water until the middle of the field. In the center of Tighezrane, the tree roots stood in the water, and orange trees grew in a dark grove. The orange blossoms filled the air with their fragrance. At the foot of one of the trees, Slimane had set up a small whitewashed hut where he put his fodder. There was a small spot where the earth was hard packed, and Chabha was washing some clothing there when the visitors arrived. Slimane was at the top of the field, just finishing with the plowing.

"Come here, Parisian, and plow the last row," Slimane called.

"Why not?" Amer responded.

He put down his *burnous*, took off his *gandoura*, and went over toward Slimane, sinking in up to his ankles in the soft earth, hesitating a bit to tread on it.

"Come forward, don't worry, you are not hurting the earth."

"The rows are so clean and well-done! You're really good at this."

"So are the oxen. Come and see."

Amer grasped the rough handle of the plow in his plump and

slightly soft hand. He was moved and did not dare to speak. Marie and Chabha watched him with amusement.

"Go ahead, walk naturally . . . don't tense up. No, press . . . you are making the plow tilt. There you go. Oh! The oxen are wonderful. They show you how to do it, just follow their lead."

At the same time, Slimane was following and watching. The two women admired his confidence as he took over the plow when Amer reached the end of the row. The oxen were immediately more at ease. Slimane's arm seemed to blend right into the handle of the plow; it appeared to be made from the same wood. It seemed to form an extension designed to give more weight to the plowshare. There were no useless movements; the oxen moved with confidence. A small knock on the plow let them know that they had to pass under the fig tree one more time. When Slimane pushed the shaft straight down into the ground and extracted the buried blade, he did not need to speak. They understood that they were finished. They stopped and waited to be unharnessed.

The liberated oxen rushed toward the stream. They were thirsty. Chabha dropped her laundry and ran in front of the beasts to stop them from drinking. She brought them back to the small clearing, up against the shed, while Madame, frightened, tried to get out of the way. Everyone gathered there.

Chabha threw the oxen two armfuls of fodder with a couple of handfuls of acorns. She spoke to them and stroked them. They knew her well. They were a beautiful pair of all-white oxen, skittish and yet well-muscled, not very large and absolutely identical. "A perfectly matched pair," she said proudly, looking at the Parisians.

"Madame, do you see their long eyelashes, their slender and curving horns? They are lovely creatures, aren't they? We are the envy of the village."

"They are well trained," Slimane added. "They do not need to be led by the ear. I hitch up the one on the right, and the one for the left comes over to get under the yoke."

"Women do not frighten them either. When I change their

bedding straw, I slip under their bellies. They know me: they have eaten from my hand. Animals, as you know, Madame, are not like us. They never bite the hand that feeds or strokes them."

Madame did not answer but admired Chabha's common sense and understood for the first time how a person could get attached to an animal, not just cats and dogs, or canaries in a cage, but also to a large and dangerous steer with horns. Kabyles are not attracted to cats, dogs, or canaries, but they are especially attached to their oxen. The oxen labor for the survival of the family; they are fattened up to be sold for a profit. The *fellahs* love and spoil their oxen. The men, their wives, and their sons refer to "our team, our pair"; they take care of their "couple," speaking of them with love and pride. The daughters braid wreaths to place around their necks, and the boys lead them to drink at the best spring and find them the best place to graze. The man behind the plow does not spare either his strength or his knowledge; he valiantly does his share of the work, only satisfied if he is more tired than his beasts. Then he is certain to have treated them well, and thus he is happy. The mother takes care of their food at home, getting up at night to check on them in their stable. Our men and women are very fond of oxen. Chabha and Slimane are no different in this respect. Perhaps they are even more affectionate than any others, as if they had a surplus of unused affection.

The field was indeed well kept. It looked as if it had just gotten spruced up, like someone getting ready for a wedding, a spring wedding. The fig trees, having been pruned in the winter, were now sprouting vigorous, brown shoots. Some of the shoots even sported a dozen or so wide dark-green leaves; this was the "healthy" green color, because before they had been pale, almost yellow in color. Above each leaf was a small bulge, like a large grain of couscous, as we say, promising a fig for July. No more bare stumps were to be seen, no breaks in the cactus hedge; the orange trees were bushy, the old oak tree had returned to life. The cherry trees, which had looked a bit abandoned and had suffered even more due to the frailty of their branches, their early fruits stolen by shepherds, appeared happy and reassured. Their small cherries were already losing their greenish color, growing lighter under the leaves, hastening to ripen.

There are signs of the season that do not lie; they can be seen, but not explained: it is the harmony between the people and the soil. Amer felt this perfect balance between Tighezrane and Chabha and Slimane. Perhaps, for their part, they were unaware of it. Perhaps he was also thinking that instead of Slimane, he would have been welcomed by the field. Yet he had the impression that neither he nor his cousin Hocine was right for Tighezrane. Our land is modest. She loves and rewards in secret. She recognizes her own right away: those who are destined for her and those for whom she was made. It is not only "white hands," those soft, untried hands, that she rejects, or lazy or weak hands, but even those mercenary hands that seek to force her to yield without loving her (take, for example, the pitiful state of fields owned by the wealthy but worked by day laborers). She does not even want those hands that seek to embellish her. She wants nothing to do with straight and groomed paths, or strange flowers, or rectangular enclosures with wooden fences. The land's beauty must be discovered, and for that, she must be loved.

Amer, with a heavy heart, understood that he loved Tighezrane well but that it was over: they were strangers to one another. Tighezrane was not angry with him. Slimane was suited to the task: he could work her, take care of her like a lover, and harvest the fruits like a miser because our land loves rough and miserly *fellahs*. As for Amer, even if he cleared, hoed, worked, and pruned, it would have all been for nothing; the harvest would have been wrested from the land, not gathered. He would have remained an arrogant and distant master. Tighezrane would have been trampled under by all the bad *fellahs* who work for wages and rush through the job to spend their time on their own fields. Slimane was really the one he needed.

But with a character like him, there could be no question of playing the master. One was not the tenant and the other the owner. The uncle was so thin-skinned that their roles were practically reversed; every time Amer felt intimidated and would wait for his uncle to speak to him of the land. In short, Slimane had to feel that he was the real master of the field. It was something he just had to accept about his uncle, Amer thought philosophically. But neither Chabha nor Kamouma accepted this meek role for Amer. For Kamouma, it was because she disliked Slimane; for Chabha, it was because she admired Amer. Marie did not usually take sides in this question as she was not overly concerned with these subtleties. It was enough for her to know that they had indeed paid for Tighezrane from their savings.

As for Amer, it bears repeating that his uncle's attitude was of no consequence. He completely understood the people of his village and found their particularities to be amusing since he saw in most of them the same veneer of attitudes and behaviors: an illusory self-esteem, a gruff stubbornness, a simplistic logic, fierce mistrustfulness, not to mention jealousy, selfishness, and fear. They were just like children, really. "Easy enough to manage, but sulky; they sulk all the time," he thought. Some of them were perhaps noteworthy, some were moneylenders, some were sly old foxes: farsighted people who knew how to lay their traps. All the rest were as pliable as a herd. Amer was proud of seeing through them and sometimes thwarting their plans. He felt that he was "up to the task"! He had become a regular at the village councils. These completely disorderly meetings were held every two weeks on a Friday. They were held in the only room of the mosque, on the rough straw mats covering the earthen floor. The first meeting enlightened him by its disorder. Everyone yelled and spoke at the same time. It was a boisterous cacophony that ended like a nervous breakdown, like a firecracker going off, or like a cloud of starlings leaving an olive tree. The *tamens* of each *karouba* left without resolving anything, leaving their own projects to simmer, speaking to each other in pairs, trying to figure out their neighbors' intentions, the *amin*'s plans, and the desires of the moneylender. Everything happened off-stage; practically the only result of the general meetings was to allow the *fellahs* from rival *karoubas* to size each other up and insult each other, or for the entire herd to cry out their unconscious and unorganized indignation. None of them knew, in fact, where the money went from the fines that were paid, from the *mechmels* or the *sadakas*. Hours of labor for public works required by the French [*corvées*] and taxes were demanded of them without any explanation. Water distribution was poorly done, regulations were not respected, and agreements between *çofs* were overturned without notice. It was a raging torrent of questions that fell upon the smiling *tamens*. Then everyone went home, the clan chiefs with their paternal smile, the others red from anger, their eyes ablaze, but proud to have dared to speak. They walked home repeating their refrain until they arrived there and could say it one more time for their wives' benefit: "I am a man, and I say what I think."

The following meeting would start in the same way. The *amin* opened the session, and immediately voices rang out from all sides.

"Speak, in the name of the Prophet!"

"No, wait, Ahmed, speak in the name of the Prophet!"

"So, now listen to me, first I will say to you: speak in the name of . . ."

Then it was the usual, inevitable commotion. The loud-mouths always managed to be heard, as well as the patient ones who knew how to take advantage of a lull to put their arguments forth. There are some clever men who win out, triumphing with little effort.

Amer knew how to take advantage at the right moment. He calmly stood up, and without rushing, or taking sides, he began to explain how French workers organize a meeting. He did not yell, he did not rush; he explained with conviction what he found to be good about those meetings, and since he had not taken anyone's side, they all listened to him. What he said made sense. Slowly, each listener was able to envision in his mind a gathering of the sort where wise men dressed in dark clothes, seated in front of a proper orator, would listen attentively, their hand resting on their cheek or knees. Indeed, that would be a real meeting: with an agenda, a presiding official, speakers listed in advance, taking turns to speak in front of a respectful audience. There would be a silent and honest vote, a dignified adjournment; it would all be a pleasant and profitable undertaking. Of course, all this could not be expected from these bumpkins in Ighil-Nezman, but a few of the main points of the process could be retained.

"That is all well and good," said the first *tamen,* "but in the name of the Prophet, I ask that, to start with, a list of every man in the village, of each *karouba,* be drawn up. Amer will keep the list, and he will read it at the start of every meeting, and a fine will be imposed on any man who is absent without a good excuse."

"Agreed," the *amin* exclaimed. "That will save us time. We will only need to take attendance. We will think about that someday. You are right, Amer."

"I would also advise you to write down all the rules in a notebook. In France, this is called the code," Amer added.

"Yes, yes, we shall see . . ."

The meeting was not much better than previous ones. The following meetings did not improve much either. Nevertheless, Amer came out of them with increased stature, and he boasted of this to Marie, who thought it was a very good thing that Amer pitted himself against the village notables. The Aït-Larbi, who had been a bit neglected in the village of late, realized they now had a new leader. Slimane, who was despised, now had a nephew to rely upon.

For Amer, it was also, in a small way, a matter of vanity, as well as a desire to show that by living so long in France, he had acquired experience that the others did not possess and that he also had gained sufficient broadmindedness and enough money to do without hypocritical ways. In this way, he believed himself to be above all the trivialities of this minuscule town, but now that he was being drawn back into this community, he felt himself becoming once again a true child of the Aït-Larbi, nephew of the Aït-Hamouche.

Land and Blood

It only took twelve months for Amer to forget his past, to feel happier than he ever believed he would again. He pushed bad memories out of his mind each time they crept back in and found enough in his new existence to occupy his mind completely. In this way, life seemed simple to him, happiness within reach. Yet one cannot be too demanding in Ighil-Nezman. Happy is the man who has no money problems—as it is often said: money *is* everything. Amer knew how to live in style. No one knew what his savings were, but he spared nothing. At regular intervals, a sack of semolina was delivered to his house; he purchased some meat each Friday like wealthy people did, and he returned from the market with a full basket. His large build, his happy and optimistic countenance, and his satiny *gandoura* and clean *burnous* all indicated affluence. It was known that he was helping his uncle Slimane. As for the Aït-Larbi, they could always hope for something from him! If only they had helped Kamouma when they had the chance.

They were both aware of the opinion that people had of them, and it had to be upheld. People told them: "You are happy." At the end of the first year, Amer and Marie said to each other: "We are happy." The small room at Madame Garet's was just an old memory. All the rest was just an old nightmare. Everyone had their own fate, but that was all done now. Let the middle-class Kabyles live with their daily dish of couscous and their weekly meat stew, these lucky men who drink their coffee each morning, who wait for feast days without concerns and who wait for the winter without fear, these big loafers who can hire fieldhands, who pay a woman to carry water, and who buy their firewood instead of cutting down a tree. Well, indeed, Marie and Amer knew they were happy in the midst of the others because happiness is relative. Amer was good-natured, and all of Kamouma's reproaches about everything she had endured could not change that. These were old stories for him. One person or another had scorned his mother or rejoiced in her misery; well then, he promised to keep it in mind and if need be to get revenge, but after all, she could not expect to make him hate the whole village! If only she would stop thinking of Slimane as an implacable enemy. On this point, he was firm; she would not convince him. He found Chabha to be an excellent woman, and he said as much on numerous occasions. Whenever his mother insisted that Slimane was deceitful, he answered that Chabha was honest, and Kamouma would nod her head.

XX Amer and Chabha got along well. It was Chabha who, in the beginning, tried to please, with no other plan than to make a good impression upon this beautiful Parisian and upon Amer, whom she naturally held in more esteem than Slimane, quite a bit higher! Usually, women who play at dangerous flirting games know how to stop at the right moment. Our women especially understand perfectly that they cannot venture too far down this road, and the most serious among them prefer to never even attempt it. They remain on their guard; they avoid looking at men or joking with them. They expect neither refinement nor self-control from a man, and they are never shocked at being deceitfully provoked if, by chance, they forget to be on their guard. In short, honest women are mistrustful.

Chabha was neither too young nor too naive. She was not unaware of these risks. Slimane had, until recently, complete confidence in her. He even used to find her too reserved.

She had changed, of course; she had not even really realized it. But since she had been going to Amer's home, she took great pleasure in speaking to him, in joking and being pleasant to him as well as to Madame. It was irresistible. Even so, she did not have any firm ideas in this matter. At first, it was the fact that he treated her like a sister. Simply stated, that made her happy and warmed her heart. She never blushed when the three of them were together (Kamouma with her lashless eyes like a sick goat did not count). She did not blush; instead she felt fine. All that was good within her appeared there on her face, making her smile, making her eyes shine. These Parisians also liked her, and she took comfort in that. When she spoke, she simpered just a bit without even being conscious of it; she had a way about her that was charming. She was pleasing to them, and Amer did not even realize it. In the beginning, she thought of the spouses together in the same surge of kindness, but then Amer won out over Marie. It was a slight nuance that Marie did not sense right away, but one that Chabha in vain tried to hide. No, each time Amer was absent, she showed less spirit; she became reasonable, sweet, and melancholy. It was because of this that the old woman was the first to uncover her secret while Chabha was not even aware of it herself yet. But what exactly would she be aware of? Her intentions were pure, Amer was serious, and Marie was young and beautiful. She had nothing to reproach herself for, even after she finally understood that for her, Amer was no ordinary friend, but rather the man she loved; he attracted her and made her heart beat faster without his even knowing it. "Will he ever know it?" she wondered to herself. This happiness she took from them, stole from them, it seemed to her, was visible on her face and revealed itself in her bearing and in the tone of her voice. If she washed herself meticulously, it was to be clean, of course, but also because it was a spontaneous manifestation of her internal contentment. If she changed her clothes, it was so as to not appear negligent, but also so that he would find her attractive. She became indulgent and kind with Slimane. It was not hypocrisy on her part; she was not forcing herself. She felt a particular tenderness toward Marie, a bit whimsical even, causing the Frenchwoman to sometimes burst out laughing. When this occurred, Chabha would adopt a pitiful pout that Marie erased with a touch or a kiss. She tried to hide her love from Amer, and she encouraged sharp criticisms from him that secretly tickled her. But her cleverness did not prevent her from showing him each time with a touching and unplanned refinement the passionate élan of her heart.

Sometimes she was afraid of being totally exposed. She would panic, believing herself to be dishonored and lessened in their eyes. She would become morose, depressed, feel ashamed and remorseful. Her imagination would take flight, being more audacious than even her wildest desires: she feared Amer hated her and thought her capable of the worst. At other times, she was despondent precisely because she thought that he did not understand and that he would never come to understand. Then this happiness that overcame her in secret became as fleeting as a mirage for a man lost in the desert. She would then take on an obstinate and unhappy look. She called Amer's image to mind to examine him in a critical light and only saw him as a smiling fat man, fleshy and self-confident, someone she could easily dislike. Why, he did not understand a thing!

But her feelings changed as soon as she was with them. Her apprehensions disappeared; she no longer feared being found out or not being understood. Everything seemed clear, simple, and wonderful to her. What others might say, or do, or think, no longer mattered. It was as if her love was returned. Her love was known and thereby authorized, since love was not a crime.

Of course, the Parisians had guessed what she was up to. Madame was greatly amused by Chabha, as was her big husband, who was not in the habit of making hearts flutter. Madame was not concerned. The game was innocent. It simply brought older memories to mind. Her union with Amer was sound, based upon mutual trust. In the beginning, this union was born of necessity and the common interest of two existences that, up until then, fate had mistreated.

Marie had no more illusions. She was ahead of Chabha, as Paris was ahead of Ighil-Nezman. No, Madame would not be jealous. Would she forget her past and give in to that ridiculous rigidity that her mother had flaunted so well? Marie had never desired conventionality anyway, even if she had wished for a simple and straightforward life after having been so disgusted with herself. Here, she found herself pampered and respected with Amer. She wished only for it to continue, nothing more.

But many times, Chabha's situation worried her all the same. She was a bit annoyed with herself for not feeling even a small revolt, that instinctive reaction that drives an owner out to confront raiders because they threaten his possessions and because it is not right to raid another. But Madame understood Chabha well. She left her to her charming fantasy. She even felt a measure of inadmissible warmth for this sturdy peasant woman whose desire she could plainly see, and she thought that if "it" could be realized, she would even feel a certain satisfaction in knowing she had found happiness. A moment or an hour would be sufficient. All this was, of course, inadmissible. All in all, this was not too serious, and, she repeated to herself, there was no reason to worry.

Land and Blood

"You Kabyles have odd marriages," she said to Amer one day. "Slimane is not right for Chabha. She needs to love, it's obvious."

"But he really does care for her, you know! They make a good couple! The things you think of! And why is it 'odd'? The more you have, the more you want? They have grown on each other. Here, for us, practicality is more important than all the rest. You already know that."

"I understand, but I feel sorry for her even so. The kind of man that she needs is more someone like you."

"Ah! Did she tell you that? You are not going to be jealous now, are you?"

"Is it too late?"

"Not too late, no. But that isn't your style, as you say. I laugh and joke around with Chabha. But she is off-limits for me. Slimane and I are blood relations."

"Don't get carried away, dear, and leave 'blood' out of this," she said with a laugh. "For me, jealousy is not . . . But just look at her distress, all the same . . ."

"She loves each of us equally; in my opinion, she is just outgoing. We must not attribute feelings to her that she doesn't have. This would be unfair, given the friendship she has shown us."

"You refuse to understand, my friend. I don't blame her, and you can see that I am not angry with her. I am saying this in order to warn you about her."

"There you have it! She is already guilty!"

"I am certain that she herself does not know where she stands in this. She is innocent, if you'd like!"

"Her first affair, is that it?"

"Exactly. So, if you care about her friendship, 'their' friendship, you'll need to watch out. You should make sure that everything is as it should be, that these 'blood ties' you speak of remain sacred, precisely so. Do we agree?"

"Don't make fun of me, and leave Chabha alone. She is not as troubled as you make her out to be. You are just getting jealous, and for no reason. I am a . . . let's just say, a respectable man."

"An Ighil-Nezman notable!"

"Well-dressed, not working in the fields . . ."

"Not doing anything at all," she said with a smile.

"Seemingly rich . . . married to a real lady, with an honorable family . . ."

"Like all the others, an irreproachable past . . ."

"Just like his spouse."

"A reputation solidly built upon several months of good conduct. Listen, Amer, we did the right thing coming here. We have changed so much from living here. Let's try to imagine ourselves *back there,* in room number 4. No, even so, she is a silly fool, our little Chabha! But I would prefer that you leave her alone, that you put her in her place. We cannot have any complications here. I feel a little sorry for her, but we will always like her."

Amer shrugged his shoulders, and that also was one of his arguments. Usually, it was the last one, the one that ended the entire discussion. But this time, he left in a pensive mood. The shrug of his shoulders was for Marie.

He admitted to himself that Chabha's attentions flattered him. His heart was filled with a kind of tenderness for her that was neither love nor affection. It was an intermediary feeling that was difficult to define, that made him want to kiss her tenderly and murmur touching words to her, words that issued directly from his heart, sweet words that would be good for Chabha.

"Oh, my little sister, you are so kind to love me, so intelligent to find me so pleasant, so beautiful in my eyes to find that I am handsome enough. Do you know that I have known many women, foreign women, who only wanted my money? Do you realize that you are the first one to love me for real, to love me in secret, and without hope or gain?"

He would whisper this and more. It would be a chaotic and confused outpouring. He would pour out his heart into hers.

Then he told himself that after all, true love is only found at home. It is quite normal that a girl from Ighil-Nezman knows how to love a boy from the same place and that the boy get to taste of this love. Naturally, there was no question of preferring anyone else to Marie, but he had missed out on an experience, and now he was already living that experience, and it had not taken long to happen. He took great pleasure in it because, for him, it was an awakening. He had believed himself to be jaded, but here he was, rediscovering the world as if with a child's heart. A mere glance could enliven his heart, a smile could fill it with joy; his heart was attuned to the smallest wishes of another heart that resembled it, ready to grasp the smallest signal, to hear the faintest call, to interpret the slightest gesture. This reasonable man, on his way to becoming one of the sages of the *djema*, began—with a shrug of his shoulders—to taste of the sweet, youthful, priceless emotions that he had been deprived of until now. In some moments, his soul sang out in happiness. This happiness transformed him, filled him with optimism. But his joy also had to be selfish, hidden, made stronger from others being unaware of it. Marie and Slimane had to remain unsuspecting. All in all, this happiness was fragile, abstract, and almost unreal. It was a dream. When he awoke, he would feel light and happy. He certainly did not hope to make this dream come true, but he would have been unhappy, for example, to find out that he was mistaken, that Chabha did not love him in the way he thought.

That is why, in a certain sense, he was annoyed with Marie for having said anything. He was irritated by her frankness. It had all been so peaceful, darn it!

It was all Marie's fault. It was really too bad that some other mouth had not revealed this truth. Marie having said this took away some of the charm of this whole affair. Marie had also said that what Chabha needed was *someone like him*. She was nothing if not realistic, Marie. His own desires were a bit unclear. He dared not wonder if maybe they could not be realized. He had stupidly believed that her love was different from any other, but Marie was right: Chabha was young, strong, and stubborn; she had certain needs. Now, because of Marie, he saw her in a different light. But too bad if that was how Chabha really loved him; he too was ready to desire her . . .

XXI

"I always thought that Kamouma had her secrets. All the medicine in the world is not worth a single one of her remedies. She succeeded, didn't she?" Ramdane said.

"Yes, Madame is expecting. Kamouma saw to it because, without her, they would have waited a long time, those Parisians! Good for her, the poor woman. She is an orphan, after all. Amer deserves his good fortune as well."

"You know, I do like him. But all the same, I wish it were Slimane in his position and that our Chabha could be so blessed. My God, what have those two done to be punished in this way?"

"God does not hear our prayers. It is too unfair. On the one hand, Chabha and Slimane have been waiting for years; they have tried everything, visited all the *koubas* and left numerous offerings. On the other hand, here are these two nonbelievers who just start to desire a child, and they are going to have one just like that. I am jealous, husband. I am angry with all of them right now; it is not fair. Even with that, Kamouma is not content! It serves her right if she's sorry for helping her daughter-in-law!" Smina said.

"Do you know the remedy she used for them?"

"You are mistaken, Husband. Kamouma does not know any more than the others. She just succeeded, that is all. I know these things."

"Well then, you can pull it off too."

"You are a fine one to talk. What has it gotten you, all of your prayers, *marabouts*, and dervishes? Say, your Si-Mahfoud who saw a lamb behind walking Slimane? It is behind Amer that it will follow, that little bleating lamb; it will be all white and adorable. He must have mixed things up, Si-Mahfoud. You promised him a real sheep, but he won't get it; at least that consoles me."

"You are getting carried away, Wife. You wish to penetrate God's plans. Are you truly certain that she has not done something that you did not try with Chabha?"

"It was the big pot."

"Did you see how she did it?"

"It is very easy! Everyone knows how to do it: three days of fasting, place the pot under the waist, starting with the right side, twice. Then the left side, also two times. Lie down for a long time. For the rest of the day, drink nothing more than herb tea made from forest plants."

"I know, a bud from all the plants that can be found in the fields. Everything is in it."

"That's it."

"Nothing else?"

"No, Husband. Believe me, Kamouma is not going to outdo your old Smina. I did not forget anything for our Chabha. There must be a spell hiding the solution for her or Slimane. If only I could get him, this grandson, blood of our blood, I would gladly give up all the days that remain of my life just to see him come into the world."

"Yes, I believe you are capable of anything."

"I am not speaking of the grilled hedgehog intestines in honey that Chabha ate for seven mornings, or the crêpes prepared by a stranger sprinkled with dog's milk, or even of the special weeds that few people can recognize. I obtained all of these things for Chabha without difficulty. But even so, these things do not grow on trees. I don't see how Kamouma . . ."

"But she isn't her daughter."

"Madame got lucky. As for the rest, can we know for certain that she never had a child before like our Chabha? Our poor daughter! Who knows? She is healthy and capable too. I want to believe it. The unfailing remedy, the most difficult one to find, I got it, me, your wife. At the cost of how many prayers, how many discussions . . ."

"Not to mention how much you had to pay, right?"

"Yes, I paid. It is for our daughter. I don't have the habit of acting secretly, you know me."

"I thought I knew you, Woman! What is this no-fail remedy?"

"I challenge anyone to obtain from the sheikh the foreskins of circumcised boys."

"Did you get any?"

"Three, not seven, but it was enough."

"Miserable woman! My daughter ate human flesh. You're crazy! Poor Chabha! I pity her. You are pushing her too far. You will have to answer for this in the hereafter."

"All will be as He pleases. I did no wrong. I was told that this remedy is so radical that if it doesn't work for the woman, then there is nothing more to be done: it is the husband's fault. Now, I have my proof."

"It does you no good to have your proof!"

"I guarantee that any other woman in my position would not take more than ten months to have done as much for her daughter and son-in-law . . ."

"What, she would have bought it?"

"No, husband, you do understand me. It is night, and God sees us. He knows just how much I want this happiness for my daughter, how much her fate worries me. When we are dead, she will have no one. Where will she turn? When we are in our graves, we will bang our heads in vain against the slab. You will be a helpless witness to her solitary and miserable old age. You will regret having brought her into this world, and you will be trembling in fear in your grave that she will come to ask for an explanation. You are not thinking of death, Husband."

"It is you, Woman, who is not thinking about it, at least not how one should. We say that the dead watch what the living do. Perhaps they also watch over them and protect them. I don't know. But all of this is not important. In the end, we are all joined together, we meet again forever. There are no parents, no children. No individual love, hatred, or gratitude. You must envision life differently than you do; otherwise, gradually, we go back to the single ancestor, and he would be the one to bear the weight of human rebellion or ingratitude. No, my wife, you imagine that life continues on the other side. You do not know what death is."

"That's good reasoning to let you leave this world with an easy conscience! Be sure that she will be crying on that day and that her lamentations will shred your dead man's soul."

"Do you believe that your parents are very worried about you in the cemetery of Tarzout?"

"But me, I am fine! Anyway, it doesn't matter. I will never abandon Chabha. I will always be at her side, and she will always feel that I share her misery. Oh God, forgive me!"

"For *Him*, all is settled . . ."

"I have not had my last word."

"Listen, Woman. You chased Adam from Paradise. We have been married for forty years. We have been happy and unhappy. People never gossiped about us. Our strength has slipped away; my sight dims. Soon I will be a wreck, and you, you won't be much better. Let us finish our days in peace. What did you used to say about honest women and all the others? Do you want to have regrets? Too strong of a desire is always unhealthy. Chabha is healthy; she is my daughter! Do not push her to extremes. Be careful not to tarnish my remaining years. No, God has no need of men and even less of women, I tell you again. Think about what is happening here with us. Family is like an old tree, and an old tree always dies, and I am not speaking of the ax. It dries out from the top on down. It is the center of the trunk that dies first, while the circumference and branches resist. Look at all the families in the village that are dying out! It is the direct descendants that are collapsing, the Aït-Hamouche, the Issoulah, the Aït-Larbi! The ones who hardly mattered, who were scorned, who barely had a name, they are flourishing, growing rich, and becoming strong. We are witnesses to this stupefying thing; this is what makes, as you say, the dead bang their head against the slab: these second-rate offspring raise themselves up to the level of the ancient ones, they continue the traditions of the uncles, they are enlivened by their spirit, their name does not disappear thanks to them, while their own children collapse and allow themselves to be discredited. Look at Hamid Issoulah, the widow's son. Who speaks of the other Issoulah, the son of Ouachour, who was a real lion of a man?"

"Oh, that one . . . times have changed too."

"They aren't the only ones. The Aït-Hamouche, the real ones, will disappear after Slimane if this continues. But there are the cousins. Even myself, I have no heir, but my young nephew already has six children."

"He is waiting for your death. Chabha can really feel like she has a brother in that one!"

"I have no reason to reproach him. He is hardworking and honest. He is the son of my unfortunate brother. He is a decent man."

"He will bare his teeth when needed."

"Yes, you don't like his wife. I go to the *djema*, and I am always happy to see him there. He and Slimane are all the family I have. There is Amer, too. I helped him, before, in France. I have maintained a bit of my influence on him. I was able to make peace between the two of them."

"Me too, I like him very well, this boy. He is not sly like his mother. Don't you think that people will find something to talk about if Chabha spends too much time at their place? I have been tempted to talk to her about it, but I did not want to annoy her."

"That's all we need, for you to grow suspicious about Amer or that Slimane could become jealous. It would be an insult for him and especially for our daughter."

"Well, now you reassure me. You know very well that Slimane is quick to take offense, and people are mean-spirited. We are from an honorable family."

"Sure, that's it. Only thieves raise suspicions."

The conversation went on like this for a long time between Smina and Ramdane because it was night, and they were not sleepy. They slept so little and so badly. For them, nights were always too long, always interrupted by periods of wakefulness: they were old. They liked to go to bed late, to wait for the tiny, blackened, tin coffeepot that only held two cups. One or the other of them would watch over the pot, putting in the precisely measured dose of grains, then pour out the thick liquid into two cracked cups with no handles. They drank carefully, inhaling the aromas, sipping each drop while clacking their tongues in satisfaction. They recognized this as being a luxury that was granted to them. They did not ask for anything more than this; they had spent their lives working and counting pennies. The result was not brilliant, of course; they found themselves alone, just as they had started out alone too. But back then, they had their entire lives before them. Now, life is behind them, and if they think about it sometimes at night, before going to bed, it is not with regret or to find comfort in it. They know the past belongs to no one, and as for the future, they are no longer afraid of it.

Ramdane believes in God. He says his prayers. He does not cheat the Creator and only wishes for what he believes he deserves. Death does not frighten him; of course, as he often tells himself, everyone has to die, from the bravest to the most cowardly person. But from his present perspective, he has, all the same, come to understand what it is to be alone.

It is precisely this solitude that he has come to know with Smina, who is also alone, but who does not completely realize it. She wants to remain attached to their daughter, Chabha, who is young and strong, since she represents life while they are death. He feels sorry for her; he feels sorry for Smina, who might perhaps outlive him and who will be unhappy. He also feels sorry for his daughter, because Chabha will be an orphan and she will have no heirs. How many of them are they, in the village, who have sons, daughters, daughters-in-law, sons-in-law, and grandchildren but who, nevertheless, are still in the same position as he, living with their old spouse in the oldest of homes on a small pension provided by their sons and whose only satisfaction is to ramble on, just the two of them, in front of the small coffeepot and the chipped cups? What good has it done for them, to be the fathers of an entire *karouba*? Still, it would be best if they did not insist upon living for too long because the children are always in a hurry to share in the inheritance, and the daughters-in-law are impatient to vent their enmity. This is why he wishes that Chabha had a son and other children after that. But his desire does not prevent him from sleeping or from thinking about himself. When he speaks of all this with Smina around the *kanoun,* he shows no emotion; he is calm and appears indifferent.

They sit there in the reddish glow from the embers covered by a layer of ash. The small house is plunged into darkness. He has the impression of being in a tomb where the only living thing is this hearth that dwindles and dies out little by little. They do not speak to each other anymore. Ramdane forgets his tired, old carcass. He is absorbed in observing a small flame that dances between two embers, hesitant, diaphanous like the shroud of a ghost, full of mystery and capriciousness, since it takes shape more clearly and greedily swallows up the rest of a twig, and then its efforts only produce a small spiral of smoke. Then Ramdane notices that now even more ash covers the embers. Indeed, life is like that as well. There are flames that spurt, climb, climb, and illuminate everything. There are some that go out or smolder in an unpleasant way, but in the end, soft ash covers the embers, and the next morning, the housewife gathers up a shovel full of whitish dust and then fills her *kanoun* with dry wood to make a new fire, new flames, and new ash.

Smina was accustomed to her old husband's silences, which always followed any conversation. She let him have his way. Often, facing Ramdane sitting heavily upon her old cushion stuffed with rags, she tried to meditate to gain insight into one of those eternal truths to which, for a long time now, he himself was able to rise. But she never managed that. She was too heavy and glued to her cushion. Her large thighs rested on the warm ground on either side of the hearth. Her cheeks sagged as usual. Her thoughts seemed to flee in order to take refuge in her belly, which the soft warmth caressed. Sleep finally overcame her. She dragged herself over to the small slate slab attached to the bench that provided access to the loft. She rubbed her hands together in preparation for the last prayer, recited while seated, the evening *sura,* and took her place on the mat. She had prepared the bed ahead of time, at dusk. Oftentimes it was Chabha who came, in between the chores of her own household, to throw two sheepskins, then two old rugs, onto the mat; then she put down the pillows and blankets. Smina always took her pillow to sit upon it. She would return it to its place on the bed after having said her prayers. She slept next to the *kanoun*. Ramdane slept closer to the door. It could only be thus. He only had to climb over his wife's body to be in his home. One misstep would cause him to fall against Smina's soft flesh. In the past, this happened often, and then it was a pretext for certain games. He often falls now too, but it is no longer a pretext. He cannot see well, and the incident makes both of them grumble.

Underneath the blankets, Smina began to snore right away. When Ramdane goes to join her, she does not even notice. In the past, her snoring would exasperate him, and he would nudge her with his elbow to wake her up. But he has finally grown accustomed to it, and now it was Smina herself who would wake up from it. She would suddenly open her eyes right in the middle of an unfinished dream, and the dream would remain unfinished, leaving her to feel sorry, or angry, but rarely pleasant. When she had a bad dream, she was content to wake up, but she believed in dreams more than in soothsayers. She knew how to interpret them to her advantage. She was unmatched at this game. She confidently sifted out the dreams that had to be interpreted directly from those that were obscure, the negative symbols that indicated good things and those that meant nothing. She was never troubled when the dream was muddled, inexplicable, or frightening; she would say with confidence: "It is a good sign, God willing!" and she thought no more about it.

Each morning Ramdane listened patiently to an account of her dreams. This was her weakness, and he liked to please her in this matter and encourage her to get the coffee ready. As a reward, he received his cup in bed. He inhaled the aroma silently, propped up on his pillows like a real pasha. Smina would end by saying: "All this is for the best, God willing." He would answer, unperturbed: "God willing!" And that was it.

When Smina startles awake from an unfinished dream, at first she does not fully understand what happened, and she tries to go back to sleep to catch up to it. She tries to pursue the last image of the dream, but it escapes from her. Then she says to herself: "Let me see, what was it about? I want to run after my dream! Well, go ahead." It is at this moment that she wakes up completely. Many times she is furious with herself; a small piece of the future, one that she could have known about, has gotten away from her. She hates her snoring and complains about it as if it were an illness.

"But you have always snored," Ramdane tells her, with his morning coffee.

"But before, it did not wake me up."

"It used to wake me up. It is your turn now."

"Don't joke about this; tell me, what causes this?"

"It's easy. I think it is the dream waking you up, not the snoring. Besides, you always have bad dreams of late, but you interpret them as you wish."

"Like I always say, the night is evil, and the daytime is good."

"Then bear with the bad until the end of the dream! It is fear that wakes you up."

"I saw the dwellings of people in Tzrout, under the ground. I saw everyone: my mother, my brother, your father. I visited the houses. I jumped with fright when my grandmother tried to shut me up in a small room just for fun. 'This is your room,' she yelled. I told you, it was just for fun, so see, it is a good sign."

"No, it is fear. Don't worry; the dead on the other side are calling for you; you'll be teasing them soon enough."

"Do not joke about this, Husband. You know that my dreams come to be."

Indeed, the dreams of all elderly Kabyle women "come to be," and for a simple reason: the ones that do not come to pass are easily forgotten. Whatever Smina tells Ramdane in the mornings remains unheeded. It is never thought of again. But it often happens that this woman recalls a dream after the fact. She then finds the explanation of what is happening.

"Yes," she tells Ramdane, "all of this was foreseen. I saw it while I slept. I did not want to tell you at first. You are too

Land and Blood

skeptical, and I was wrong to keep silent about it. You must not doubt it anymore: my dreams come to pass."

Lately, Smina has a "split personality." There is the heavy, good-natured Smina, naive and mischievous at the same time, whose candor and affability have won her the apparent esteem of all the other women because they all, deep down, know her to be sensitive and shrewd. Then there is the nighttime Smina: the one who snores and dreams. During the night, Smina is transformed. At first, she is not aware of it. She is in a blurry and nonsensical world where everything is a feeling. The indistinct forms that surround her end up impregnating her, dissolving her, and carrying her away in a whirlwind. She flies; she soars cheerfully in order to alight in another land that has nothing in common with our own and where, not surprisingly, she has the most unexpected encounters: with the dead, the living, people she likes or hates, people she knows, or that she only thinks she knows. Then the dream takes shape. But is it a dream? She is transformed, yet always as naive and mischievous as the other one. But her behavior, as well as her words, is crazy. She can no longer control herself. However, she knows that she is talking nonsense; she is aware that she cannot stop raving, cannot avoid being ridiculous and saying or doing something idiotic. She says: "Fortunately, I am dreaming . . ." And it continues. Then, as if she were an observer, she hears her own snoring. Then she wakes up, more or less quickly. Sometimes, she feels herself returning very slowly, like a paper airplane tossed by a schoolboy, landing softly after a graceful pirouette in the air. Now and then she dreams that she is being strangled, she is suffocating; she groans instead of snoring, and she quickly opens her eyes in terror. On these occasions, she does not try to "catch up to her dream." But in any case, she pursues this dream once she is awake. Her imagination works on it, and then she reasons, rectifies, arranges, adds some coherence where there was none, and then finishes what was sketched out. In the morning, the tale forms a whole whose evident meaning is right there in plain sight. Even when she presents an unfinished account, whether on purpose, or from caution, or from lack of imagination, she only leaves out the answer to the question, but the question itself is always put forth. Smina's dreams always have a meaning! Of course, the dream must be worth correcting. But it always is worth the effort because she has a choice: the nights are long. Her hopes and plans form a whole that will come to fruition in order to ensure her daughter's happiness.

Chabha is the only thing that worries her. At night, Chabha is always present. She sees her. Sometimes she thinks she is dreaming, but really she is just imagining. She really could not say. She has been thinking about it too much since learning that Madame is pregnant. Why can it not be the same for her own daughter? And thanks to Amer as well. But it is only just a wish. She knows that she cannot interfere with Chabha, who would refuse, who would spit out her indignation. Chabha is honest, like her mother. Nothing should be rushed; it is only a question of preparing for the right occasion. She sees Kamouma, that treacherous woman, who has already gauged Smina's despair and guessed at her plan.

"Oh, Smina, God has opened the door for us! Rejoice with us. You are on our side; there isn't a jealous bone in your body. Madame has not had her period this month. The 'big pot' worked."

"Yes, my dear, I rejoice with you. May God open doors for us as well!"

"It is from His hand that those who wait will receive. You will be happy, just like me. Let me tell you, I was worried that maybe Amer is sick. But that is not the case. Now I have the proof."

"That is true."

These allusions, these signs of interest, these secrets, this friendly and trusting attitude, when Smina analyzes them at night in her semiconscious state that is extremely lucid for her, she understands that Kamouma is her ally, that she can count on her discreet intervention. They are in complete agreement.

In the darkness and silence, under the blankets, lying between the sleeping Ramdane and the cold *kanoun* now filled with ashes, everything is simple. She constructs a stack of plans, demolishes all the obstacles, and slips unaware into a sleep that will be bothered by another dream . . .

The difficulties reappear with the morning, when everyone awakens, moves about, and yells. She is once again just good, old Smina who fears scandal and loves her daughter.

XXII

That evening, Amer returned home a bit late. It was a beautiful, moonlit night, the paths and streets were dry, the evening was cool; it was pleasant to linger to discuss serious matters under the hesitant light of the night sky. A few village notables were speaking together in front of the café door that had just closed for the night. They strolled around before going home and they ended their day with the words of wisdom that flowed effortlessly from their mouths, as if they had been dictated by some divinity in this serene night. It was, all things considered, a good way to part company.

Amer started down the alley of the Aït-Larbi, with the men's voices still within earshot. He was "a young notable" for good. He had figured out the mannerisms; he knew how to find the correct answer, to understand an allusion, and to respond by another, to cite the moralizing fable or parable, to present a real or plausible fact, thereby earning their astonishment or esteem, easy enough to detect on the falsely indifferent faces.

He found his mother curled up in a ball at the foot of the bed. Madame was waiting for him to serve him some couscous and to eat with him. The two women were not speaking to each other. When he entered, Marie had a newspaper folded up in her hand to fan the steaming-hot couscous placed on the table.

"I am late," Amer said. "Are you sleepy, Mother?"

"I am settling in for the night, son. You know that I am sleeping here tonight."

"Oh, right. But under the loft is better perhaps . . ."

"No, no. The Aït-Hamouche have not chased me away, I am going back there tomorrow. You are supposed to go over there tonight."

"What has happened?"

"Nothing serious, it is just that no one is there, that's all."

"Slimane did not return home? Ah, I see. And Chabha?"

"Chabha is sleeping at her parents' house; it's just right next to it, of course."

"Is this *marabout* far that Slimane went to consult?"

"A day's walk. He is attending a *zaouia* gathering for the whole night. He returns tomorrow. He will be back before nightfall."

"A lot of good it does him. I don't know what use all these pilgrimages are to him."

"You should pity him, my son."

"Do you really think I have to spend the night there? And you, Marie, what do you think about it?"

"Oh, as for me . . . Your mother thinks there are burglars around."

"It is just a kind gesture that they would appreciate," the elderly lady said. "Ramdane is too old to look after the house. I suggested that my son would not hear of Ramdane being obliged to keep watch."

"You were right, Mother. Okay, then it is agreed."

"It is above all for the pair of oxen. The thieves would be after nothing else. Eat, my son, eat. Then you can head over there. You will certainly find that Chabha has prepared your bed. You can sleep on the ground tonight, but Chabha keeps it clean, and they have lots of blankets. You won't be uncomfortable, take my word for it. Of course, I don't believe this business about thieves either, but one never knows. Your friends will be very pleased. Madame, don't worry, I am not putting Amer in any danger . . ."

Amer found himself again in the deserted alley, which he retraced back toward the *djema*. The shadow of the houses obscured the paving stones, the furrows, the hollows, and the bumps, but only reached midhigh on the row of houses that faced the moonlight. Amer wisely walked along the lit side of the street, and his silhouette was cast, larger than life, against the walls as he passed by.

When he passed in front of his cousin Hocine's doorway, he happened to be standing on the threshold. Amer walked by without speaking because he did not see anything: the house was in the shadows.

Not a soul was at the *djema*. The stone benches, all lined up in proper fashion, seemed to enjoy the quiet. Moonbeams shimmered here and there, glancing off the paving stones of polished slate. Amer felt this restfulness from afar as soon as he spotted the *djema,* but when he arrived there, he felt something heavy, painful, and sad as well. In spite of himself, he thought of those who had passed through there, who had the habit of holding forth there, those for whom this *djema* represented a public forum: the ones so long ago who had built this place and never even saw the Moorish café and never knew the seasonal emigration. Then, in more recent times, he thought of his grandparents who had no other entertainment than to go there and talk after a day of hard work. For them, the *djema* was a noble place where everyone had a place as well as a status that he had been able to win. All those people, now departed, whose memory was forgotten, he felt them sitting there on those benches, invisible, in their usual seats. Their presence suffocated him. They were taking back their legacy, one that was a bit disdained nowadays. A multitude of eyes fixed him with angry gazes. Amer crossed the *djema,* making an effort not to quicken his pace, looking straight in front of him.

When he had passed the *djema,* he shrugged and calmed down. He had felt this same silly anguish, these fears common to nervous young girls or simple-minded boys, when he was a child. Here he was feeling this way again, now as a grown man! It had only taken two years for him to become totally Kabyle once again, as if he had never traveled nor skirted death. The camps, the war, the mine: all those memories came back to him. Yes, the mine and Rabah's smashed face. "This night was not off to a good start," he thought. Now he had to watch over Slimane's house, which had also been Rabah's home. Amer had come armed. His hand automatically felt for the revolver he was carrying in the pocket of his *saroual.* Thieves were not the only problem!

"Well, fine," he told himself. "It is quite simple: I will spend the night in the old house of my uncles, Slimane and Rabah, yes, Rabah, but it was my grandfather's home too. I am not to blame for anything, and I have no reason to be fearful. As for the bed Chabha has prepared for me, will it have any special sign of her feelings for me? I am certain to find some private and delicate message, like a tender thought or some small sign that no one else could notice, like a discreet appeal from her heart."

He pushed on the old door that opened without a sound. In a few strides, Amer found himself in front of the large room that served as the living space. The other two rooms that enclosed the yard were always closed off, serving as storage and a hayloft. To have an exact idea of the dwelling, just picture an incomplete square with one of the small houses leaving a narrow corridor between its gabled wall and the neighboring house. This corridor, closed off by a reed screen, was a discreet lavatory for the women. It had been well laid out. Slimane had plenty of room, naturally. He was quite proud of his home, just like the Takat family who had the property bordering the road, or the Aït-Hamouche who had their café (that old, broken-down building that sat next to the new café, at the entrance to the village). Slimane could sell one of the rooms, or even both, and wall up the courtyard. He had no need of so much space. But he would rather die of hunger than sell! His cousins understood this and teased him a bit about it with their air of saying with confidence: "Watch over all that. You are a good watchman. But eventually, it will be ours."

This is what enraged Slimane the most. They had even tried to get close to Chabha, to make an arrangement with her, since Chabha's childlessness suited their plans. They praised her, said what an excellent wife she was; they insinuated they did not want Slimane to remarry. Slimane and Chabha both knew what they really thought. Chabha rejected their hypocritical compliments and would proclaim, just to annoy them, that she was not a suitable wife for Slimane and that one day soon she would pick a new one for him and this would spoil their hopes and plans within a year's time. Slimane loved her all the more for this. The cousins saw that she was not about to abandon her husband, and so they began to hate her as much as they hated Slimane. They all avoided each other; it was better that way, especially since their home was separate and closed off with a courtyard big enough to arouse anyone's envy, since normally our small courtyards are crossed not by several strides, but by a single one.

The door to the house was open, and Chabha, seated by the *kanoun,* jumped up when she heard steps.

"Who's there?" she called out firmly. She stood facing the door, her heart beating as if to break, her eyes wide with fear, but in control of herself enough to wait to recognize the intruder before calling for help.

Amer's heart was also beating loudly. He had not expected to find her there.

"Don't be afraid, Chabha, it's me, Amer."

"Oh! Our Amer, you scared me with the noise from your shoes. I was expecting my mother, so I haven't closed the gate or the door. But I never hear her steps since she is barefoot. Come in then, Amer, what is it?"

"What? You were expecting your mother?"

"She is sleeping here tonight. Slimane is away, and Kamouma is staying at your place."

"I know. Your mother is supposed to come here to sleep?"

"Yes, to keep me company. You can see that I am not all that brave."

"Was that the arrangement? So she knows Slimane is away?"

"Yes, of course, our Amer."

"Ah, good. I came to keep watch, thinking that you were at your parents'. You never know what might happen. There are the oxen, the supplies. And as you know, between my uncle Slimane and his cousins and even with the others . . . Well, I thought it best to be here."

Amer spoke, became confused, and grew more and more embarrassed. He did not know how to get out of this. It was ridiculous. When he saw on Chabha's face a sad and pitiful pout, he became angry with the two old women; his heart overflowed with tenderness for his friend. He dared to look at her with a gentle smile. She blinked her eyes and turned her head away, but in that swift movement, the tears welling up in her eyes ran down her face. He caught sight of them just in time. Then he did not hesitate any longer:

"Listen, Chabha, I have to tell you: my mother sent me. She urged me to come. She saw your mother; she warned her. It was arranged between them: I was supposed to come. Your mother knew, didn't she, that you were alone. What is she waiting for to come over here?"

"Kamouma and my mother! Oh! Those old ladies, they are like harpies, that much is true."

"There has been a misunderstanding, I think. Your mother will surely be coming over. I am leaving, Chabha. Come and close the door behind me while you wait."

"No. She will not come. Go in peace, Amer. Too bad, I will sleep alone."

This time, she looked him directly in the face with her eyes still welling with tears, yet threw him a challenge: it was a challenge and a prayer, an invitation to rise to her level, to be worthy of her love, of the high regard she had for him. The pout had disappeared. A smile hovered about her lips but did not manage to take hold because of a remaining bit of mistrust. Her gaze was eloquent, irresistible. Amer understood. He clung to that gaze, docile, fascinated, oblivious. This may have lasted a long while. They had no way of knowing; it was as if they were no longer mindful enough to find out.

Amer stood in the doorway, blocking it with his bulk, his beret touching the door frame, his feet slightly apart in a stance of uncertainty. He remained astounded, his eyes fixed on Chabha's face, which he thought he knew but which now revealed to him undreamed-of charms in the pale light of the flickering night light. The expression on her face changed several times, successively reflecting the contradictory feelings she experienced since Amer's unexpected appearance. But he thought that these changes made her more attractive each time. She stood there, close to him, a bit taller than him since the interior of the house was raised. His eyes could examine her, take her measure, undress her in her lightweight cotton *gandoura* printed with little blue flowers, without a shawl or a belt, having only a small

braided ribbon tied around her sinuous hips. Then he no longer saw anything. He was lost in Chabha's gaze and no longer
had control of himself: his mind became cloudy, confused; elu-
sive ideas churned around in it, his heart pounding, sending his
blood rushing to his temples; his cheeks began to tremble in a
quick motion that, in a flash of clear-sightedness, he thought
was disgraceful, but he was powerless to stop it. The thought
of his unattractiveness frightened him and suddenly imposed
itself on him. It was as if he was returning from afar and recov-
ering his senses. The charm disappeared; he saw Chabha as she
was: undecided, anguished, and perhaps afraid. She had one
arm leaning against the edge of the loft; with her other hand
she absentmindedly kneaded her belt. Her fingers trembled. He
felt ashamed of the image he had just presented to her, because,
as he thought, she had shown him nothing comparable to it:
emotion had not altered her features.

Yet, she hadn't noticed anything. She had not been expecting
Amer. When she had seen him at the door, she had been upset, of course. Above all, she thought that some serious matter
must have brought him there at that hour of the night, and she
was awaiting a suitable explanation. Then he would be gone,
leaving her to dream at her leisure, her heart full of his image,
of his voice, of an impossible and jealously guarded secret love.
Then she suspected him of having bad intentions, and she was
flooded with anger and sadness: he dared to take advantage of
these circumstances to try to dishonor her. When finally she
understood the trap that had been laid by the old women, she
looked directly into Amer's face to reassure herself that he too
understood. This gaze was as long and limpid as her heart. It
met Amer's gaze, and they told each other of their love. She did
not notice he was trembling.

"Follow my lead, Beloved," she was saying. "Never mind
this stupid and useless trap. Scorn your mother and mine. Oh!
If only I could hate them and rush into your arms. The trap is
too well laid. Go away, I am afraid. Leave me. I love you."

"But you can't stay here alone all the same! Listen, Sister,
come with me. Your parents are close by. I will take you there
and return here to keep watch."

Land and Blood

"No, our Amer, I can't bear to see her tonight. It's impossible. And my elderly father, what will he think? No, I am brave. Go in peace."

"Well, there is another solution. We will go to my home. You will spend the night with Madame and my mother. What do you say?"

"That's an idea, our Amer," she said after a moment.

Certainly, she was thinking, Kamouma will be quite surprised by it, Madame as well. But my father, no. He must assume I am already at your home. That must be what she told him. Well, fine, Mother. You told the truth after all. The old man can sleep peacefully, in spite of your nasty plans. Another one who suspects nothing is Madame. Then I will go to her place, and we will sleep side by side like good girls.

"I will arrange a bed for you, our Amer. It will just take a moment. Then we will leave."

Amer went out and waited for her in the courtyard. Then she quickly followed him. She was in an extraordinary state of elation. It seemed to her that her heart was wide open and that her feelings had spread out across her body that was soaked through with them. Her entire body vibrated and palpitated from a mixture of joy and sadness, of anger and sweetness. She wanted to laugh and cry at the same time. She felt herself to be light and ready to faint, to sink into a never-ending drowsiness.

They were walking, as silent as their own shadows. When they crossed the *djema,* she had to run a bit to catch up and walk beside him. As they entered the Aït-Larbi alley, she went first, and he was following. They had to descend the entire alleyway. Shadows drowned the houses and stopped on the one side level with the roof tiles. All of the doorways were closed. People were sleeping. Chabha slowed down. He was almost touching her. He was not thinking of anything. She stopped; with her feverish hand she took hold of his and brought it to her lips. He did not have time to react: she threw her arms around his neck and kissed him. When he realized what was happening, he responded ardently to her passionate embrace, and they drew apart trembling, without having said a word. Just at that moment, Hocine's gate, which they had passed a few meters back, squeaked with a bizarre music that could have been a whistle of astonishment, a mean laugh, or a cry of amazement. They quickly turned around, but they listened in vain: the gate did not move, and they did not hear any footsteps.

"The sky will fall down upon us, oh my God," Chabha murmured, covering her face with her hands.

"Let it fall!" Amer replied with a low and resolute voice.

They arrived in front of the door, standing next to each other, not looking at or touching one another. Amer knocked, entered first, and declared in a single breath, stressing each word and giving his mother an ironic look from the foot of her bed:

"Here is Chabha. She hadn't yet left for her mother's place. She prefers to sleep here."

He turned on his heels and disappeared.

He spent a never-ending night of bad dreams. Before he lay down, he remained awake thinking, squatting near the hearth, with his pack of cigarettes on his knees. How to explain everything he was thinking, all the arguments he raised, his remorse, his anger, his fear, his scruples as a wise and noted man of the village? But there was also this intense and crazy happiness that flooded him, this blinding, commanding desire that had taken hold of his flesh and blood, a feeling that all the logic in the world could not appease. It made him feverish and muddled his thoughts. He lay down fully dressed under the blanket, roughly blew out the lamp and closed his eyes.

When he reopened them in the darkness, he saw two parallel lines of dim light that came in through the cracks of the door. Right there at the threshold, within this frame of eerie light, in the same spot where he had stood just a short while ago, his overwrought imagination suddenly presented him with a precise vision: Rabah-ou-Hamouche immobile, dressed in dark clothes, stood with his powerful silhouette in front of him, with his face splattered black, and the white of his eye hanging out of its orbit.

XXIII Amer examined his conscience in vain; he could not quite think of himself as guilty, nor did he manage to condemn himself with any sincerity. He could not condemn Chabha either. He thought about it constantly and suffered because of it. But he wanted this suffering, he needed it. It was different from any he had known previously, because this particular suffering reconciled him with life. This was life: piercing doubt, torment, remorse that prevented you from sleeping or startled you awake from your sleep. Life was also this image, so sweet and smiling that it brought tears to your eyes; it was the trusting and determined face of his friend.

Sometimes, he tried to reason coldly, but he did not fully understand himself. He was no longer master of his thoughts. Contradictory arguments came to him. They came and they went. At the *djema,* while he spoke on some subject, he suddenly thought that if his listeners knew, they would perhaps listen to him scornfully. At the meetings, while supporting a point of view full of good sense, it came to his mind that, really, he was in no position to lecture other people. This would come to him in a flash, sometimes at the same moment he was defending honesty or giving a lesson on wisdom. Then, in spite of himself, he would lower his voice, pout a bit, and his conclusion would waver. He also began to listen indulgently to the stories that were going around. Knowing that some austere man was guilty of something consoled and reassured him. He saw how some of the others acted, and their appearances hid everything. It was enough to make one wonder if they were truly capable of behaving badly in secret and on other occasions, showing so much simplicity and naturalness! They did not seem to know what remorse was. No internal voice murmured in them. Or, Amer mused, it was as if they had completely changed who they were. There was nothing in common between the man at the *djema* and the man by himself. Why could he not manage to completely forget too, to feel at ease in the midst of others since he knew they were themselves not above reproach? Was it a question of habit? There is a learning process in all things.

Certainly adultery dishonors a man as it dishonors a woman. But how many of them really felt themselves to be diminished? Why did they remain calm and continue to arrogantly play a role that should no longer belong to them?

Each time, he would pass from doubt to certainty: certainty that his behavior was not really dishonest. The essential was to conceal it well, to not make his uncle unhappy. All that mattered was that Slimane not suspect anything. In Amer's mind, Madame was not at all an obstacle. No remorse on that account, because he still felt himself to be hers, entirely hers. He could not even envision that she might have a complaint. At the very least, he was certain of this: he knew that he had not forgotten her, his Madame. He had not changed toward her. What would she complain about? No, Madame had no reason to complain. It was likely that Chabha had the same thoughts as far as Slimane was concerned. In mulling over all his arguments, he ended up all tangled, thinking only of their moment of mutual intoxication. But this feeling aside, his thoughts became clearer, as did Chabha's, no doubt.

Their love became less beautiful, of course, since they knew each other, since their bodies had come to know each other. They were each disappointed, but with an attachment that did not diminish. On the contrary, in the beginning each one feared having disappointed the other, and this made them mistrustful, unsatisfied. Then, they understood better; they discovered that their love was also based upon indulgence, affection, and blindness. They accepted each other as they were, happy even to find imperfections, faults, and weaknesses in each other. Between them, there was no longer any shame or modesty, but from that moment onward, they could not envision any possible separation. They did not think of the consequences of their behavior either. All that mattered was fooling other people, always hiding while increasing their meetings. It was an ardent life, insane and imprudent. Amer needed this in order to find his balance again. He had never before known anything like this.

So, they went along blindly. They lived totally for the present moment. When they parted, replete from each other, they knew that another moment, just as happy, would come.

They were never lacking in caution or sensitivity. This was necessary in order not to raise anyone's suspicions. It is not that easy to go unnoticed in a land where suspicion is the first sign of wisdom. Amer and Chabha could see each other at her home when Slimane was out. The young woman could, in certain instances, skillfully provoke an absence. But that risked arousing her husband's suspicions. They met at Tighezrane, which was not wise, because since the fields hummed with workers, the paths were always used. Amer was not exactly a *fellah,* and Chabha was neither his sister nor his wife. They could be seen returning from the same place once, and nothing would be said. But if this were repeated, if they acted indifferently, or if, by way of precaution, they returned separately, no matter how long the interval, people would begin to understand. There was a small path across from the garden plots, behind the houses, which led from Amer's house to Slimane's, a private path. During the night, the two mad lovers met there, in the darkness, embracing, full of fever and anguish. There, they exchanged kisses and disconnected, unfinished words, words that rushed out because they had been burning on their lips for the entire day.

"I am afraid, my friend. We are being spied upon. Hemama and Hocine suspect us."

"No, you are always thinking of the noise from the gate that evening. There was no one there; I am certain of it."

"There is something else. Hocine looks at me in a strange way every time I see him. And me, ever since I have noticed these strange looks, I pass without saying hello."

"You should not do that. He will perhaps be surprised by that. It is better to act natural."

"No, I am not mistaken. I know him well enough. His smugness makes him think all women are secretly attracted to him. He maybe thinks that . . ."

"Oh, that animal!"

"I know what I'm saying. He must think that now I have

become easy. All he has to do is show himself. So, he shows himself."

"Has he been disrespectful to you?"

"No, but I have met him three times now on the path to Tighezrane. He must have been waiting for me."

"I will watch for him."

"No, I can protect myself. But try to find out. He may start to talk."

"We'll see. Don't worry about it."

"I am afraid he will do something about Slimane. He could manage to arouse his suspicions. But he will wait until I have denied it. Oh, my Amer, do you think I am not suffering enough in this way? But no matter, it is my doing. Shh! Let us not speak any more."

She pressed herself against him for a long moment, took his arms, which she placed around her waist that was both sturdy and delicate, the waist of a young woman that pregnancies had not thickened. Then she placed her hands on the man's shoulders and brought her face close to his. Her caution, her worries, and her regrets transformed themselves into a soft murmur and disappeared in a breath.

It was the cruel reprobation that they feared, even more than the danger. Chabha was honest. She was honest from force of habit; she derived no vanity from it, but she could not stand certain women who were talked about. She never pitied them. Since she had known Amer and had given herself to him, she imagined that she was like them. She suffered because of this. She knew, however, that the happiness she tasted each time might one day be paid for in suffering. So she accepted her self-contempt: she managed to overcome the kind of instinctive repulsion she felt at meeting certain women. She no longer avoided them. She became very gentle toward Slimane, gentle to the point of astonishing him. Since it would not do to astonish him, she had to control herself and try to be natural with him. The women at the fountain, on the paths, in the street, at the neighbors', also noticed this change of character. Chabha seemed perhaps wiser, more reasonable, or happier, but it was felt that this calm happiness hid something more melancholic, resigned, and mysterious. Her eyes shone with a special brilliance, but her gaze dropped too often; her smiles did not tell of her joy but instead begged for sympathy. It was obvious: she wanted to be seen in a favorable light.

With Marie, she almost ruined everything by being too kind. From the very first day, she imagined that the Frenchwoman read her face like an open book. She made herself humble, no longer daring to joke as before; she grew embarrassed and blushed as soon as she spoke about Amer, and she avoided meeting him in his home, slipping away whenever he appeared.

Amer was sure of himself. He did not get flustered, and he managed not to let anything show; he rebuked her often so that she would know how to behave. Yet he also, to a certain extent, felt this need to be forgiven by people even though he was not as foolish as Chabha. Chabha now saw herself as a criminal. Not him. Not Amer. He told himself he was no different from the others, and after all, other people were more or less guilty; they owed each other leniency, and instead of condemning others in the name of some theoretical justice, a judge should always take a look at himself first and imagine himself in the place of the guilty.

Amer may have been right. But we do not grant any legitimacy to clandestine lovers. They are cheats, nothing more. They are watched, they are mistrusted, and if by some chance they are not condemned, it is preferable that they have the courage to hold their heads up and look people in the eye. This is fair, after all, because they would be asking too much to be happy in their hidden affair, all the while continuing to put people off the scent, fooling good people who, in their blind faith, let them live without bothering about them. Once trust vanishes, then it is too bad for the lovers: they become a target. Nothing in their actions or gestures escapes attention. Usually, it is from this point on that they are then oblivious, whether because they knowingly flout opinion or they are really smitten with each other to the point of madness. This is how they become completely ridiculous and other people laugh at their expense. However, sometimes when serious risks await the lovers, people begin to feel sorry for them and to tremble at what fate may await them, all the while really wishing that their fears will turn out to be justified one day, thus proving that they were correct to predict misfortune.

Amer and Chabha soon found themselves in full view of public opinion, like nocturnal game caught in the glare of a brutal light. They clung to each other in vain; they had to put on a show, to answer insults and threats. Then the scandal broke. Naturally it was Hemama who provoked it. Chabha was afraid of this from the start; she felt it brewing and avoided annoying this woman whose indignation had reached its limit.

From an early age, Chabha and Hemama were a bit like rivals and had always had difficulty tolerating each other. Hemama always thought of herself as more beautiful. In reality, she was simply more jealous and proud. At the fountain, Chabha inspired more warmth because of her simplicity, her candor, and her cheerfulness. She had faithful friends who sought out her company, and when they returned together to the house, with the full jug on their backs, her group was always the liveliest. They laughed and joked until they reached the edge of the village. They hardly noticed the weight of their load, or the length of the path, or the ruggedness of the hill. Hemama was rarely in this group: she had her own.

In a public place like the fountain, there is no lack of disputes. It is actually an ideal place for sorting out any issues: far from the men, with all the women present. One's reputation can be demolished in front of witnesses who will not ask too many questions before they return home repeating the story. The demolisher can return home victorious, elated, and popular! It is at the fountain, of course, that one lays out "the dirty linen" so that it can be beaten with a vengeance. However, echoes always end up reaching the men's ears. Sometimes it goes quite far. Often, the *djema* punishes the wildest ones, and their husbands feel the humiliation of having to publicly pay out a fine imposed upon their wives. Once the fine is paid, some angry husbands head straight home, and in a few minutes the wife has a pretty good idea of how much they just had to pay out. Some women, who in a manner of speaking have no master, whether because they have no one to fear or because they dominate their husbands, are truly feared. They are handled with care; they do not have to wait their turn at the fountain to fill up their jugs; they have their say, and they reign over the place. They take part in all the fights. Like knights of old, it so happens, they take part simply to defend the weak, to right a wrong, or to express a neglected truth. As for their own reputations, they could not be more indifferent: their own past has been an open book for a long time and is constantly being updated by a chance adversary. It was precisely one of these women who restored Chabha's courage:

"She is talking about you. Don't you understand?"

"I just let her yap. She is more vain than any of the others."

"She said that you have been paying attention to your appearance of late. Is it Madame whom you are trying to imitate? What business is it of hers, this arrogant woman? Everyone knows Hemama, after all. She would be better off to leave you alone."

"Oh! You know, I am like a wide open space. I don't have any quarrel with her."

"You are wrong to fear her. If she notices, she will come after you. I know all about her. Here, you go after me, it's your turn to fill your jar. You can listen a bit . . ."

The fountain resembles a small *kouba* with its white dome held up by three brick pillars. It has recently been restored. The interior is clean and lined with cement. Two large shiny faucets can fill two jugs at a time. It is located a few meters from the road; a small path leads there, hollowed into a ditch, bordered by brambles, shaded by large fig trees. The small courtyard paved with uneven paving stones is always filled with women who chat, laugh, and argue while waiting their turn. Groups constantly form and then scatter. If the courtyard is blocked, then the women spill over onto the path or climb on top of the fountain's dome; they squeeze in, sitting anywhere. They

Land and Blood

listen, they talk, and they yell. A serious conversation takes place alongside one that is unkind, confidences are exchanged in a low voice in the midst of a sassy group, and coarse remarks are tossed out in a loud voice that neighbors hardly hear. There is something for every woman in the unruly tumult: the serious women manage to speak reasonably; friends are free to tell each other their remarks, their hopes, their worries; family members who meet there can always find a corner where they can feel a bit sheltered; the young women who want to show off succeed in wooing the mothers of young men; the women who come to have fun are naturally the least inhibited and the noisiest.

In such an atmosphere, disputes first go unnoticed. But usually, they rapidly dominate the chatter and the jokes because the others always more or less know the grievances of the antagonists. The spectacle begins: everyone remains in their place, they do not interrupt, they are all ears. Chabha knew that already. Hemama leaned against a pillar, facing her listeners. Chabha went by, followed by her companion. The three other women snickered.

"I am in a hurry, Sisters," said Hemama ironically.

"Is he waiting for you?"

"Yes, he is waiting."

"Is he the reason you've changed your clothes?"

"Yes, for him, Sisters. What my husband has not done, I hope that he will do. Ah! If only he could give me a son."

"You are clever. And Hocine?"

"He agrees. We are tired of waiting."

"Spite will finish off that old woman," murmured Chabha to her neighbor. "Help me carry the jar."

"Who asked you?" yelled Hemama, all red faced.

"She is not talking to you. You are the one provoking her," said the neighbor.

"I see. She is counting on you to defend her. Stay out of it, please."

"I don't have to defend Chabha. We all know her. Your jealousy cannot take anything away from her."

"Is this true, Chabha? Do you think I envy you?"

"No," Chabha answered. "But everyone sees your spitefulness. Your face tells the whole story."

"In that case, yes! I live out in the open, with my head held high. I don't walk around at night when the gates are closed. Indeed, everyone knows me. But you, people don't know about your dirty secrets, right, Chabha? At least that's what you believe. Does this face of mine scare you? Look at me, everyone, and compare."

"Never mind about anyone's face. Chabha is not ugly either," said her new friend.

Hemama was annoyed at Chabha, and the others all saw this when she refused to answer the other woman. They could all tell that Hemama had some news to relate, so they settled in to listen. Chabha grew pale. She stood facing Hemama, holding the full water jar on her back. Her friend shut off the faucet with a brusque gesture and pulled her still half-empty jar between her legs. She held it by the handles and was listening like the others.

Chabha kept her wits about her. She knew that her adversary would see this quarrel through to the end and that her love, her peace of mind, and her honor were all threatened. In the space of a few seconds, her heart knew extreme suffering and saw the extent to which spite and hate were implacable weapons, against which neither tears nor cowardice could be used. Every fiber of her being was shaken and appalled. So Chabha raised her head and faced her enemy. She did not feel anger since it was imperative to remain calm and answer the accusations right there on the spot, to refuse to admit anything.

"What do you mean? You see we are all listening. Go ahead," one of the ladies urged Hemama.

"You don't worry me with that tone of voice. My husband has forbidden me to talk to you. You are wasting your time looking for a fight. I don't have to listen to you," said Hemama.

"But you are the one looking for a fight," said Chabha's friend from before. "Chabha was over there minding her own business; I was with her. You were talking about her."

"That's right. Come to her rescue. The two of you are the same. I will not say anything more."

"We are better than you, you old windbag."

"You share the same secrets, I know. Watch out, or she will steal your lovers."

"Your husband, brothers, or shepherds aren't among them."

"They would not want you. My husband is honest."

"You can claim that," Chabha said to Hemama calmly. "Hocine never lifts his head since Fetta's death. You know how to keep an eye on a man. As for your lovers, you enslave them."

There were a few laughs among the women, which exasperated Hemama. Her mouth twisted with rage, and she began to yell:

"Come and listen to Chabha-ou-Ramdane, the friend of Amer-ou-Kaci. She wants to slander an honorable woman and to deny what everyone knows. Just leave me be, in God's name. Go to him. We don't want to take him from you. You can have him. Do you think we are all in love with him? Calm yourself. No one is interested in your affairs. Just wait until you get what you deserve for insulting honorable women and calling them names that come back to stick on you . . ."

This came out of Hemama's mouth in a boiling rush that didn't want to stop. Her mouth twisted, gesturing wildly, Hemama stood facing Chabha and let loose like a madwoman. She told in detail all that she knew and what she supposed to be true. Everyone was listening and waiting for Chabha to respond. But Chabha burst out laughing. Confronted by such vulgarities, she remained calm. She had the conviction that she was better than this mean woman, better than all these curious women, eager for scandal. It seemed to her that the insults hurled at her were cleansing her of any wrongdoing and that the revelations she had so feared had just relieved her of an enormous weight! So this was what she had been afraid of. It was done. Her guilt was exposed now to anyone who cared to hear of it. Why this fury? What had she ever done to Hemama? It was, apparently, simply that they did not want her to be

happy. Her happiness was forbidden, and for that, it was necessary to scream out loud. So Chabha began to laugh, and the
result was that the fiery torrent of words suddenly stopped.

"That's it?" she asked. "You are not telling anyone something they did not already know. Besides, I cannot either reveal
anything about you because there is nothing hidden in Ighil-
Nezman. You have wasted your time."

"I have nothing to hide."

"Nor do I. You see, Amer is my friend. We have been caught
in the act a hundred times. I go out at night, leaving Slimane—
his own uncle—to sleep alone. As for Amer, he abandons Madame, who is ugly, as you all know. He gets up wearing his
gandoura, and we behave like dogs right in front of your gate.
Or we meet in the daytime at Tighezrane, an isolated field that
no one knows of, and it's Hocine, of course, who catches us
there. Hocine, his own cousin, who has done so much good
for Kaci and who returned Tighezrane to the son. A good soul,
Hocine, just like you."

"You mock me, but I know I am right."

"So much so that Madame cannot stand the sight of me. You
are the one she admires, right?"

"That woman! I don't need her friendship. God alone knows
where he got her from."

"And she is ugly as well, is that it?"

"Do not make jokes. I will catch you like a thief, and I will
alert the whole *karouba.*"

"Do not wave your arms around. I am carrying a heavy
load."

"Put down your jar. I am not afraid of you!"

"We shall see."

With a quick twist of her arm, Chabha slid the amphora
onto her thigh and grabbed it with both hands, placing it carefully against the pillar. She stood up, arms hanging, with a
fiery look in her eye, and she advanced confidently toward Hemama, who drew back without even realizing it, mesmerized
by the look in Chabha's eyes that clearly spelled her defeat. A
few reasonable women intervened, surrounding Chabha, who

Land and Blood

was smiling, though pale, while several young women furtively picked up pebbles, spat on them, and replaced them on the ground with the wet side toward the earth; such is the custom when one wishes to see a dispute grow even more vicious.

The argument did not get out of hand, because at the last moment Hemama lost her nerve and showed herself to be so cowardly that deep down inside, the other women at the fountain all despised her. She did not dare to say another word and went off sulking to the far end of the little courtyard. Meanwhile, two older ladies calmed Chabha.

"Don't listen to such insults. Who could believe them? When anger speaks, only madness can come of it. We are not crazy and you, you are so reasonable . . ."

"But I didn't say anything. Why does she insult me?"

"The devil himself turned over a pebble for you. Curse him in your heart. Let's both curse him, and just imagine if the men could hear you. How complicated things can become . . ."

XXIV

"God's portion, O believers!" sang out a rough voice one evening at the threshold of the half-opened gate of the Aït-Hamouche.

Chabha grabbed the ladle, filled it with couscous, and quickly carried it over to the elderly beggar; this was the portion for God that he requested. Slimane, out of boredom and almost without thinking, followed her out into the courtyard. He heard the old man say to his wife, as was no doubt his usual way of thanking her: "May God protect you from catastrophe, my daughter." It was as if he had been struck by lightning. That night, he remained awake, stretched out and rigid as a board, unable to control himself. He began to toss and turn, shifting his position endlessly. He closed his eyes and tried to picture himself lying under the ground in a narrow hole. It was indeed a question of catastrophe. A catastrophe hovered nearby, and he did not want to admit it to himself. The voice of the old beggar rang in his ears like a supernatural voice; he was certain that he would never forget that voice, and it would torment him forever. In the darkness, under the covers, he drew near his wife and felt her warm, firm body against his. She turned her back to him, and at that precise moment she pressed up against him in her sleep. "She is mine," thought Slimane. He slid his hand underneath her and turned her over. He heard her softly murmur words of support. He waited until she was completely awake. He wanted to remain lucid to catch her. Neither one said a word. He had something in mind. His hands caressed her, moving from her hips to her chest, then to her throat and her face. Slimane placed his fingers on her eyes: they are closed, he said to himself, and she is thinking of the other.

"Should I turn on the light?" he whispered.

"No, later."

He became brutal, squeezing her as if to suffocate her. Ah, to destroy her, as when one destroys a precious and expensive object in a fit of rage, a total destruction that soothes the soul. He only succeeded in exciting her. He had the impression that she was revealing herself to him for the first time and that she was giving herself to him completely. This is how it must be for her with the other, he thought. When they turned on the light, she returned his hate-filled gaze with a look of defiance and a devilish pout, an expression so irresistible that he almost threw himself upon her a second time. Her smooth arms were visible against the fabric of her sleeveless *gandoura*. At the top of her left arm, near the shoulder, a red spot appeared.

"It will be a bruise tomorrow," she said, rubbing it. "You're playing the young man again, Husband."

They took up their masks once more, smiling hypocritically at each other as they prepared to return to bed. She turned her back to him again, leaving him to his thoughts. Not so long ago, Chabha intrigued him. No more. Now he was jealous. He knew that she wanted Amer, that she loved him and sought his company. It was torture for him. It was torture for him to know this and to continue to doubt. It was vital for him to doubt. He needed to tell himself that it was not possible, that neither one could betray him. Slimane was tormented by imagining her in Amer's arms. Amer, taller and stronger than he, enfolding her, caressing her until she was black and blue. All of the advantages were on Amer's side. Slimane himself was not worthy of any consideration; he was a pest to be squashed or despised. In the past, he would even be moved to self-pity since he had no one to love him. He had at least been certain of Chabha's affection for him, and together they could hold their heads high. Now he despised himself, he was an object of ridicule. He thought that perhaps his wife's affection was still there, but he no longer wanted it. It was all over, and he knew that he was absolutely alone. The idea of death haunted him and always came to him as he finished his brooding, in the same way that rain purifies a darkened sky. This notion of death cleansed his sad soul in the same way. Sometimes he told himself that there was nothing to any of this—that death was the only unavoidable conclusion for everyone. He was unhappy. He would never have the strength to be done with it all. Despair, not sadness, would be his lot in life. He knew that suicide was not an act of courage, but rather the act of an insane person that, someday, he might still carry out. He had to resign himself to living with Chabha, always suspecting her, loving her, hating her, sensing her affectionate pity for him and yes, sometimes feeling her contempt. He would have to accept the supposed friendship of the other and his hypocritical attentions. Finally, he would have to endure his fate like a sick person who gives up on expecting a cure to come to him. Yet, it was not a cure that came to Slimane that night when the beggar spoke, but a remedy to apply, an illuminating response to his hesitations, to his uncertainties, and to his trouble. It was indeed a matter of catastrophe, but the catastrophe would be for Chabha, Amer, and himself. This seemed to be totally logical to him. As he had drawn close to Chabha that night, he needed to touch her, he imagined her dead, her body decomposing right alongside his own, and not far from them would be Amer's corpse lying under the wide slab of the Tazrout. The old beggar's voice was that of justice: simple, clean, and sparkling like a new dagger.

Then his thoughts took a different direction. He admitted to himself that killing was not easy. Would it not be better to keep doubting and to find in this doubt a harsh sensation, a passion that his wife, to all appearances, could not resist? To enjoy her and, in turn, scorn her little by little? Should he wait for everything to return to normal and for her to return to him? Unfortunately, that was not possible. It did not take long for Slimane to realize this. He enjoyed jeering at others; he was the most spiteful gossip in the village. He knew all the secrets of Ighil-Nezman. He soon realized that all three of them were dancing to the same tune. Others shared his suspicions. For some, it was already a certainty. At the *djema* and the café he had noticed a group of men, always the same ones, surrounding Hocine and laughing. They joked in his presence, discussing willing cuckolds. It was clear: the allusions were for him. On several occasions, concerning ordinary matters, Hocine had uttered a meaningful proverb: "What do you expect? The world is cruel, but God watches over our secrets and our wives' lovers, as the saying goes."

Land and Blood

One day, Hocine and Slimane spoke to each other a bit more frankly. They were alone.

"Your nephew has rediscovered an interest in the land. It is obvious; he often goes to Tighezrane."

"You seem to be very interested in him, I think."

"I am an Aït-Larbi, but he loves you a great deal."

"I don't need anyone to get along in life. If you think for a moment that I am making any profit from Tighezrane . . ."

"In any case, you are the one he prefers. The field is well taken care of. Your wife is always there, cleaning up; it is a real garden. Don't neglect your fields for the sake of Tighezrane! But all the same, Amer is quite happy."

"Mind your own business, Hocine. You know that no one jokes about me and gets away with it."

"Calm down. I am pleased for you if you both get along so well. Amer is like a brother to me, after all."

"Do not forget that we have all lived here together in Ighil-Nezman. I knew you as a child, right? Do you recall? Fine, now I know that all the Aït-Larbi are bursting with jealousy to see that I am friendly again with Amer. There are others like them too, I know it."

Yet the sarcasm and allusions troubled Slimane a great deal. He became stubborn and responded aggressively as soon as he felt himself targeted. Slimane was no longer certain of anything. He tried to behave as if the gossip had no effect upon him. He held his head high. This was in keeping with his temperament. But secretly he was suffering greatly. Sometimes he thought to himself that since Amer's return, others were determined to poison his existence. What they thought and repeated now was nothing more than slander designed to revive his hatred and push him to carry out the vengeance they were all hoping to see. Next, he would be seized with a desire to run to Amer and Madame to pour out his heart to them and to tell Chabha to brave the gossips and continue to visit Kamouma and to speak openly with Amer anywhere at all, at home, in the street, or out in the fields. Continued contact between them would be the right response to all those who snickered out of spite.

Land and Blood

Invariably, when Slimane got to this point in his reasoning, he would break down. He would be terrified by the idea that behaving in this manner would encourage the clandestine meetings of the lovers, who would then be the first to mock him, all the while taking advantage of his naïveté. Next, he would choke on helpless rage and feel that he despised all mankind. Then he imagined that one day he would get his proof, and he would no longer be in doubt. Everything would be clear, like a bolt of lightning. It would strike all three of them. The catastrophe! People would talk about it for a week. They would all spitefully reproach him for his actions, but he would no longer be there to insult them tit for tat or to uncover their own nasty secrets. There was no way out: they all wanted to crush him. He saw enemies all around him. Finally, he thought that his uncle Ali would welcome him in the next world as a beloved son who had avenged his blood. His brother Rabah's opinion, or that of his other uncle Slimane, Kamouma's father, was of little concern to him. He forgot about them. Only Ali's soul, he sensed, would welcome his own. In the same way that Slimane cared nothing for the opinions of the living, he scorned those of the dead. If need be, he would give them a piece of his mind. In order to criticize someone, whether dead or alive, he believed, one had to be above reproach, and in Ighil-Nezman, he did not see anyone in that position. However, when Chabha told him of her fight at the fountain with Hemama, he reacted with indifference.

"Would you like me to go and fight Hocine?"

"That is not what I am asking!"

"Well, that's good, because you see, it really is a matter for the . . . other one. I am not involved in this."

"But you are mad, Husband."

"No, Wife, I do not like to be insulted, and I know how to respond. Why didn't you answer back for yourself? Hemama is not above reproach. You can tell her a thing or two."

"I already know all that. Don't worry: she got what she deserved."

"Fine, then what are you complaining about? You had an

argument, I don't care about it. But all the same, you see what people are thinking. Do you think people are blind? Too much familiarity surprises people, especially with an enemy."

"An enemy?"

"Yes, Wife, an enemy."

"Please don't yell. Your cousins might hear."

"Yes, they can spy on us too to find out whatever they wish. Given your behavior, people are talking about us, and soon they will all be laughing at us."

"What wrong have I committed, husband?"

"You have just been told, it seems."

"And you believe it?" she murmured softly, in the grip of a sudden emotion.

"Who do you think I am? Would I accept my own dishonor?"

Chabha collapsed near the *kanoun* and began to cry. At first she cried silently; then, her shoulders began to shake with harsh sobs. She lowered her head, holding it in her hands. Her scarf was on the floor, and her long black hair hung down to her hips. He looked at her for a moment with alarm, but then he misunderstood the reason for her tears. His gaze became penetrating, his face beamed, he saw a glimmer of a beautiful life with his sweet Chabha, innocent and slandered. She did not seem to notice him. Quickly he repressed his joy and said in a gruff voice:

"What I think doesn't matter. But you have always allowed me to hold my head up high in public, and now others insult us. Think about what must be done."

She raised her eyes, drowning in tears to him, a pitiful face upon which no injured pride was visible. Her gaze was submissive and resigned. Slimane grew bitter. His joy evaporated on the spot, and an overwhelming sadness enveloped him next.

XXV

Kamouma and Slimane were too similar to really like each other. They exchanged a few words when it could not be avoided. They knew each other too well and mistrusted one another. Slimane went out every morning before the old woman. As for her, she patiently waited for him to go before she left the small room where she slept. Chabha had gotten in the habit of stopping her each time to offer her a cup of coffee. Kamouma and the young woman grew accustomed to living side by side. For Kamouma, Chabha could have been her daughter-in-law; she would have never wished for another, and in her mind, knowing "what she knew," she considered her a bit like a daughter-in-law. A daughter-in-law who is respected: "There are some like that, after all," Kamouma thought.

That is why she was distraught when Chabha told her about her fight with Hemama and her confrontation with Slimane afterward.

"Does he suspect you, my girl?"

"I am afraid so, Aunt Kamouma."

"But he is out of his mind! You, so honest. And with my son Amer, who is respected by everyone, who is so wise. Oh, Hemama is evil. She knows that it only takes a spark to light a fire, and she does not hesitate to set the spark. She forgets my kindness toward her, my words of advice and my discretion. She is an ingrate that I have helped before. No, Chabha, I know that you have not done anything wrong. She is not after the Aït-Hamouche. We are her targets. Hemama and Hocine envy us Tighezrane. So you see, they would like to get Amer killed and then take his land. They don't know that Kamouma keeps watch. But you are silly, my girl. That is what you must explain to Slimane. You have done nothing, understand? Nothing! You are innocent. Amer is your brother. We will proclaim it to all. Hold your head up high. I will discuss this right away with your mother."

The old ladies met at Smina's home. It was important to reach an understanding.

"I am glad to find you alone here," Kamouma told her.

"What is it, sister? Welcome! It is good news, right?"

"Yes, Smina, with me it is always good. May God reserve misfortune for those with bad intentions. Do you know that our Chabha had dealings with Hemama?"

"At the fountain, was it? She did not stop by last night. I have not seen her yet. What caused this dispute?"

"Your daughter did no wrong."

"She never does anything wrong, you know."

"I know. The other one provoked her and insulted her in front of everyone. She said Chabha was Amer's lover."

"Oh! Is it possible? What did Chabha answer? The others will not believe her. Hemama wants to slander us all now. She forgets our blood ties. I am from her family, after all. What have we ever done to Hemama?"

"That's right, snivel like your daughter!"

"I am not sniveling! I know that she is on the side of all the Aït-Hamouche; your cousins' wives are all so jealous of Chabha. They encouraged Hemama in this, I am sure. I will speak to her husband, and if need be, I will lay out all of Hemama's business in the street and the *djema*. They must not attack my daughter."

"What you are saying is true, I hadn't thought of it. I am naive, Smina. Everything is clear now. This is actually a good plan."

"What is?"

"We are good people, Sister, and we fear God. But there are some who do not. While we old believers prepare ourselves for the afterlife, others are laying a trap for our children. You must speak of this right away to Ramdane. He must warn my son and my cousin."

"You see how I am trembling, Kamouma. Tell me exactly what is on your mind. You frighten me."

"I advise you to remain vigilant."

"My daughter has been careless . . ."

"She has not done anything, your daughter."

"I answer for her as I would myself. It is in our blood, this reserve that characterizes us. We can walk with our heads high when we go out to the market."

"You do not need to convince me of that."

"I know. Ramdane can be certain of us."

"Good. But he must explain to the others that the Aït-Larbi, on one side, and the Aït-Hamouche, on the other, want a scandal to break out. Slimane is mean and quick to take offense like the others in his family. They know full well that it would not take much to rekindle all his hatred. Now they have found something important. Do you think he will put up with having his honor insulted after having allowed his brother's blood to be 'spilled'?"

"Yes, you are right: they are going to destroy both families at the same time. Then they can inherit. I always thought that if they could arrange his death, they would do it, these Aït-Hamouche. Besides, Slimane says as much himself."

"And Hocine-ou-Larbi, do you think he would not stand to gain? Our children have no heirs. So . . ."

"My poor daughter. Look what has she been reduced to, my God! You see, the worries she causes me will be my death."

"Would you bring about her end by your inaction? We must fight, not wail and lament. We must strike the serpent's head. Yes, it is the head we must crush, without hesitation. After that, there are no more worries, it hisses no more."

"Your words give me courage."

"Slimane must not know that these explanations come from me. He would be suspicious; he doesn't like me."

"You are imagining things. He has a bad personality, true. But what you have just been saying is so obvious. We have seen the real nature of this affair; they need only think about it, and they will see it too. It may be a good thing for Amer to talk to Hocine, man to man. That would settle his wife down."

"You realize that I cannot speak to my son Amer about any of this."

"And what about Madame? She frightens me as well. I don't see that she is very accommodating. Let us hope that she, at least, will have an heir."

"I will deal with Madame. As for an heir, nothing is less certain . . . fate can be fickle."

"My esteem for you will increase tenfold."

"Our children need us. The trap is too well laid for them to avoid it on their own. Let Ramdane know right away. He sees a lot of what goes on. Tell him I want to stay out of all this. I am an old *tharoumith* who is not frightened of the devil's plans. I fear only the Lord."

"Yes, Sister, you are lucky not to have daughters."

But I have a son, Smina! In this affair he is the one who risks the most."

"Then it should have been prevented . . ."

"Prevent what? You are out of your mind, Sister. Truly, you don't realize what you are saying. Calm down, and wait for Ramdane. I will be on my way then."

When Ramdane was told of this matter, he just shrugged his shoulders. For him, this women's business did not concern men. He was certain of his daughter's conduct. "It is always the same," he thought. "Slander falls by itself upon anyone wise enough not to be worried by it." His favorite saying was "The truth will always be known." He was not worried by any of this.

"Listen," he said to his wife. "Men take care of their hunger. They may, deep down, covet Slimane's or Amer's land, but what you are telling me is just madness. Would they really be pushing for a crime that would tarnish them all? They are too reasonable to think about taking advantage of an unsavory remark."

"Oh, really? Would they hesitate one bit?"

"They know that Slimane is not a child or a blind man to be led to the edge of an abyss. Do not repeat such things. People will say that your story is a coverup for your daughter's bad behavior. The women had an argument. I hope that Chabha knew how to defend herself. Now they will behave; they will not speak to each other again. All of this is of no concern to men, I tell you."

"I will be vigilant for my daughter's sake, you can be sure that."

A few days later, Ramdane had to acknowledge that this affair did concern the men after all. It was a Friday evening, a market evening. He was calmly making his way to the *djema,* leaning on his oleander-wood walking stick that never left his side. A young Aït-Hanouche man was waving his arms about in the midst of a group of young men; he had lost his *chechia* and his *burnous;* his shirt was open, and an open bottle bounced inside of his pocket. He was drunk and had just come from the market. As soon as the old man approached the group, the young men moved aside for him. The drunkard rushed forward to greet Ramdane.

"Uncle Ramdane," he said, hiccupping in a tearful voice, "I like you a lot. Here, I swear by all the saints of the land that I must kiss you. Yes, I am a good fellow, I like respectable old men. But Uncle Ramdane, I am sorry. Yes, I ask your forgiveness in advance. You have a bitch for a daughter. That's right, a bitch."

Ramdane's face flushed, and he pushed away the incoherent man.

"There is no worse kind of dog than you. You stink of wine. You don't know what you're saying."

"No, Uncle Ramdane, don't push me away. You can beat me, but don't push me away. I must tell you. I have to unburden my heart. We are a good family, the best family in the village. Everyone must know it. Yes," he yelled, "I want everyone to hear. It is your daughter who decided to dishonor us. Do you know what she is doing with that puffed-up Amer? Oh, as for him, if I get my hands on him . . ."

Ramdane lost control. In an instant he was as drunk as the young man—drunk with fury. He felt his heart beat forcefully as the blood rushed through his veins, giving him back the vigor of his youth. The others tried to intervene, but he pushed them aside easily and pounced upon the man who had dared insult him. He tried to strike the fellow with his wooden stick, but the other young men seized it in midair. Throwing down his stick, Ramdane seized hold of the young man's face, ripping into his cheek with his nails. He stood aside a moment and snickered while the young man howled in pain and dabbed at his cheek. The others restrained Ramdane. Children came running to the scene, rousing other adults. The old man then screamed insults at the whole Aït-Hamouche family. Level-headed bystanders tried to calm him and find out what had caused the fight. The first witnesses obligingly repeated what they had seen. Earlier, Chabha had passed by and was insulted by the young cousin.

"You know, she just lowered her head without responding. Then he began to shout. Dada Ramdane arrived just then and was insulted as well. The old man is right: these are not things one should say."

"What things?"

"It is too filthy to repeat. Things would get even worse if Amer-ou-Kaci happened along. That would not be good."

"Ah, and what about Slimane?"

These remarks circulated in hushed tones. The young Aït-Hamouche man hiccupped and wiped again at his face. He looked at the assembled crowd and sputtered his remarks again, imagining himself surrounded by adversaries, that is, anyone not happy about his behavior.

"Since we are a good family, one bad female cannot dishonor us. The women in other families ... we ... Well, as for our own, we get rid of them."

Two of his brothers, their mouths set in anger, parted the crowd and threw themselves on him. No one tried to stop them. They gave him a thrashing and dragged him away like a criminal, glaring at the assembled group. The brothers wanted to smash the wine bottle over the other's head, but in the end, one of them angrily threw it down on the ground. Then the *djema* emptied out, and the men walked off, commenting upon this new scandal.

It is certainly true that the Aït-Hamouche held a meeting the following day, without Slimane's knowledge, of course. One of their own had behaved badly. The matter was definitely a worry for them. They had to decide on a stance to take. They all agreed that the best way to ensure peace of mind would be if the whole matter was snuffed out immediately, that all remain silent on the matter. "Let Slimane deal with his nephew," they reasoned, since any publicity would hurt them in the same way and would, in the end, get all of them involved. The elders knew that by pretending the matter did not exist, they would only be doing what most people do when faced with such a lapse by one of their own. Was there a family in the village whose reputation was spotless? They also told themselves that, as for Slimane, that fallen and detested member of the group, what had happened was not so surprising. One day he would find out about this, and the good family "fiber" would resonate within him. This was to be hoped for in order to cleanse the family name and honor. So they decided upon a strict quarantine. Forget about Slimane, act as if he wasn't family, but do it in such a way that the rest of the village would not notice. With Amer-ou-Kaci, they would act with hypocrisy. As for the young man, he would apologize if need be.

"No," one of them argued. "He will say that he was drinking with Hocine-ou-Larbi, that it was Hocine who gossiped and who spurred his anger. This way, Amer will have to talk to his cousin. His enemy will be in his own family. For everything else, it will just be hello and goodbye when you meet him in the street. Slimane is his uncle. He is the nephew of all the Aït-Hamouche, do not forget this. But our wives will avoid speaking to him; he will understand that he has offended us.

They did not discuss Ramdane. They shared the same contempt for him. This contempt dated from his alliance with Slimane, but now it was twice as strong, as if the old man were responsible for his daughter's behavior. For his part, Ramdane expected some sort of consolation, a few soothing words. He was ready to forgive the affront. When he met up with the oldest of the Aït-Hamouche, they crossed paths without exchanging a greeting, and at that moment, the plot imagined by his wife jumped to mind, and he felt as if this encounter was proof of it. He nodded his head, and he then swore to protect his daughter from this, to enlighten Slimane, and to strengthen his friendship with Amer since the others were obviously so jealous of it.

Amer, Madame, and Kamouma knew in detail what had transpired at the *djema*. There was a heated and chaotic argument among them. Madame was truly angry, and this alarmed Kamouma, who realized that her daughter-in-law had been told of the matter by a neighbor. Amer and Madame shouted at each other in French, while the old woman yelled in Kabyle. The two spouses calmed down afterward but sulked for the entire day. They were both annoyed with Kamouma, who never did learn what they were yelling about. Taking advantage of a brief absence of Amer, Kamouma tried to explain things as best she could to Madame. She explained in her fashion how the whole affair had been set up, begged her to take Amer and Chabha's side in order not to make the gossip seem credible and thus to avoid stirring up Slimane's rage.

"You know that Amer has to be careful not to arouse his uncle's animosity, Daughter. If he had remained in France, for Kamouma he would be lost, but no one here would have asked for his blood. Now that he is close to the trap, you must be as careful as he. You would lose more than I, Madame. Kamouma does not matter anymore."

"He dares betray his uncle!"

"It is a rumor, daughter. Chabha is honest."

"He has cheated on Chabha too."

"Do you really think she is so fickle? Amer is no fool either."

"I know him."

"All men are like that. It is up to the wife to forgive."

"Then you admit he has . . ."

"No, nothing happened. Everything came from Hocine and Hemama."

"They would not have made this accusation if they did not have proof. What you are telling me here is just a story. You are trying to cover for your son. I see it clearly. All old ladies are devils! As for Chabha, this is the price of her friendship."

Madame went and sat down on her bed and began to weep. She cried in spite of herself, ashamed of her tears, but feeling relief in letting them flow. It had been a long time since she had cried like that. In the end, she felt lighter, almost happy. At first, it was her solitude and her exile that caused her to feel sorry for herself, since she lived here without protection, without a friend, abandoned in the midst of this society that suddenly seemed so hostile to her. Then it was her husband's and her friend's betrayal that hurt her, like an injustice too heavy to bear. Tearfully, she thought that not so very long ago, in another place, what was happening to her here would not have bothered her in the least. Having lived beyond reproach for the past two years in such special circumstances, that is, in such primitive conditions, it seemed to her that she had rediscovered all of her former simplicity. The tears had come on their own, washing away the sad past, restoring her in her own eyes. She was no longer the humiliated girl who put up with mean boys. Instead of anger, she felt a certain compassion for her rival, Chabha, as well as sadness. Madame decided to hide the compassion and show only the sadness that she felt. But she knew that it would only take a glimpse of an equal sadness on Chabha's face to bring her compassion to light.

Amer and Chabha's names had been on peoples' lips for several days. Then, people busied themselves with other things. As soon as others were informed about their situation, nothing more was asked. They were forgotten. Chabha suffered greatly but held her head high and managed to believe that she was somehow victorious even after all of the insults. Amer was not suffering: he vented the anger welling up inside of him on Hocine, and then he calmed down. Amer sorted it out with his cousin at Tighezrane. Amer had the upper hand; they did not come to blows, but Amer stood his ground. Hocine lowered his eyes before Amer. They were standing near the spring, under the largest of the orange trees. Hocine was returning from his field, located further below. Amer had been waiting for him in order to have his say. He came directly to the point.

"For a month now people in the village are talking about me. I owe that to your wife."

Hocine's face grew red, and he looked off in the distance.

"Your wife, Hocine!"

Hocine would retain a very bad memory of this day. His hypocrisy was of no use to him that day. He could not make

Amer believe that he and Hemama had acted out of a sense of offended propriety. Amer was too furious and the matter too serious to attempt an evasive falsehood. Amer stood in front of Hocine as an implacable enemy, and he was afraid. Afterward, he went off cautiously, red in the face, sweating from fear; he climbed the narrow path that led to the village without turning around. He was in a hurry to get home and to forget Amer, Chabha, the threats, and the danger; Hocine was defeated, tired, and sad. He was angry with himself, not for having spread the stories, but for not having managed to stand up to Amer, for not having been seen by the other as a virtuous man who could criticize others since he was beyond reproach himself. Amer had told him he was despicable. It was true; he did feel despicable. It was almost a revelation for him. Hocine was accustomed to throwing others off the track, but he had never doubted himself. Amer's clenched fists had made an immediate impression upon Hocine, making him feel guilty. He had noticed the grip of a revolver visible in Amer's pocket. This had greatly disturbed him, and he lost all dignity; his gaze became subdued, imploring. When his cousin pointed to the path, Hocine practically ran away.

When they saw each other the next day in the village, they did not speak to one another. From now on they were enemies. But Hemama and Hocine put an end to their spying and their slander. They became more discreet. Hemama avoided Chabha, and Hocine fled from the sight of Amer.

From that moment, everything fell into place as simply as could be. Chabha again began to visit Madame without any worries. She no longer blushed in Amer's presence and spoke to him quite naturally, allowing herself to look at him and tease him without feeling that Madame was studying her and without fear of being caught. Madame was in fact watching Chabha and was soon surprised not to discover anything alarming. As for Amer, he had maintained his easygoing manner from the start, and his uncle did not notice anything suspicious. For some time, the guilty couple no longer saw each other in secret and, not having anything to reproach themselves for, proudly wore this look of innocence. Their love had changed into affection, and this affection could be seen in their way of looking at each other, giving them self-assurance, enabling them to restore the peace. It so happened that even without discussing it, they decided to resist the temptation to meet alone. Every time they passed up such an occasion, each one felt the same relief; they loved each other all the more for it, and their eyes exchanged a look of gratitude.

In order to prove that the gossip had had no effect upon them, the three families grew even closer. Indifferent people grew accustomed to this; this was also the way to stand up to anyone else who was unhappy about the situation and to no longer fear scandal.

XXVI

Chabha removed the teapot from its tripod and set it on the edge of the *kanoun*. Then she took three tea glasses and the box of sugar down from the shelf and placed them on the tray in front of Slimane.

"You can serve the tea," she said.

She went and rejoined Kamouma in the small room. It was nighttime. Slimane had invited Amer and Ramdane. They stayed after the couscous was eaten in order to drink a glass of tea.

"Give me your advice, Amer, you are our nephew. It is my only revenge," said Slimane.

"It can be done, in any case. But I think the two of you are young. You might regret it later or have children . . ."

"No!" cried Slimane suddenly, fixing Amer with a penetrating gaze. "Children? It's too late now."

Amer blinked as if he were upset, and he gently replied:

"What will people say? They will think that you were bewitched, that you have lost your mind. It is not good for the family name. Your cousins will think they are being insulted. Do not be angry, but I prefer to say what is on my mind."

"Fine with me if they are unhappy. They are truly looking out for my well-being, is that it? You're clever to defend them. Isn't it so, brother Ramdane? They will see that Slimane is outsmarting them. Don't you think so too?"

"I know they await your death to inherit, but it bothers me to push you to give up your property for the benefit of my daughter . . ."

"I have had my fill of their traps and their hatred. They will get nothing, and in my own lifetime they will lose all hope. I could die suddenly. Then they would inherit, all the while cursing my memory. They would send your daughter away with nothing but the dress on her back. With nothing! She would be destitute."

"I ask for nothing more, you know. But I too would have liked to have had grandchildren."

"Yes, this desire is a strong one, but it is over. I accept my fate. It is agreed then, right, Amer? This matter must be settled. I cannot rest until it is."

The two men were wary of continuing the discussion any longer. Slimane was in an agitated state akin to madness. For a few days, he alternated between melancholy and exuberance. He showed great affection toward Chabha, Amer, and Madame and even had a kind word for Kamouma. He drew his happiness from the knowledge that there had never been anything between his nephew and his wife. To reward himself for having arrived at this certainty, he wanted to punish those who slandered him, and he had found the means to do so all by himself. First, sell Amer all his property, a legal matter, notarized by the *cadi*. Then, Amer would resell everything to his wife, Chabha, with a duly notarized act. The two transactions would be completed at a one-month interval. The cousins would be taken in. They would not know anything about it. If he died, they would open their rapacious jaws in vain. They would come to dislodge Chabha from her home, and then she could derisively wave her deed in their faces. Slimane imagined himself watching the whole scene from under the earth, rejoicing at their belligerent, mad-dog faces.

The matter was, in fact, settled quickly. Amer accompanied Slimane to the city to see the *cadi* and to agree to the purchase. As soon as they affixed their thumbprints at the bottom of the document, written in Arabic by the heavyset *cadi* who wore an impressive turban, Slimane became melancholy and did not even attempt to hide his sadness. Because of this, Amer's mood also darkened. But he noticed that his brusque tone seemed to calm his uncle, who had a distraught and subdued look when speaking to him.

"Do not be angry, Amer. This is God's will. Do not think that it is with a light heart that an Aït-Hamouche decides to 'save' his property by putting it into the hands of a woman. Thank you for being the instrument that enables me to do this. Do not be angry."

"I wanted to make you happy, yet I see that you are upset. Do you already regret this?"

"This is a matter between fate and myself, but you don't expect me to be laughing about it, do you?"

"Well, fine then. It is your business after all."

Each man returned home unhappy with the other. Amer suspected that Slimane did not fully trust him. He would now be in a hurry to turn back over the property, to be free of it and to prove that he was worthy of Slimane's trust. Slimane spent a difficult month. His suspicions, fears, and dark thoughts returned, and he lost sleep over it all. One fear dominated everything now: that Chabha might be pregnant! This would be an appalling proof of his misfortune. What if fate chose precisely this moment and decided to give him an heir who would not be his own at the very moment he had divested himself of his property? He was anxious that she have the menstrual period that he had so despised. He began to spy on his wife and on Amer. Slimane tortured himself by imagining their rendezvous, and then he shrewdly kept watch over what each one of them did, since he could not remain at his wife's side all day long. He tried to find out how many girls were ahead of Chabha in line at the fountain, at what time she visited her parents or Madame, whether she had seen Amer at his home or not. As for Amer, Slimane also tried to stay informed. He questioned the waiter at the café to learn if his nephew had played dominoes for very long. Sometimes he could stand it no more, until he went to see Madame in order to get information from her.

One day, Chabha had gone to Tighezrane to wash out their *gandouras*. He thought he was going to catch her once and for all. He returned home by a different path and found the gate locked. He left to pick up the key from his mother-in-law, Smina. He came back to his house in a state of anxiety. The couple was in the habit of leaving the key with Smina if they went out. Then Slimane ran straight to Madame, finding her in the small courtyard.

"Hello, Brother Slimane, welcome."

"Thank you. I have come to see Amer. Where is he? In the field, right?"

"But no! He is in bed. A bit tired, come in."

Slimane wanted to run off, but she held him by the *burnous* and obliged him to come in. They looked at each other; for just a fraction of a second he read gentleness and pity in Madame's eyes. His throat constricted. He pouted like a child. He was certain that she sympathized with his misery and wanted to put his mind at ease.

Slimane was happy to find Amer in bed. They chatted and drank tea, and then Slimane returned home beaming, once again reassured. In this fashion he went from one extreme to another, torturing himself without cause, next telling himself he was mad, and afterward calming himself once more. At times he was angry with himself for his mistrust, making up excuses in his mind—mental wrangling, going so far as to accept that his fears were well-founded, telling himself that after all, it was not worth killing for, or killing himself over it, as long as it all remained a secret. Slimane would feel so reassured that he would allow them their forbidden happiness, the very idea of which was causing him such unhappiness.

Slimane and Chabha earned profit from Tighezrane. They thought to themselves that Hocine, the Aït-Larbi, and the Aït-Hamouche were all jealous of this fact. It might have been true. In addition, they benefited from the field, more than the time and energy spent on it. Amer was happy to help his uncle, to loan him money, to let him enjoy the use of the pair of oxen. Slimane no longer felt alone at meetings held at the *djema*. People saw that he had support. Sometimes this exasperated Slimane, strengthened his suspicions, sparking his hatred for Amer and his contempt for himself. It would often happen that Slimane would find an excuse to steal from his nephew, to cynically take advantage of his generosity and avoid doing a favor for him in return. As for Amer, he gave the impression that he allowed himself to be swindled and that he actually enjoyed it. Then Slimane would imagine that his nephew was perhaps seeking his compensation for this elsewhere, and Slimane would become angry with him. Chabha herself appeared to understand this arrangement and be complicit in it. She took his side against Amer, just as she did against the others. But he was not proud to have her on his side in such shady transactions. He would have preferred, for example, that she encourage him not to take advantage of the trust Amer showed them. No, she did not say a word, pretending not to see anything, accepting it all. Of course, later she had to pay, secretly!

Amer had the *cadi* come to the village in person. This is something Slimane himself never could have obtained from the fat official. Thanks to Amer, the second bill of sale was drawn up in Ighil-Nezman. No one suspected a thing. The *cadi* was seen going to Amer's house, but the others could only guess at the purpose. Generally, people thought it might be some type of loan agreement. If the Aït-Hamouche suspected something, it was vague. They scornfully told themselves that their cousin's business was no longer their concern, especially any matter that linked him to Amer.

The deed was drawn up on Madame's table. Two elderly, trustworthy friends of Ramdane served as witnesses. Then they all ate lunch together, at Amer's expense. Grandma Smina showered Amer in blessings, Chabha was radiant, and Madame was proud to show off her cooking skills and her beautiful dishes. Slimane felt a bit like a stranger in the face of all this joy: things had been settled without him. He no longer mattered. He was nothing now. He observed that the apparent seriousness on Ramdane's face hid the same triumph that was visible on Smina's good-natured face. Only Kamouma, to her credit, was the same as she always was, and she did not pass up the opportunity to show her bad mood and say what was on her mind.

"You can be happy," she said to Ramdane. "I like your daughter, but this affair cuts me to the quick. Our parents would not be proud of what is happening to you, right, cousin?"

"Be quiet," Slimane responded. "Your white hair is straight out of hell."

"I am not dead yet! Girls are only entitled to a third."

"Usufruct, just the use of the land, Sister, and that is only for those who have no home of their own."

"In that case, you are creating two victims," she said, indicating Madame.

"You are not entitled to anything, understand? I inherited everything from my uncle Ali. It was all his. You're stuck, aren't you?"

They looked at each other with nasty expressions. Their reddened eyes, clouded by tears, glowered equally with hatred and anger. Amer burst out laughing, and the others started to incite them even more for their own amusement. After lunch, the two men accompanied the *cadi* back to the café, from which he took the taxi back into the city. The matter was truly settled.

It was a miserable day for Slimane. The sky was dark and clammy like his soul. It was not raining, but the weather was sad. He was bored at the *djema* and at the café and returned home early. Chabha prepared his couscous. To avoid looking at her, he settled himself on the mat, far from the hearth, and dozed with his back against the wall. His wife ignored him; she bustled about a bit too feverishly. This was his impression. She seemed to be in a hurry to finish: he could tell this from a few of her gestures and from the quick way in which she put away the utensils and stoked the fire. Slimane thought he noticed she was in a hurry, but he did not think too much about it. It was nothing out of the ordinary, really. But when she spoke to him, he stopped dozing and had what seemed like a fleeting vision of the future that awaited him, and he began to think again of the old beggar in spite of himself. Once again the gloomy words rang in his head: "May God protect you from catastrophe, my daughter!"

"See," Chabha said, "everything is ready. You just have to keep an eye on the couscous pot, Husband. Take it off the heat when the steam starts to rise."

"Are you going out?"

"Yes, just stopping by my mother's place to make up the bed. I'll go to Kamouma's to bring her over here. Just a few minutes, okay? I'll be going then."

She was tapping her feet and mumbling. It was alarming. She might have trembled and blushed in the darkness, he sensed it. And the voice of the elderly vagabond punctuated Chabha's last words: "God . . . catastrophe . . ." Slimane saw his image reflected alone in the couscous pot perched over the flame.

He waited, sullen, for the steam to appear; then he carefully took the couscous pot off the stove, put it aside, removed the tripod from beneath the pot, and stood up without thinking and went out into the courtyard, where he stood for a moment, undecided. He felt tired and sad. He wanted to go back inside, light the lamp, stretch out on the mat, and wait for her to return. Ah! To not have to see that old hag Kamouma pass by and to not have to return her greeting. An idea came into his mind: he had to leave, to meet them in the street. The street was deserted. He avoided the *djema,* taking the small path that ran between the nettle bushes, the women's path that hugs the walls of the enclosure, running through small garden plots. This was the hidden path that led to Kamouma's. There was moonlight, but the sky was still cloudy. Sometimes the puffy crescent moon pierced through the dirty clouds, then disappeared again behind them. Slimane managed to follow the path alongside the nettles quite easily; he knew the way.

Below Amer's house was a threshing floor. The area belonged to the Aït-Larbi, who had access through a small door in the enclosure, a few steps from Amer's house. For some time now, Amer had been storing stones there. He was getting ready to rebuild his old home. It was, in fact, Slimane, with the help of a specialist, who quarried this stone for his nephew. Slimane was in charge of supervising the quarryman and the women porters who carried the stone. He was paid the same as the quarryman. Amer depended a great deal upon his uncle to help him with advice, as well as relying on Slimane's physical strength, since building was a serious undertaking. The pile of stones had been stacked up against the house. It was already as tall as a man. Each day, Amer busied himself with the placing of the stones.

When Slimane arrived at the site, he was struck dumb with astonishment. They were hidden behind the pile of stone and were speaking calmly in low voices. He listened, his mouth agape, eyes fixed in their direction. From deep down in his throat, an enormous burst of laughter rose up, just one single burst, like a thunderclap, capable of pulverizing them and himself along with them. His head was empty; his limbs were as stiff as wood. Slimane was like a statue. There was only this monstrous laugh that filled his lungs yet refused to come out. He could close his eyes, the moon could drown in the clouds, he saw them clearly all the same. It was daylight in his mind: a cruel light of day, with no shadow, without ambiguity, a glacial and implacable light. Instinctively, he drew back several steps. His feet were then bolted to the ground. He did not want to leave, abandoning her to the other man completely. He remained not in order to learn more but to protect her, to not totally give her away because she was his. He thought to himself that just his presence there alone, near them, without their knowledge, spoiled their love, depriving it of its meaning. They were absurd, both of them. Absurd and cowardly. He was the master! He called to her with his entire soul, inhaling violently with his mouth open, as if he could snatch her from the other in a single breath. Then he crouched down on the path, hiding between the nettle branches. A few words came to him clearly.

"Yes, the door is open, I've checked. Go first to take my mother. She and Madame think I am at the café. I'll be returning from the café."

"You'll wait until we have left . . ."

"It doesn't matter, I tell you. I am back from the café. I prefer to rejoin all of you at the house."

They left through the small doorway, one after the other at a one-minute interval. Slimane saw Amer's large silhouette framed in the doorway, waiting for the minute to pass. He bit the palm of his hand in agitation. A target! It was a perfect opportunity. But he did not have a weapon. He would have to forget about it. Perhaps it was better this way. Now his head was heavy, and his ideas came undone, slipping down to his lips, which moved silently to punctuate his mental workings. His thoughts slid down, but that was it. Nothing came up from his heart. He was lucid, calm, and cold, like everything around him. He mulled things over in his mind but felt nothing more. He rose and quickly left in order to arrive back home first. He was rather calm. What had happened no longer concerned him. It was in the past, and the past could not be changed. The future was there before him, gaping open like an abyss; this abyss was inside of him, for himself and others. Once again he felt himself to be the master. The master? What a joke. Before he arrived home he had ample time to feel the unbearable weight of supreme despair upon his shoulders. He stood again in his courtyard, bent over and weak. His elbows were drawn fearfully into his sides, under his *burnous;* he bent over double to cross the threshold, which was not low to begin with, and he·moved toward the mat in this wretched stance like a beaten animal, his face haggard, his heart constricted, and his hands trembling. Chabha found him sitting exactly where she had left him. The couscous pot was on the ground, a ways from the hearth. The pot was on the trivet; the fire was banked with ash. She glanced at everything with a satisfied look. He had taken care of the housework!

"Could you get me some water from the jar?" she asked. "My hands are dirty. I will serve supper right away."

He filled up the old jug for her. She went out to the courtyard to wash her hands. Slimane felt a sudden rush of disgust. She was soiled. He heard the water splash. She used the water to clean herself up. When she returned to the room, she seemed to see the disgust in his eyes. She turned her head away in spite of herself, but did not suspect anything.

Slimane knew he had to act as if nothing were wrong. His efforts, however, were limited to maintaining a cold silence. He answered in one word, or a growl, or a gesture to any questions she asked. Chabha tried to get him to talk, to cheer him up to end the day in a pleasant fashion. He was not able to swallow the first spoonful of soup he brought to his mouth. Slimane stood up to go out. As he passed, he took the revolver down from where it hung on the wall in its holster. Her head bent down, Chabha did not pay any attention. She assumed he was headed to the *mechmel* at the end of the village to attend to his needs. The village men always went to the *mechmel;* it was where they relieved themselves. They usually went there at night. She was not unduly worried. She was glad to be alone for a moment. She made up the bed on the mat and calmly went to sleep.

Land and Blood

Slimane started down the main street of the village. The night was dark. No one was at the *djema*. He sat down on a stone. Vague images danced before his eyes: his uncles, his brother, Madame, Chabha, and Amer. They filed past at a great speed, became muddled, dimmed, and returned again. He endured these visions without being able to react, to organize them, or to hold on to them. Then the threshing floor and the pile of stone stood out against the shadows in his mind's eye. The voices rang in his ears, pounding against his temples. The old beggar's words: "God . . . catastrophe . . . my daughter . . ." Slimane stood up like someone who was sleepwalking. Several moments later he found himself at Kamouma's gate, and there, he came to his senses. His chest burned, and the heat ran down into his arms, nourishing them with great strength. He grasped the revolver, then let go of it to grab the sides of the gate. He tried to raise it from the rusty hinges. He could have torn it right off its hinges, but he thought better of it and remained motionless for a moment. He told himself he was out of his mind, and he fled. He went to the *mechmel*. His belly churned and caused him pain. The pain went away as soon as he reached the spot. He felt as if he were suffocating, and he had no desire to return home. He already felt like a prisoner in his own body. He needed space, some cold fresh air, not the four walls of his home: that tomb with Chabha innocently stretched out on the mat. He had to flee from that prison. He went out to the road and hurried toward the cemetery. Again he gripped the gun and thought about returning to Amer's house, knocking on the gate, waiting for his nephew on the threshold, seeing him come out dressed in his silk *gandoura* holding a lamp, his big belly offered up trustingly. And yet, here was Slimane, practically running to the cemetery.

A riot of noise, like an outdoor market, stopped Slimane in his tracks as he reached the first tomb. The cemetery was animated. Thousands of voices, deep or shrill, overlapped each other. He could make out strident cries, desperate appeals, sad and gentle chants, growls, sobs, and snickers. He stood petrified, head up, hair standing on end, trying to make out a sentence or at least an intelligible word, but he could not perceive anything clearly. The heat he had felt earlier in his chest drained out of him from between his shoulders, as if a door in his back had just opened to let in an icy draft—the coldness of death. He began to shudder. He cursed the devil, raised the revolver up in front of him, and gazed out toward the cemetery. This time he saw something, in spite of the darkness: over there between the tombs, a human form loomed up and made its way toward him. It only lasted a second, but he did in fact see the ghost take a few steps in his direction. There was no mistake. It came to him in a flash. It was his uncle Slimane, Amer's grandfather, with his old turban, his muddy *gandoura* cinched at the waist with a wide strap, carrying the old pouch woven from ash tree saplings, just as he had dressed in his lifetime. A sound that was not quite human came from Slimane's throat. He closed his eyes, turned around, and an extraordinary force propelled him back to the village. Slimane found himself once again in front of his gate, trembling like a leaf, face haggard, in a cold sweat. He went inside quickly and pushed the latch and stepped into the courtyard. Only there did he stop to gather his wits. He felt as if his legs were still moving. Then he recalled that as he was running away, his anguish was intensified by the impression that his feet were moving in a void, that they did not touch solid ground, and he could not move forward. He took a deep breath and went over to the water jar, filled the old jug, and washed his face. Chabha was sleeping; the small lamp burned next to her.

The next morning he was able to laugh at himself about his nighttime terror. For him, a new day dawned, as if the night he had just experienced became a screen shielding from view his entire existence. Suddenly, everything seemed as if it had changed; people had mean and suspicious faces, objects around him mirrored his shame, everywhere he went he felt that insults, mockery, and challenges confronted him, but nowhere did he sense any pity. He was cornered; he was forced to acknowledge it. This impression was so strong that it seemed incontrovertible and filled him with revolt. No, he was not a coward. He was not afraid in broad daylight, but his anger hardened, settled itself deep inside him. He needed to think for a moment, to weigh everything, to set his trap. As everything around him had changed, he had to become different too when faced with the hostility that surrounded him. Once again he felt master of his own life and of the other two lives as well. He was on the edge of a precipice, but he held three lives firmly in his grasp.

"Are you going to the quarry?" his wife asked.

He looked at her coldly and answered her in a harsh and somewhat haughty voice:

"Yes, Wife, I am going to the quarry."

XXVII

The news spread quickly. People ran to the quarry. The entire village was in a state of shock. A hundred or so men and children stood packed together at the edge of the crater, watching intently as the men who descended worked to clear the debris. Others arrived, their faces anxious and flushed. A few bold ones tried to cross the edge of the circle to descend as well, but the others pushed them back, scandalized.

There were about ten men inside the quarry: the *amin*, the miner Lamara, Hocine-Aït-Larbi, two of the Aït-Hamouche, and a few others who had been the first to arrive. They worked in their shirtsleeves and pants: *gandouras* and jackets were thrown in a heap on the stones. Their feet, hands, and faces were splattered with wet earth. The wounded had been laid out side by side, while the others continued to move large pieces of rubble and to mindlessly throw shovelfuls of earth from one spot to another, without it doing much good, but so as to not stand there doing nothing.

"Okay," yelled the *amin*, "let's take care of the men."

Hocine sat beside Amer and held the injured man's head on his lap. He was crying and leaning over his cousin. From above, the others called down to him: they were impatient, they wanted to come down. The Aït-Hamouche crowded around their injured.

"Bring the stretcher," ordered the *amin*.

Two young men ran off to the village. Next, the men went about moving the injured out of the quarry. They were carried up carefully and laid down one next to the other, waiting for the stretchers. Onlookers formed a circle around the two unfortunate men. Off to the side, a small group surrounded Lamara, who related what had happened. People moved from Lamara to the injured and back again.

They were not dead. However, no one could know the extent of their injuries. Amer's face was smeared with earth, and there was a large blood clot on his temple. He had been trapped beneath an enormous slab; they had used extreme caution to extricate him. They had ripped open his *gandoura* and shirt to examine his body. No wound was visible, but his chest may have been crushed. Amer had been struck by a large block of stone that knocked him flat onto his back; then an avalanche of earth and rock had buried him. The wound on his temple was no doubt from a projectile. The explosion had hit him at point-blank range. He was wet and covered with earth, blood, and sweat, which made him a terrible sight. He was not dead, but his eyes were closed. Blood no longer flowed from his wound. A reddish foam escaped from the corner of his mouth; one nostril was blocked as well. An elderly *marabout* murmured the *shahada* to him with his mouth pressed up against Amer's ear, right next to the black clot. The others did not dare touch him, afraid that they would finish him off. They just stood aside shaking their heads. Hocine, desperate, tried to open Amer's eyes and leaned over his face to blow into his mouth.

Slimane seemed less affected. There was no visible wound. They had found him lying on a pile of stones at the quarry's edge, his *chechia* pinned under a block that must have fallen on his head. His breathing was more labored than Amer's, and his eyes were also closed. Someone felt the top of his head, and it was as soft as a newborn baby's. Slimane uttered a feeble groan, half opening one eye and shutting it right away again. Then his hand began to move up and down the length of his body. Only one hand moved in this way, the one in which they had just discovered a fracture. It was as if a mechanism had been set off: the fingers splayed out as his arm straightened and then clenched back up into a fist as his arm traveled toward his chest. The movement was repeated over and over, as a group of men stood stunned in front of this inexplicable motion. When they tried to immobilize the arm, it felt as if all the remaining strength of this poor man was concentrated in his arm. For fear of causing Slimane to suffer more, they decided to leave him be.

When the stretchers arrived, the men took care of Slimane first. He was placed with his head resting on his folded *burnous*. They used a turban-winding cloth to tie him to the stretcher, leaving his hands free alongside his body. His arm continued its traveling motion up and down his body, and when the stretcher was raised to carry him, it seemed to signal to the bearers to go.

While the others looked after Slimane, only Hocine and the elderly *cheikh* remained, bent over the dying Amer. The faint breath that came out from the single nostril was rapidly fading, his chest was collapsing, and his face was turning yellow. Hocine noticed that his hands were icy. Yet, at the instant he noticed this, Amer opened his eyes wide. The *cheikh*, fascinated by the dying man's gaze, began to recite his prayer more quickly as if he knew what was about to happen. Amer's eyes remained open a few seconds, fixed upon a mysterious point far away from the useless bustle of the living. Suddenly his eyes rolled back, and only the white globes could be seen from under the half-open lids. At that very moment as well, his lips swelled, and in an almost imperceptible breath, his last puff of air formed one last pinkish bubble in the middle of his mouth. The *cheikh* closed Amer's eyelids, pressing down firmly with two fingers to keep them shut. Slowly he repeated the formula: "There is no God but God and Mohammed is His prophet."

They placed the corpse on the second stretcher, and the two processions followed each other back to the village. The strongest men carried the bier of the dead man, taking turns in groups of four to shoulder the bier. Those who followed at the rear sang the gloomy chant that everyone knew and that no one could hear without trembling. Blood seeped out from between the planks of the stretcher, thick and black, as it had pooled under Amer's back and now finally found a means of escape.

They arrived at the village, which was in a state of great confusion. A crowd had gathered in the street; women had come to meet the procession; children threaded their way in between the adults' legs. There was chanting, yelling, the issuing of orders. The women of the Aït-Hamouche and the Aït-Larbi lamented, while Madame, Kamouma, Smina, and Chabha waited at home. The bulk of the crowd stopped, however, at the *djema*, unsure whether they should accompany the dead man or the wounded man. Lamara, his eyes still dilated from the shock, explained one more time what had happened:

"O believers, it was written! You will all see that it was divine will. We wanted to blast the rock. Amer was not there. It was my task. I hollowed out the blasting cap and filled it with powder, a triple dose. It was midday, and the porters had gone to lunch. No one was around. We lit the fuse, and Slimane and I ran behind the large ash tree. That was it. Then the explosion! Slimane stood up all of a sudden. I didn't hear anything, but he thought he heard a cry. I followed him. He rushed down to the quarry. There was still so much smoke that I couldn't see anything at first. Slimane was already inside. I arrived just in time to see an enormous piece of rubble come loose on top of the poor man's head. A stroke of fate, friends! You would have thought it was dropped by an invisible but firm hand. There was a great roar, and Slimane could not even make a move to avoid it. When everything settled, I began to call for help, not even realizing that Amer was trapped under a heap of rock and earth. It was only after Hocine arrived first, and we went down together, that we saw Amer's feet moving slightly. Oh brothers, I will never forget the sight of those feet, awkwardly planted like crooked stakes in the ground. That's all there was. The rest of him had disappeared. The two men were speaking: I swear to you, I heard them crying out in pain, calling for help, hanging on to life. It was Amer's soul that had sought refuge there and did not want to leave. In an instant, I forgot about Slimane lying there close by. We both forgot about him. The others would have to arrive to look after him. I called out for the others to come and help me free Amer; I tore at the rock and earth like a maniac. What a day, my God! Why do catastrophes like this happen?"

"How is it that Amer did not hear your warning? You call out a warning each time you light the fuses," someone asked him.

Lamara hesitated a second, then nodded his head with a sad look.

"But yes, of course. 'Fire in the hole!' 'Fire in the hole!'

Right? You know that. It is our signal. The kids make fun of us when we go by in the evening: 'Fire in the hole!' they call out. Slimane would even get angry about it sometimes. Their voices would follow us. But you see, when it is written, what can we do?"

At that moment, old Ramdane appeared, coming out from his daughter's home. He was solemn; he did not look at the others but went straight up to Lamara and motioned for him to follow. They went into the alley leading to the Aït-Hamouche houses. In front of the gate, Ramdane stopped and looked at Lamara.

"You, along with God, are the only witness. Tell me what happened!"

"I will tell you, Ramdane. You found me here doing just that. I will tell you everything. I was the first one to get behind the tree, and Slimane was right behind me. I crouched down. He was standing facing me and could see across to the entrance from the field. Then he bent down suddenly; his hands were trembling, and with them he grasped my face to make me look at him. He was babbling, stammering, repeating: 'Quick, look in my eye, there is some dust, get it out, blow on it . . .'"

"'Fine, take it easy. Let go of me first.'

"'Oh my God, it stings, hurry, blow!'

"His hands, placed upon his knees, trembled. He pressed up against me. He spoke the entire time. There was no chance to call out the warning.

"'Look in the other eye. I can't see. Take a good look, Lamara,' he said.

"Then in an instant, there was the explosion! He jumped up, told me heard a cry, and ran without worrying anymore about his eyes."

"So you think he saw Amer come out of the field near the quarry?"

"Yes, on the path. Amer was supposed to meet us there to see the midday's work."

"This is your opinion. Nothing proves . . ."

Land and Blood

"Indeed, there was dust in his eyes. I mean, it was all written. That is what I think."

"My thoughts as well."

"Now, Ramdane, everything I told you, it is just between us, naturally."

"I think you must keep your impressions to yourself. Do not try to understand God's plans. Our judgment is so weak!"

"No, Ramdane. It is not a question of judging. You have a daughter. I have three daughters. The evil one sows, the children harvest it. One man is dead; the other is in the hands of God now. It is not right to poison the lives of the survivors . . ."

Ramdane was silent; then he lowered his gaze, and the two men stood like that for a moment. Then the older man pushed open the gate and went inside without inviting Lamara to follow. Lamara, a worried look on his face, returned to the *djema*.

Inside, the Aït-Hamouche surrounded Slimane. They were all there, the men and the women. They felt themselves to be in their own home, and they tolerated Ramdane's presence. Slimane was laid out right in the middle of the room, on the large red carpet. An old Aït-Hamouche woman had made up the bed. She had taken hold of the mat, two sheepskins, the best blankets, the carpet, and the large pillow. She placed all of this down to get ready for the visits they would receive, without a single word to Chabha. The woman did not even hesitate to climb up into the loft in order to inspect things, touch them, and take inventory of what was there. She had made herself right at home. In addition, all the others were busy fawning over their "poor Slimane," visibly ignoring Chabha, slumped in a corner of the room. Smina paid no attention to her daughter; she carefully noted the comings and goings of the others. She took note of her enemies' ploys. She saw them taking over the house. Already! Of course this was an affront to her daughter, but from this insult they would both have to draw courage and strength. They would need courage to bear this twist of fate and the strength to confront these intruders and not back down. Right there, in front of this inanimate body soon to be drained of life, she felt a secret joy in thinking that Providence had, with the stroke of a pen, secured her sterile daughter's future. Let them ignore the two women, those Aït-Hamouche, their disappointment will be great, their anger will be all for nothing when they see the house and the land escape their grasp. Without thinking, Smina drew her daughter to her withered chest and began to rock her tenderly. They sat in the darkest corner of the house, and yet, the others saw them and took the opportunity to insult them again.

"Our poor son," an elderly Aït-Hamouche lady cried out. "You lived alone and died alone."

"Shut your mouth," her husband yelled at her. "We are all here with him. We are all he needs."

Chabha stood up, closed her eyes, pressed her hands to her eyes, then reopened them and looked at the cousins proudly. She brushed aside her mother's arms and made her way through the group to take her place at the head of her husband's bed. As two of the women were getting up to leave, the men, with a look, obliged them to sit back down. The eldest of the men in the gathering turned to Ramdane, whom he seemed to just notice standing there for the first time.

"I don't think he will last the night," he said. "There will be two burials tomorrow."

"Let God's will be done."

This brief exchange calmed the others. They understood that they would have to tolerate each other's presence.

"Ramdane," he said again, "we Aït-Hamouche have another duty to fulfill. We have an injured man, they have a corpse. It is up to us to visit the Aït-Larbi. Brothers, do not forget that Kamouma is our sister, and her son is our nephew. We will go to see him in spite of everything."

His gaze traveled across the faces of the assembled men, but no one answered. They had all understood that the last reticence was an additional insult directed at Ramdane.

"Amer is dead," Ramdane replied. "Speak as you wish. His uncle will not be long to follow suit. Look at him."

In turn, they swallowed the insult and leaned over the injured man. His arm no longer moved under the blanket. His body sagged more and more and seemed to gain in length what it was losing in volume. His face took on a waxy look, and his chest did not move with any breath. They decided to leave him in this state.

"Let us hurry," said the eldest man. "We will all go there, men and women together. Ramdane, would you stay here with your son-in-law to wait for us? Your daughter must come too, I think. The people at the *djema* will see us pass by as a family. This is very important."

Ramdane did not answer. He looked at his daughter, who stood up with an effort, drew away from her husband's body, and went to the door to go out first. She knew that her father would have preferred her to stay, but once again she rose to their challenge.

Kamouma's house was full of people. The procession of visitors had begun even before the body arrived. People came to express a few comforting words to Kamouma and Madame; then, one by one, they moved closer to the dead man, standing a moment on the threshold, then gave up their place to other visitors. The cousins and the entire *karouba* were there too. Some of them remained in the courtyard. They were the first to receive the condolences, and each time they displayed a serious countenance. Those who were the least touched by sorrow were quick to respond with well-turned phrases, as if to prove to everyone and to themselves that they were affected. But everyone knew that only the two women were really deserving of pity and that the blow that had struck them did not affect the Aït-Larbi. Yet even the most reasonable among them deplored this premature death and thought that it was a loss for the family. Hocine said as much as he sobbed out loud, in front of the assembled family members. But as far as Hocine was concerned, there was perhaps something else. No doubt his tears were sincere, and his pain was evident. Each time a group of notables arrived, the cousins drew attention to Hocine to show the strong family ties with the Aït-Larbi.

Hemama was with the crowd of women who wailed, and her cries outdid all the others. Each time she gave the signal; she chose her moment to cry out, and the others followed. She watched for the visitors to arrive, and when an important group blocked the door, she deafened them with her noisy despair.

Madame was seated on the chair, positioned next to Amer's corpse, her back to the door, head in her hands, and she sobbed softly. She gave herself totally over to her sorrow and paid no attention to the group assembled there. It was plain to see that she had completely detached herself from this group who no longer meant anything to her. Yet nothing would tear her away from this inert body that she gazed upon in fright every time she raised her eyes from behind her hands. Then she would nervously shake her head as if to deny the evidence, wringing her hands and lowering her shoulders to sob even more.

Kamouma paced around the bier in the small space people had left open for her; she appeared to have suddenly grown shriveled, dried out, and twisted. Her bony arms had slipped under her belt and buried themselves in her hollow belly. Her spine, standing up in broken lines, was all one saw of her. There was something both ridiculous and sinister in her movements, which prevented anyone from feeling much pity for her. They could see that she was edgy with anger and rebellion; they could sense her blaming Satan, God, and men. They saw how she did not bend under the weight of her misfortune; instead she had seized hold of it and confronted it directly.

In the presence of her dead son, the Aït-Larbi feared her. They dreaded an outburst of irreparable words that would complicate things. When the body had been brought in, she had thrown herself on it with ferocity in tears, and she spat out her hatred in front of them all.

"You are happy now! You bring him to me on a bier."

People acted as if they did not understand her, and the *cheikh* rebuked her.

Land and Blood

"Do you think, infidel, that he is your son alone and not a creature of God? He wanted him and took him. Accept this. You are too old to blaspheme. Do you think you can change the course of destiny by your petty scheming? Mourn your son, and resign yourself to this, and then perhaps He who took away your son will bring you consolation. Only He can!"

The old *marabout* held her by the arm and shook her with all his strength while Amer's body was placed on the bed. He forced her to listen to him. Unknown to him, he struck a chord in her. She looked at him as with the gaze of a cornered animal, and then she turned away. From that moment on, she no longer cried out. Her plans had been foiled. Who was to blame? Who had killed her son? Slimane? Chabha? Hocine and his wife? Perhaps even herself, along with that stupid Smina? Or was it maybe Amer himself who had hastened his own death by his behavior, all due to an unpaid and unyielding debt? A debt that might well have been forgotten! The *marabout* is right: God mocks our petty plans. He decides, He alone lays out the path each one follows.

When the Aït-Hamouche arrived, they were received by the Aït-Larbi with obvious satisfaction. On both sides they felt at ease; they felt united by this common misfortune, which, in truth, had hardly touched them. The glances they exchanged seemed to congratulate each other on saving face in this way and getting out of a difficult situation without there being any bad blood between them. They would bury their dead, who in turn would be quickly forgotten, and everyone would feel at ease.

The Aït-Hamouche women mingled their lamentations with those of the Aït-Larbi, and the cries reached their crescendo, filling up the entire house. Kamouma understood that in reality, these lamentations proclaimed their tacit agreement.

The sight of Chabha arriving at the head of the procession bothered Kamouma greatly. She despised her like an enemy and felt pity for her. She was the living image of her own pain and guilt. The young woman moved forward like a sleepwalker, and yet they saw each other clearly. Kamouma turned her head away; Chabha grimaced in pain and went toward Madame. Kamouma came around the bed to get there first. So the three women found themselves together at the head of Amer's bier. About twenty other people were crowded around them in the home, crying and gesturing, but watching what would happen next. The men were grouped behind, blocking the door. At that precise moment, a young Aït-Hamouche cried out that Slimane had died. Chabha, terror in her eyes, leaned slowly toward the bed and collapsed in a faint against Madame's knees. There was a loud tumult. Kamouma straightened up. For her, this was good news. Both of them dead! She dared to raise her eyes to look at the Aït-Hamouche gathered there. They turned away to go to their dead, while Chabha remained at Madame's feet, forgotten by all. Suddenly Kamouma felt Madame take her hand to place it on her belly. Then she shuddered.

"Did he move?" she murmured to her.

"Yes, when Chabha came in."

"God be praised, my daughter. We will have an heir."

Then she bent down and helped Chabha back up on her feet. She forgot for a small moment her son, her pain, and her anger.

"Tomorrow," she thought, "when they come to take him away, Madame will throw her red flannel belt onto her dead husband's body. Then everyone will know that she is carrying his child!"

Glossary of Arabic and Kabyle (Tamazight) Words

Achoura: Muslim holiday marking the tenth day of the new year

Aït: from the family of. The two main Kabyle families in this novel, for example, are the Aït-Larbi and the Aït-Hamouche.

amin: an elected village official or notable, similar to a mayor. He is an agent who executes the decisions taken by the *agraw,* the *djema.*

baraka: benediction or blessing (like a wish for good fortune)

belboul: pancakes, crêpes

burnous: a man's long cape, an outer garment, usually made from white wool with long sleeves and a hood

cadi: a traditional judge who represents customary law as opposed to French law

caïd: a leader or chief

chechia: knitted skull cap worn by men (often underneath a turban)

cheikh: a title given to the head of a tribe, or more commonly, a respectful term used to designate an older man of status

çof: an alliance of clans or a league of tribes

dada: a term of respect for an older man ("elder brother")

djema: akin to a village "square" or meeting place, it also means the elected men of the community who meet there to discuss issues and problems in the village. The term can also stand in for the elected assembly of male villagers (*agraw* or *tadjmaat*) who advise the *amin.*

fellah: a peasant or agricultural worker

gandoura: a traditional North African robe (for men or women), usually made of silk or cotton, with a v-neck embroidered around the opening

ima (yma): "mother" in Kabyle, often shortened to *ye* or *ma.* (Note: the Arabic word for "mother" is *oum.*)

Glossary

kanoun: a fixed hearth inside the home used for cooking; also may refer to a portable earthenware brazier used to hold coals for cooking

karouba: an important term for Kabyles, meaning the clan or large extended family. The *karoubas* form the base of any village; they have blood ties usually traced back to a common ancestor.

khaounis: women mourners hired for wakes and funerals

kouba: a dome; by extension the domed shrine of a *marabout* or holy man

marabout: a holy man who provides interpretations of dreams and protective charms

mechmel: a field for grazing animals held in common ownership

mektoub: fate or destiny ("written on the forehead")

nana: a term of respect for an older woman ("elder sister")

nif: the Kabyle concept of honor

ou: used as part of a man's name: "son of." Amer-ou-Kaci, for example, means "Amer son of Kaci."

ouada: a small offering of money brought to the *marabout*

roumi (tharoumith) (originally "Roman"): a term used to designate the French (i.e., Christians) or a word to designate "a foreigner"

sadaka: an Arabic word for charity and alms, a duty for all Muslims. *Sadaka* also calls for hospitality to strangers.

saroual: loose-fitting trousers

shahada: Muslim profession of faith

Sura: a chapter of the Qur'an

taleb: a student or a learned person with knowledge of the Qur'an

tamens: the leading members (elders) of a *karouba*

thadjmaat(or *agraw*): a Kabyle village assemble of elected men

tharoumith: a term indicating a foreign, European woman (see *roumi*)

tazrout: a cemetery

zaouia: a religious brotherhood or fraternity

Afterword

PATRICIA GEESEY

Mouloud Feraoun was born on March 8, 1913, in the village of Tizi-Hibel in the mountainous region of Kabylia, Algeria. The Kabyles are the largest group of North African Berbers; they refer to themselves as "Kabyles," the descendants of the "Imazighen," meaning "free people." Their presence in the region predates the Arab conquests of the late seventh century and can be traced back as far as the Roman era. Feraoun's mother tongue was Kabyle, a form of Tamazight, and he also spoke and wrote in French, the official language of Algeria during the colonial era. In the work *Journal: 1955–1962* (1962, 2000), Feraoun laid bare the paradox of his identity as an indigenous, Muslim Algerian of the colonial era, educated in French schools: "When I say that I am French, I give myself a label that each French person refuses me. I speak French, and I got my education in a French school. I have learned as much as the average Frenchman. What am I then, dear God?" (65). He felt himself to be both Algerian and French at a time when the label "Algerian" usually referred to inhabitants of the colony with European ancestry. During the period of French rule, even French-educated, indigenous Algerians were called "Muslims" or "Natives."

Born to a modest family who farmed and herded, Feraoun attended a French-language school in a nearby village, and thanks to a scholarship, the gifted young student later pursued university-level studies at the prestigious École Normale d'Alger-Bouzaréa in the capital city of Algiers. Feraoun relates much of his own childhood in his first novel, *Le fils du pauvre*, first published in 1950, then reedited in Paris with the prestigious publishing house of Éditions du Seuil in 1954. The English-language translation of this poignant account of growing up in a Kabyle village is entitled *The Poor Man's Son: Menrad,*

Afterword

Kabyle Schoolteacher (2005). Greatly admired during and after his lifetime, this autobiographical work traces the trajectory of Fouroulu Menrad, the author's alter ego, from life as the poor child of a typical Kabyle village to the early years of his career as a schoolteacher in rural, colonial Algeria.

Mouloud Feraoun worked as a teacher after completing his schooling, and he held various teaching posts in small towns in Kabylia throughout the years 1936–52. Then Feraoun moved to the town of Fort-National (in the Kabylia province) to teach. In 1954, the Algerian War of Independence against the French erupted. In 1960, while the war still raged, Feraoun accepted a post as a school inspector for the French educational organization in Algiers, called Les Centres Sociaux. This humanitarian institution had been founded by the French anthropologist Germaine Tillion, herself a member of the French Resistance and a concentration-camp survivor, its purpose to improve educational opportunities for impoverished indigenous children in Algeria. It was during an administrative meeting of Les Centres Sociaux, on March 15, 1962, that Feraoun and five other school administrators were brutally murdered by right-wing, French paramilitary terrorists (members of the O.A.S., or the Organisation de l'armée secrète), in the final days of the French-Algerian conflict. The objective of the O.A.S. was to create an atmosphere of terror during the last twelve months of French rule. The O.A.S. was responsible for the murder of hundreds of civilians—indigenous Algerians, as well as French liberals who supported independence—and for the destruction of government buildings, including schools and hospitals. Bridges and roads were bombed by O.A.S. commandos in order to punish the Algerians for breaking away from France and to make life in the newly independent nation that much more difficult.

Mouloud Feraoun was one of the most well-regarded intellectuals of colonial Algeria. He wrote fiction and essays and translated Berber oral poetry, and he maintained a friendship and correspondence with Albert Camus. He counted several other well-known writers as his friends, foremost among them the "Pied-Noir" novelist Emmanuel Roblès, a friend since their college days together. Roblès's moving preface, first published in the posthumous 1962 edition of *Land and Blood,* is included in this translation. As a young teacher, Mououd Feraoun began to write in his spare time, and his friend Roblès encouraged him to pursue this creative outlet and publish his work. According to literary historian Jean Déjeux, Feraoun began to write in late-colonial Algeria during the era and ambiance of a literary school known as the École d'Alger, whose other famous members included Albert Camus, Gabriel Audisio, Emmanuel Roblès, and Jules Roy (135). These fellow French-language novelists wrote of Algeria, its peoples and landscapes; in addition, they were known to encourage Muslim Algerian authors to publish their own works as well. Feraoun recounted that these authors were an inspiration to him. In an important essay entitled "La littérature algérienne," first published in the journal *La Revue Française* in 1957 (reprinted in the posthumous *L'anniversaire,* 1972), Feraoun described his own literary endeavor as a response to what he felt was missing in the writings of the École d'Alger novelists. Feraoun appreciated the fact that these writers had broken with cheap exoticism in order to portray a more accurate and true picture of the humanity that could be found in Algeria. Yet, as Feraoun noted, "One encounters in their works a warm sympathy for the Native, sometimes even friendship, but in general, the Native is absent, and if we all deeply deplore this fact, it is not due to the writer, it is not a matter of a regrettable literary deficiency, it is simply one of the sad, Algerian realities" (54). Feraoun also referred to "the honorable modesty" (55) that prevented some Algerian-born French authors from testifying in favor of the Muslim, Arab-Berber population during the Algerian war. This then inspired Algerian authors like himself to take up the pen and make their thoughts and beliefs known. To rectify the absence of Muslim Algerian characters from the novels of the Ecole d'Alger writers, Feraoun was determined to focus attention on the lives and psychological makeup of his indigenous characters and on a realistic depiction of the Kabyle human condition.

La terre et le sang (Land and Blood) was first published in
Paris with Éditions du Seuil in 1953. This early date of publication makes Mouloud Feraoun a pioneer of North African,
French-language writing. Along with Feraoun, other novelists who began to publish during the early years of the 1950s,
such as Mohammed Dib, Mouloud Mammeri, Kateb Yacine
(Algeria), Albert Memmi (Tunisia), and Driss Chraïbi (Morocco), would later collectively become known as "The First
Generation." In addition, in 1953 *La terre et le sang* won the
renowned Prix du Roman Populiste, a French literary prize
that recognizes works of fiction depicting the true humanity of
modest social classes.

Feraoun was aware of his unique situation as a Muslim-
Berber, French-language novelist in those years. He wrote of
the "paradoxical" situation that he and his fellow Muslim-
Maghrebian authors faced, desiring above all to document
their societies from within and to bear witness to the reality of
their lives under French colonial rule. In "La littérature algérienne," Feraoun described the role he felt called upon to play:
"We are intellectuals from a separate world, and we possess
French culture. Our paradox—or our drama, as it is commonly
referred to—is readily understandable. Attached by every fiber
of our soul to a fixed, backward, and poor society on the mar-
gins of the new century, we are perfectly aware of what we lack
and of our duty to claim it. The militant aspect of our work
is therefore not surprising" (57). Feraoun's intention was to
transmit an authentic message from the colonized, dominated
culture of Algeria to the reader—most probably at that time
a resident of metropolitan France—and to depict the reality
and the fraternity of humankind among the Kabyles as he had
experienced it. When he states that his work has a "militant"
quality, he refers to the fact that a work of fiction by a colonial
subject of Algeria of this era, depicting indigenous inhabitants
in an accurate, humanizing manner, is in itself a form of protest
against the political and economic status quo of French-ruled
Algeria.

Set between the years of 1910 and 1930, *Land and Blood* is

the fictional tale of Amer-ou-Kaci, a young man who returns to his Kabyle village named Ighil-Nezman after several decades of living and working in France. As recounted in *The Poor Man's Son*, Feraoun's own father also made numerous trips to northeastern France to work in the coal mines as a last resort to support his family. The novel therefore reflects a historical accuracy: the Kabyles have been one of the first and the largest ethnic groups of North Africa to immigrate to France. France is presently a multiethnic society with several million citizens of Muslim, Arab-Berber heritage. Feraoun's novel, therefore, illustrates the long-standing ties between France and Algeria, ties that date from the 1920s and 1930s, as reflected in the migrant labor force that crossed the Mediterranean Sea each year to work in the factories, mines, and fields of metropolitan France.

While in France, Amer inadvertently kills his uncle in a mining accident. World War I soon begins, and Amer is taken prisoner by the Germans. He remains in France to work for several years and finally returns to his village accompanied by his French wife, Marie, to take his place in his society once more. *Land and Blood* is a hybrid text: it is a work of fiction depicting a gripping story of murder, revenge, betrayal, and adultery; yet great attention is also paid to presenting and explaining traditional beliefs and customs of the Kabyles. Robert Elbaz and Martine Mathieu-Job suggest that the dual nature of this text—both fiction and anthropological treatise—is an ideological choice on Feraoun's part, carried out in order to forge a new territory of literary expression for the North African novelist (86). These authors point out that since Feraoun was a pioneer in the field, there were virtually no existing literary role models for him to emulate. The creative strategy employed by Feraoun in *Land and Blood* is to briefly suspend or interrupt the novel's narrative with a digression about farming practices, the meaning and origin of a saying, an account of the power structure of village life, or a meditation on the fate of the poor in a typical Kabyle village.

Furthermore, *Land and Blood* in the present translation

maintains the use of Kabyle Tamazight and Arabic words (itali-cized, as in the original French publication), as this was also a stylistic element of Feraoun's writing. The original French edi-tion did not provide a glossary for the reader (one is included in the English version to assist readers). The non-Kabyle reader would have had to approach Feraoun's text on the author's own terms, perhaps as a metaphorical "stranger" in a foreign land—which was how the French in Algeria were viewed by many indigenous Algerians.

The documentary and ethnographic aspect of the Feraounian text is essential since it situates the novelist as an insider, some-one who presents both the story at hand and the necessary cul-tural information that will enable a non-Kabyle reader to fully appreciate all the elements of the drama. The reader becomes acquainted with the most vital landmarks of Kabyle culture: the *djema,* the village square where men meet; the fountain, where women gather to collect water for their household; the Moorish café—only men are to be found there; and the vil-lage cemetery, a space the living use for strolling and meeting. As Feraoun noted in his essay "La littérature algérienne," the Algerian novelist seeks to enact a paradoxical movement: by insisting on an accurate portrayal of the unique customs and beliefs of Kabyle culture, Feraoun achieves his goal of human-izing and universalizing the colonial, indigenous "other" to the European reader by portraying village life as nothing excep-tional: people live and get along with each other, they struggle to survive hardships, and they plan for the future of their chil-dren. As he wrote in "La littérature algérienne," "The recog-nition that each of us needs is that the most banal of human truths is stamped like a watermark on the pages of our works: we are men, nothing but men; we need friendship, tenderness, and brotherhood. If we possessed all that, our bodies would no longer hunger, our spirits would no longer thirst, our hearts would beat like all others: there would no longer be anything special about us" (58). As the French reader comes to know the Kabyles within the parameters of their own culture, the reader will appreciate the shared humanity between French and Kabyle alike.

Feraoun's writing of his Kabyle homeland in the early years of the mid-twentieth century could also link him to a literary trend found within metropolitan France at that time, which sought to celebrate and nostalgically look back upon French regional differences. This type of literature was popular just after World War II in France, since French society was then undergoing radical shifts from a largely rural to a predominately urban society. In Samira Sayeh's study of the first generation of French-language, Algerian writers, she notes that Feraoun's writings, published when Algeria was still a French "département" (an extension of France itself), highlight the fact that the author's sense of identity, grounded in Kabyle culture, was also a means by which he could assert his regional identity. Feraoun's insistence on both the specific and the universal aspects of Kabyle society may be read as a counterweight to Paris's overarching centrality in notions of French identity, in both the *métropole* and its colonial territories.

The style of Feraoun's writing in *Land and Blood* favors the insider's perspective. The narrator is virtually omniscient, in the grand tradition of nineteenth-century, French realist fiction. Mathieu-Job and Elbaz point out, however, that Feraoun employs narrative strategies to subtly undermine this traditional narrative practice. Indirect discourse is, naturally, the favored tool for this style of literature. But they suggest that the author's habit of including the adverbs "perhaps" and "no doubt" again and again points to a possible uncertainty as to the narrator's omniscience (66–67). They suggest that Feraoun used this technique to create a tension between "knowing" and the impossibility of "knowing all." The "native informant" narrator, who knows Kabyle culture from within, is at times uncertain: to depict and to sum up this vast, rich, and pluralistic Kabyle culture is a nearly impossible task. The reader might also infer from this narrative tactic that the author may have, to some extent, fallen away from his own culture, because of his time spent away from the village at the French school. The resulting acculturation of the French colonial school could also be thought of as having provoked a feeling of distance from the author's cultural origins: this in itself is a common theme of early French-language writing from North African novelists.

The first-person plural often introduces information about Kabyle traditions: for example, "As we say among ourselves . . . ." or "As for we Kabyles . . . ." This technique highlights the narrator's stance as speaking from *within* Kabyle culture. The "we" of a plural, omniscient narrator in turn evokes the presence of a "you" plural, hence the French readers whose implicit presence is required in order for a cross-cultural dialogue to occur. Indeed, transcultural encounters are an integral part of the novel. Amer joins up with other Kabyle workers in France and grows accustomed to their way of life, yet he also notices how the miners from Belgium or Poland work together more effectively to make demands for better pay from the mine operators. Amer laments the fact that the Kabyles working in northeastern France, although numerous, argue among themselves and bring their *çof* or clan alliances with them to France, thereby limiting their group cohesion and preventing them from speaking to their employers as a single voice.

Land and Blood illustrates the many cultural and religious beliefs that characterize the Kabyle worldview. The residents of Ighil-Nezman are of course Muslim, as is the Arab-Berber population of Algeria today. The men may attend prayers in the small village mosque, but women pray at home. The *marabout,* or learned and devout man of a neighboring village, is consulted on many occasions to interpret dreams, to seek a cure for sterility, and to advise a villager on any number of personal matters. Folk beliefs related to the weather, farming, and marriage coexist with more orthodox Islamic beliefs and prayers. This is especially true in the scenes in which the elderly women discuss "recipes" that may help a woman conceive a child. Feraoun's novel accurately depicts the presence of prayer in the villagers' daily lives. As Amer dies, a *marabout* recites the *shahada,* the Muslim profession of faith. Islam for the residents of Ighil-Nezman even may be seen as affecting peoples' attitudes toward their own fate. At the wake for Amer, his mother is scolded by an elderly *cheikh* since her outspoken bitterness at his untimely death signifies her refusal to accept God's will. Only God provides consolation, he advises. Humans, too insignificant to know His plans, must submit to their fate. This worldview is expressed several times in *Land and Blood*. Throughout the novel, the narrator juxtaposes the plotting and petty schemes of several villagers who seek to change the course of events with the *marabout's* wisdom regarding fate that originates in a more religiously inspired fatalism.

Amer's French wife, Marie, called Madame by the villagers, adjusts to her new life in Kabylia and finds common ground with the women there. The Kabyle women are eager to meet Marie and to view her household items brought from France. She does not represent any colonial "authority." Marie wishes above all to find solidarity and companionship with the women of the village, becoming close friends with Chabha, a young woman married to Amer's uncle Slimane. In *Land and Blood*, Feraoun shows the potential for French-Kabyle entente; however, Feraoun's third novel, *Les chemins qui montent* (1957) (The High Roads), set several decades later, tells the story of Amer and Madame's son, who is tragically unable to come to terms with his bicultural identity and ultimately cannot find a place for himself in Kabylia or France.

In *Land and Blood,* the title's meaning is made clear within the course of the story: the elements of land and blood are vital to Kabyle culture, and they form the central axis of the narrative. When Amer accidently causes his own uncle's death in France, there is a question of the blood price to be paid. The Kabyle concept of *nif*, or honor, is the dominant ethic of the Kabyle social system. Amer's role in his uncle's death is problematic, since to require that a blood price be paid would only enlarge the debt within the clan or *karouba*. The fact that the "accident" took place in France further complicates matters, since the Kabyle émigrés are subject to French laws, and revenge killing is illegal there. Amer is aware of the risk he might face upon his return to the village should Rabah's remaining brother decide to extract revenge.

Kabyle village life as depicted in *Land and Blood* is quite circumspect and operates within a narrow set of parameters. The French colonial administration hardly makes itself felt in such a small mountain village of the 1930s. Madame and Amer pay a visit to a nearby town to meet with a French official, but the experience is not a pleasant one. Feraoun's novel realistically depicts the function of the Kabyle system of the *agraw,* or *thadjmaat,* or elected village assembly. One man usually serves as an *amin,* comparable to a village mayor. The *amin,* assisted in his duties by the *tamens,* or village elders, has no religious function, and he is not paid for his services. It is an honor and civic duty to serve one's village. As Feraoun noted in his essay "L'entreaide dans la société kabyle," reprinted in *L'anniversaire,* the Kabyle village is "the indestructible entity and administrative and social unity whose existence must be taken into consideration" (94–95) if any change or progress is to occur. The village is the cornerstone of Kabyle life, and the alliances (*çof*) between and coexistence of the clans (*karouba*) who make up the population of a Kabyle village are its life force.

The narrator recounts the history of the village through the rise and fall of several important clans whose descendants still live there. This is the natural order of things according to the Kabyle worldview. In *Land and Blood,* the village of Ighil-Nezman is virtually a character of the novel, endowed with a life force of its own. In the first pages, the precarious physical position of the village, clinging to the side of the hill, is described; the visitor's likely negative perception of the state of disrepair of homes and alleys is anticipated, but the welcoming embrace of the village of one of its "prodigal" émigré sons is touching. The man who returns to his village even after an absence of many years has truly found his place "at home" again.

After his return, Amer's first objective is to buy back several fields that his father sold out of necessity while Amer lived in France. This introduces the other title element: land. Possession of the land and the blood ties between clans are the foundation of Kabyle existence. Believing the rumors that Marie is actually the daughter of the murdered uncle, Ramdane exclaims that her arrival in Ighil-Nezman will erase the debt of blood Amer has yet to repay: "Land and blood! The two essential elements in every person's destiny" (108). Writing this novel in the years leading up to the outbreak of what would be Europe's most violent anticolonial conflict, the theme of possession of the land is a politically sensitive issue. The references to land can be read for a dual meaning in the novel. After so many years of living and working in France, Amer is not suited to the rough labors of the Kabyle peasant, despite his good intentions. Amer recognizes this and reflects upon the bond between a Kabyle peasant *(fellah)* and his small plot of land: "Our land is modest. She loves and rewards in secret. She recognizes her own right away: those who are destined for her and those for whom she was made. It is not only 'white hands,' those soft, untried hands, that she rejects, or lazy or weak hands, but even those mercenary hands that seek to force her to yield without loving her" (142). The Kabyle land will yield up her fruits only to those native sons who demonstrate their attachment through careful and constant attentions. In this metaphor, the colonizer landowners who have taken lands from villages and clans in order to build large farms and plantations cannot possibly be as close to the land as the Kabyle himself. Amer continues his meditation to note that those who would fence off parcels of land, and plant "foreign" flowers in straight lines, are to be pitied, since they cannot truly know the joy of this symbiotic link between land and the peasant. Clearly, the allusion here is to the wrongheadedness of French colonial plantation practices; the French are outsiders who have acquired land in Algeria through military conquest, and they force it to yield its fruits not out of love, but out of desire for profit.

Land and Blood is, however, no pastoral idyll. Feraoun knew from his own modest childhood just how precarious subsistence farming was for the population of Kabylia in preindependence Algeria. Land is the source of life in Ighil-Nezman, but every wise, elderly villager also knows that upon death, the Kabyle peasant returns to the earth: an eternity spent under a slab in the cemetery. Earth, stone, straw, and mud are all vital elements in the construction of the Kabyle village and are present in the novel as figurative and symbolic building materials. The accident in the French coal mine from Amer's youth is replayed after a fashion in the violent cataclysm in the village quarry that brings the novel to its dramatic conclusion. Only payment in blood for the sake of honor is acceptable to settle the score between Amer and his uncle, and the Kabyle land seemingly participates in exacting the blood price to be paid.

Numerous Kabyle and Muslim social, religious, and economic practices are explored throughout the course of the novel. Much attention is given to the status of women in the Kabyle village and home in *Land and Blood*. During the colonial era, the French occupiers noted that women appeared to lead very oppressed and limited lives. Anthropologists at the time believed that Islam itself and the general poverty of Algeria were responsible for the circumspect lives of women. Feraoun actually portrays several village women in Ighil-Nezman who dominate their husbands and extended families; they are very adept at achieving their goals and setting themselves up as powerful matriarchs. The married couple of Slimane and Chabha are exemplary in this respect: they operate as a united front in the face of greedy cousins who hope to inherit their land since the couple is childless. Feraoun's work sets the record straight on the status of women in Kabyle culture. Kabyle women work in the fields, go out to get water from the village fountain, and go visit neighbors and family; they do not wear the veil, nor do they lead lives of seclusion in Ighil-Nezman. Feraoun's novel indicates that only very well-off villagers could have their women remain inside the home as a mark of their status. True to cultural paradigms in a Muslim, Arab-Berber society of the time, the worst fate for a woman is to be barren. But Feraoun does not depict any married man in this novel who divorces a wife who cannot seem to conceive. Instead, the couples of Ighil-Nezman work to find other solutions to the issue of inheritance.

Marie must adapt to the women's world; her fate is obviously more linked to theirs once she returns to Amer's homeland. Through the character of Marie, learning how to be a wife and daughter-in-law as a Kabyle, Feraoun can depict the reality of women's existence in an authentic fashion. Feraoun directly addresses a French reader's preconceived ideas about women in Kabylia when he notes that "any exaggerations about Kabyle women should be challenged" (30). As Marie comes to understand, they are not necessarily submissive; rather, their difficult living conditions tend to make them more generous and accepting of others and the reality in which they live. Again and again, *Land and Blood* is meant to be read as a novel that can bring about intercultural understanding and tolerance.

News of Mouloud Feraoun's murder in March of 1962 stunned citizens of Algeria and France. His devotion to the values of peace and humanism, his work as a teacher, and his efforts, along with those of the five other murdered colleagues at the Centres Sociaux that day, to provide educational opportunities to the youth of Algeria during the eight years of horrible war inspired numerous eulogies in Algerian and French papers alike. In the decades since Algeria gained its independence from France, Feraoun's literary and personal legacy has remained strong. Christiane Achour's study of Feraoun's writing notes that excerpts from his fiction have been included in primary school texts in Algeria, making Mouloud Feraoun a beloved founding father of Algerian national literature (18–29). Achour's analysis of school texts points out, however, that the educational authorities have edited his texts in such a way as to "de-historicize" his fiction, removing any references to the French colonial presence (24–25). Instead, passages selected from *The Poor Man's Son* emphasize the child's experiences growing up poor in a mythic, idealized Kabyle village. The Kabyle village then can become a nostalgic element in the collective Algerian identity as a modern nation-state.

Afterword

Interest in Mouloud Feraoun's life and work increased during the violent civil conflict experienced by Algeria during the 1990s. During this conflict, government security forces battled armed Islamic militants who targeted French-language writers, journalists, and teachers as part of their campaign to destabilize Algerian society. Assia Djebar, a member of the Académie Française and perhaps the most widely read Algerian writer today, linked Mouloud Feraoun's assassination by French terrorists in 1962 to the forces of obscurantism responsible for the deaths of Algerian intellectuals such as Tahar Djaout, Abdelkader Alloula, Mahfoud Boucebci, and many others during the 1990s conflict. In the elegiac *Le blanc de l'Algérie* (1995), Djebar places Feraoun into her personal pantheon of "ces chers disparus" (15) (these dear departed) and "mes confrères exemplaires" (123) (my exemplary colleagues), writers who continue to speak to her after their death through their texts, their "unfinished writing" (123).

Feraoun finds a place on the death rolls of Algeria's more recent period of terror because of the similarities between the circumstances of his murder and those of writers targeted for their intellectual stance as secular humanists between 1992 and 1995. The memory and legacy of Mouloud Feraoun is evoked by the historian James D. Le Sueur as symbolic of the cruel irony of the last days of French colonial rule in Algeria: on the very day the Evian Accords were signed, ending French rule, a memorial service was held for Feraoun and his five Centres Sociaux colleagues in a small town outside of Algiers. Le Sueur describes Feraoun's work at the Centres Sociaux as having attempted to build "a bridge of fraternity between the French and Algerians" (86). Other scholars have suggested that Mouloud Feraoun played the role of a transcultural mediator. Lucy McNair observes that Feraoun was a "cultural translator" (18), and the French literary critic Jean Déjeux coined the term "l'homme-frontière" (114) (border man) to describe him, calling attention to the fact that Feraoun straddled two cultures. The words of French sociologist Pierre Bourdieu, who did his early ethnographic work in Algeria during the late 1950s

Afterword

among the Kabyles, are perhaps the simplest and most profound recollection of Feraoun, as a "man of truth and peace . . . who, at the height of terror, managed to keep his head and even to control the violence aroused by the horror of violence" (ix).

The former French colonies of North Africa (also called the Maghreb) have undergone great political, economic, and social change since they obtained their independence from the French. In all three nations—Morocco, Tunisia, and Algeria—the novels, poems, and plays written in French, both at the dawn of the independence period and afterward, now make up what is commonly called the "national literature" of each country. These nations also face the interesting and sometimes problematic reality of having national literatures written in both French and Arabic since the French language has actually endured as a means of written expression in various segments of postcolonial society. Feraoun's fiction was sometimes criticized in the 1970s by Maghrebi literary experts for not being "revolutionary" or anti-French enough. However, most Algerians continue to admire the legacy of Mouloud Feraoun, a heroic individual whose dedication to humanistic principles and to the improvement of educational opportunities for poor children made him the target of right-wing assassination. The English translation of *Land and Blood* will enable a new generation of readers to become acquainted with the immense talent of Mouloud Feraoun, who played such a vital role in the development of French-language writing from Algeria.

Bibliography

WORKS BY MOULOUD FERAOUN

L'anniversaire. Paris: Éditions du Seuil, 1972.

Les chemins qui montent. Paris: Éditions du Seuil, 1957.

Le fils du pauvre (1950). Paris, Éditions du Seuil, 1954. Translated as *The Poor Man's Son: Menrad, Kabyle Schoolteacher,* by Lucy R. Mcnair, introduction by James D. Le Sueur. Charlottesville: University of Virginia Press, 2005.

Journal, 1955–1962. Paris: Éditions du Seuil, 1962. Translated as *Journal, 1955–1962,* by Mary Ellen Wolf and Claude Fouillade. Lincoln: University of Nebraska Press, 2000.

La terre et le sang. Paris: Éditions du Seuil, 1953.

WORKS BY OTHERS

Achour, Christiane. *Mouloud Feraoun: Une voix en contrepoint.* Paris: Silex, 1986.

Bourdieu, Pierre. «Foreword.» In *Uncivil War: Intellectuals and Identity Politics during the Decolonization of Algeria,* by James D. Le Sueur, ix–x. Philadelphia: University of Pennsylvania Press, 2001.

Déjeux, Jean. *Littérature maghrébine de langue française.* Ottawa: Éditions Naaman, 1973.

Djebar, Assia. *Le blanc de l'Algérie.* Paris: Albin Michel, 1995.

Elbaz, Robert, and Martine Mathieu-Job. *Mouloud Feraoun ou l'émergence d'une littérature.* Paris: Karthala, 2001.

Le Sueur, James D. *Uncivil War: Intellectuals and Identity Politics during the Decolonization of Algeria.* Philadelphia: University of Pennsylvania Press, 2001.

McNair, Lucy. "An Algerian-American Primer: Reading Mouloud Feraoun's *The Poor Man's Son, Menrad, Kabyle Schoolteacher.*" *Contemporary French and Francophone Studies* 10, no. 2 (2006): 183–93.

Sayeh, Samira. *La génération de 52: Conflits d'hégémonie et de dépendance.* Paris: Éditions Publisud, 2010.

CARAF Books
Caribbean and African Literature Translated from French

Guillaume Oyônô-Mbia
and Seydou Badian
*Faces of African
Independence: Three Plays*
Translated by Clive Wake

Olympe Bhêly-Quénum
Snares without End
Translated by Dorothy S. Blair

Bertène Juminer
The Bastards
Translated by Keith Q. Warner

Tchicaya U Tam'Si
The Madman and the Medusa
Translated by Sonja Haussmann
Smith and William Jay Smith

Alioum Fantouré
Tropical Circle
Translated by Dorothy S. Blair

Edouard Glissant
*Caribbean Discourse:
Selected Essays*
Translated by J. Michael Dash

Daniel Maximin
Lone Sun
Translated by Nidra Poller

Aimé Césaire
*Lyric and Dramatic
Poetry, 1946–82*
Translated by Clayton
Eshleman and Annette Smith

René Depestre
The Festival of the Greasy Pole
Translated by Carrol F. Coates

Kateb Yacine
Nedjma
Translated by Richard Howard

Léopold Sédar Senghor
The Collected Poetry
Translated by Melvin Dixon

Maryse Condé
I, Tituba, Black Witch of Salem
Translated by Richard Philcox

Assia Djebar
*Women of Algiers in
Their Apartment*
Translated by Marjolijn de Jager

Dany Bébel-Gisler
*Leonora: The Buried
Story of Guadeloupe*
Translated by Andrea Leskes